The Gleaning Time

Arc Two - Into The Fields

Angela Pritula

PublishAmerica
Baltimore

First printing

Hardcover 9781462645169
Softcover 9781462683291
PUBLISHED BY PUBLISHAMERICA, LLLP
www.publishamerica.com
Baltimore

Printed in the United States of America

To Ellda

Thanks for your support & smile ☺

Love
Magda

DEDICATION

To my mother, Elena…an immigrant and survivor of WWII from Naples, Italy who is my example of courage

ACKNOWLEDGMENTS

My thanks to author Shouji Gatou, whose Full Metal Panic light novel series gave me the idea that a plot based on an alternate world history could be a great story and helped me realize I could take biblical prophecy and do the same

The Gleaning Time

Arc Two—Into The Fields

INTRODUCING THE FULL ARMOR TEAM

PETER ROCCQUE

Called Pete by his friends. Height 6'2" Weight 197, Hair medium reddish brown, moderately long, eyes blue, age 20

Peter is the leader of the FA Team. He's intelligent, handsome, driven, courageous, heroic, has great integrity and will sacrifice himself readily for the team and the cause. He will often take the burden of missions very seriously, but due to his own desire to do everything perfectly, often comes off as headstrong or stubborn. He and Josh are best friends but often disagree about battle plans which leads to dissention between them. He has deep convictions about what God's plan is for him and his team and will verbally battle with anyone within the team who suggests any actions that oppose that. He and Angelica have a deep affection and respect for each other and it is often she who brings him down when he needs to be humbled. He can also play the piano quite well, due to his mother, an accomplished musician.

Peter's Personality

Peter has a typical sanguine temperament like his biblical counterpart. Like the apostle Peter, Peter is bold, strong-willed, and fearless but also like him, Peter is impulsive, brash, and sometimes acts before he thinks. His negative qualities come out when he discovers that the group's mentor and teacher is none other than his long-lost father. It is then that Peter's latent anger and bitterness surfaces, making him act almost irrationally by attempting to leave the group but intervention from the team members, most especially Joshua and Angelica, gets him back in focus. Forgiveness to his father is granted just as a climax is reached and his father is captured and executed. He then becomes as focused to the cause of God's will as he ever can be, to honor his father's vision and memory.

JOSHUA NUNN

Called Josh by his friends—Height 6'1", Weight 195—Hair, raven black worn moderately long, olive complexion, eyes, gray—rugged features—age 20

Joshua is the second in command of the FA team—the typical soldier with a true warrior's spirit, Joshua has the ability to plan strategies that are almost always successful—a military genius. Prior to the Rapture and his conversion, he had been in various private militia groups that trained him in all forms of combat of which he became an expert. He also has an exceptionally high IQ. He is a natural born strategist, an expert in covert operations, and a technical master besides being a fierce warrior. He's also a gifted computer hacker.

Joshua's Personality

Joshua is a choleric temperament, which makes him driven, almost to the point of obsession. He uses his anger to push himself and his combative nature comes out at times to buck authority. But he is also driven to serve God to the best of his ability, and he is tireless in his desire to do that. He is considered a hothead who can be emotional but his focus never wavers, which is to defeat the antichrist and those who have his spirit and to Joshua this means those like his parents, the academically elite, and the intellectually agnostic, which he now considers liars. The truth of the Word is sacred to him, and he is uncompromising in the application of it to himself personally and the team as a whole. On the other side, there is a deep love for his teammates and a strong feeling of protectiveness for Leah, who because of her gift of seeing into men's hearts, saw the raw hidden anguish in Joshua and reached out to him at a time when he had shrouded himself in indifference and doubt.

ANGELICA SCALES

Occasionally called Angel by the team, Height 5'8" Weight 123 lbs—Hair blonde, eyes turquoise—delicate features, lithe but shapely figure.—Age 19

Angelica is a young woman of great insight. Her former involvement in a coven and her extensive background in the occult became fertile ground for the Holy Spirit to imbue her with gifts of wisdom and discernment. And her newfound faith has given her a love of the Word and righteousness—having known intimately the powers of darkness. She has a pure heart, is an agile and capable fighter when she needs to be and is quite clever, coming up with battle plans that are successful. She is often chosen by Peter to accompany him on missions.

Angelica's Personality

Angelica is a typical melancholy temperament—deeply sensitive and introspective—as well as emotive. She has a very intuitive nature, which is probably why the Holy Spirit chose her as the vessel by which to give messages to the team. Her former gifts of divination and psychic abilities were changed into gifts of strong discernment and wisdom and she is dedicated to serving God by using them in a Spirit filled capacity. She also is driven to show her gratitude—to God, Peter and the group—for making her feel like she belonged for the first time in her life. Her role as Messenger is a burden she bears stoically.

JOHN PAX

Called Johnny occasionally by his teammates—Height 5'11" weight 170—hair, umber brown—eyes, gold—lean, but muscular—Age 21.

John is a young man with a very even temper and is always pleasant—a true phlegmatic—extremely intelligent and somewhat shy but quite scholarly about the Word—an apologetic. Since he was brought up in a commune by a father who was a pacifist, he isn't as much of a fighter as the others but if called upon he can be quite formidable, preferring to use brains instead of brawn. Although John is the oldest chronologically, his temperament makes him willing to let Peter and Josh's stronger personalities guide the team and keep him in the background. He's a talented guitarist.

John's Personality

John is a sensitive and compassionate individual, one who has a strong sense of justice and his biblical knowledge just enforces those characteristics. He is a peacemaker par excellence as he balances the absolutes of biblical truth with seeking peace. He is very protective of his sister and when exercising that he becomes formidable, as Josh finds out when he gets closer to Leah. He also is quite an adept mechanic and often fixes any vehicles the team acquires and in tense situations within the group he usually has a joke to lighten the mood

LEAH PAX

Called Leah by everyone and by the nickname "Little Bird" by Josh she's the one member who is the most sensitive towards others in addition to being acutely perceptive. She's also the youngest at 18 and is about 5'6" and 110 lbs with auburn hair worn short and an unusual eye color, a kind of periwinkle. With one eye being lighter than the other, her vision is about 65% making her partially blind. Because her mother was full blooded Cherokee, her skin tone is dark, Native American which contrasts with her unusual eye color. She and John are siblings due to the fact that they share the same father, as the commune they grew up in was very free in every aspect.

Leah's Personality

Leah is a gentle soul with an underlying strength that comes from having to compensate for her disability. Like her brother, she was brought up to accept everybody at face value and to not be judgmental. Her temperament is phlegmatic with melancholy; a sensitive soul who loves animals and cringes at the mistreatment of any living thing. Yet she is not unaware of the bold line between good and evil and her convictions are strong, belying her delicate appearance she is in fact the strongest in the group.

DANIEL ROCCQUE—BROTHER DANNY

The mentor of the team—41 years old—about 6' and 195 lbs—eyes (same as his son) vivid blue. Hair is salt and pepper sorrel brown and curly. He is heavily bearded.

Daniel was the minister and CEO of one of the largest faith and holiness ministries in Christendom at one time, with a worldwide audience through television, radio and the Internet. His ministry won acclaim not only for the miracles that took place but for his ability to bring hope to the hopeless. At first, he was very humble, giving to others and always praising God for his blessings. But as the ministry grew, his pride did as well and he began to be drawn to other women who had idolized him. And especially one woman in particular, with whom he had a very involved affair. This not only destroyed his ministry but obliterated his marriage and his relationship with his only son. So he left the ministry and his family and disappeared, thought to be dead.

Daniel's relationship with the team is that they are all his children, he loves each one as such. But he knew his son from the moment he saw him and wracked with guilt and remorse for what had driven him from his family, he keeps a distance as he sees that Peter does not recognize him. But as he and Peter work together more, he cannot help but be proud of the man his son has become and helps him all he can in the role of team leader. However, eventually Peter discovers that Daniel is his father and the relationship becomes rocky as Peter deals with his anger and resentment toward the man he feels betrayed and abandoned him and his mother. This rift adds to stress to an already stressful situation as Daniel is targeted by the UWC for his "phantom web cast" that cuts into Abram's own "Between You and Me" propaganda web casts, making his destruction a top priority.

THE STORY UP TO NOW:

The disappearances of millions foretold in the Bible as the Rapture has taken place, sending the world into turmoil and requiring that there be order restored so a one-world government has been hastily formed. Called the Unified World Community, all the world nations, are united under the leadership of the man Isaac Abram. Bringing everyone together as the chaos of the "disappearances" has created panic to alleviate the fears of the remaining people Abram has issued the directive of a universal mandatory identification system. Called the TM chip, this is implanted on either a person's forehead or right hand. Most are eager to comply with the new leader but many still refuse and become instant enemies of the UWC and are marked for execution, making then fugitives and on the run. This is the case for Peter Roccque, a 20 year old newly converted Christian youth who flees the UWF militia sent to capture the rebels.

He eludes capture by hiding in a van filled with garbage heading to a landfill out in the wilderness. After a close call at a highway checkpoint, Peter escapes the van and heads out into the woods where he finds a cave that actually turns out to be a subterranean catacomb that was once used as a military bunker for a defunct para-military group. He seeks shelter and finds evidence that it is occupied because he finds food, and a fire going. Curious yet hungry, Peter helps himself to the food and is interrupted by the inhabitants, two young men, Josh and John, a girl, Leah, and an older man known as Brother Danny. He gets a mixed welcome as they too are new Christian fugitives refusing the TM chip and after spending the night becomes part of the group as Brother Danny recognizes the young man as his son and one of a group of youngsters that he is called to gather by the Lord.

They are still getting used to each other when Peter joins them and over the following time he gradually becomes one of the group. Starting to bond with the still suspicious Josh, the two boys are doing some maintenance on the bunker's satellite dish when they spot a fire in the distance. Concerned because of the dry brush from the lack of rain they decide to investigate and then are horrified to witness a bizarre ceremony where a pretty blonde girl named Angelica is about to be burned on a cross. They burst into the circle and rescue her, bringing her back to the hideaway bunker where she is immediately grafted into the group. However, all is not completely rosy as Josh's discovery of a very disturbing truth about his past sends him into a dark rage. An argument ensues that drives Angelica off and as Peter rushes after her, Josh bares his soul to Leah who points out the need for them to stick together since they all are fugitives, which changes his suspicions about the newcomers. When Peter brings Angelica back, Josh apologizes and the group is resolved to support each other.

True bonding begins between the young adults as Brother Danny goes off into the woods to consult with the Holy Spirit as to what he should do now that the five youths are gathered. He is directed to prepare the group and gather them together and after he does, they are visited by the Spirit where they receive powers that are represented by the full armor of God. And now they await instruction as the UWC is established as the one world order…

PROLOGUE—PORTRAIT OF A BEAST

The document read as follows:

PROFILE REPORT—ISAAC ABRAM—SUPREME LEADER OF THE UNIFIED WORLD COMMUNITY

AGE...39

APPEARANCE...Height 6'0", weight 185, complexion olive, eyes blue, hair black with some gray.

BACKGROUND...Born in Innsbruck, Austria, mother of German descent, father, Syrian. Family moved to father's homeland at age of five. Family has one brother and a sister, current whereabouts unknown. Father died of heart attack five years ago. Original name Heinrich Assad, legally changed at age 21 when mother died, beaten to death by father in defiance to father's actions. Graduated summa cum laude with a Masters in political science from University of Innsbruck with a GPA of 4.00. Was awarded a Graduate scholarship to Oxford University and after a year was named a Rhodes Scholar.

PERTINENT INFORMATION...Member of Mensa with an IQ of 220 and fluent in all civilized languages. Hobbies include earth science, world history, and religion.

Isaac finished proofreading the document and smiling in satisfaction reached for an inkpad and stamp, giving his approval for the document to be sent to the media and his web site administrator for posting. Since the holocaust of the disappearance of so many last week, now known as "The Great Vanishing" and his insertion as Unified World Community Leader, the clamor for information about the magnetic man was relentless so he drafted this concise blog to satisfy the curious throng of reporters tailing him. They also wanted to be witness to any new "miracles" he might perform in the face of chaos... the widespread lawlessness, killing, disease, and worldwide shortages of food as well as natural Those who were poor were especially troubled and in many cases reduced to animalistic behavior just to survive.

The "miracles" Isaac performed covered all different types of the spectrum, from sending rain to fail on once parched lands encouraging new areas where food could be grown, to laying hands on infirmed and crippled and having them be immediately healed. Because he did these benevolent activities, his public view was one of a true savior, universally loved and revered. His pursuit of the pact between Israel and the Palestine states was historic as no other leader had ever accomplished the feat before, further canonizing him as a post modern saint. His weekly web chats, called "Between You and Me" reminiscent of the 20th century American president Franklin Delano Roosevelt's radio Fireside Chats, gave him an everyman quality that made the entire world population view him with respect and affection.

Short and sweet, just the way I want it. No need to bore the people with all the sordid details of my life. The man I am now has no bearing whatsoever on the way I grew up Abram's mind reasoned with him as he remembered his tumultuous past and the way his father denigrated his mother so she was nothing but a slave to do his bidding. He was quite young when he first realized that his father had no love or respect for his mother, a gentle woman who was dedicated to trying to please her husband and raise her children. It caused him pain to see her verbally and at times physically abused for failing to please his father, whose mercurial temperament changed when he would spend time with him. His father then would become the personification of the word father, teaching him all about the Muslim way which he accepted when young but as he grew older, he questioned as he did not see women as the third class citizens that the nation of Islam claimed they were. In his teens, he began to reject the Muslim faith and became an agnostic, moving away from every mention of Allah as his doubts grew. Disappointed by his son's rejection of his birthright his father was growing more and more violent towards his mother and because of Sharia law, his actions were not questioned so his mother endured the beatings. Then came the day after a particularly severe one, she finally succumbed. It was first and the last time Isaac would ever shed tears.

As usual, Abram sat staring ahead at nothing as the memories plunged him into the abyss of melancholy and he allowed himself the human indulgence as a break from his daily duties as UWC Leader. A cold chill in the spacious and lavish office then interrupted his reverie and what appeared as the holographic appearance of a man in white startled him from his thoughts.

"Hello Isaac."

Abram inquired in a neutral tone, "So what brings you here today, Lord Baal?"

The image solidified and stood before the vast glass topped desk and replied, "Your next task is ready for you."

Ah yes, the daily miracle "So what am I to do now?" Abram seemed almost blasé as he waited for his orders.

"The Midwest of the United States is experiencing a day of extreme severe weather. Thunderstorms with large hail and tornadoes, many EF-5s."

"I see." Abram intoned as he pushed a button on a console behind his chair.

A large high definition screen slid up from the panel and flashed on the heartland of the United States. The sky was an ominous gray-green with flashes of lightning in the multiple views that showed the various regions of the severe weather outbreak, some with vicious twisters snaking down and bearing on several urban centers. Abrams then closed his eyes and a pink glow enveloped him as he reached his hand forward to the screen to encompass the views as he spoke with authority…

"Peace, be still."

Abram then ran his hands from one scene to the other and immediately the storms abated and the sky cleared, bringing the sun out. The UWC Leader smiled and then pushed another button that hooked him into his web stream.

"Fear not, my friends in the United States for the winds have gone and again you are safe. So rest easy."

"Good work, Isaac," Baal remarked. "The Great Master will be pleased."

"Hmmm," was the reply as Abrams asked, "So what else am I to do?"

The spirit known as Baal answered, "Just your daily conference with your co-leaders from the Four Kingdoms, and Israel. I shall leave you to that and give the Great Master your report. Until tomorrow, Isaac."

The figure then evaporated as Abram reached and punched a button on his intercom to his private secretary and mistress, Thora Blackmon. She was a striking brunette with almost violet eyes who was coolly efficient at her job and morphed into a wanton in his bed when the sun went down.

"Yes sir?" The throaty alto was all business from nine to five.

Contact the branches of the Quad, Thora. And tell them the morning meeting will take place in 45 minutes in the Main Conference Room."

"Immediately sir." The office became silent as Abram then turned back to the console and pulled a microphone to his mouth then pressed a button and spoke…

"Good day, friends. This is your trusted Leader, Isaac Abram, with today's words of encouragement and support to you, wherever and whoever you are…"

PHASE 1—LIGHT AND DARK

CHAPTER 1—THE MESSIAH COMES

After lunch the Main Conference Room of UWC Command Center, located in Geneva, Switzerland was the focal point of the group of media known as the Unified World Commission of Press and Information or UWCPI, which absorbed all media outlets and news agencies around the world. This group of print, web, and telecommunications journalists' main job was to follow and report to the population on the Leader's actions and decisions, as well as the workings of Isaac Abram's right hand; the most Divine High Priest Ichabod, who was the leader of the World Faith and Belief Circle. The population, still shaken from the loss of many family, friends and neighbors had reached for any comfort and Ichabod had come in to offer that. He began to be broadcast on both the web and TV to offer sympathy and hope by brilliant preaching that brought a spotlight on the miracles performed by Abram. The two worked in tandem and everybody was enthralled, pledging total and complete allegiance to them. The UWCPI was the messenger of all this so there was no corner of the earth that did not know.

Except...

There were still some who did not take the blind devotion to the new world order as their mantle, they instead defied the order to take the TM identification chip on their foreheads or right hand, thus making them instant enemies to the UWC. These renegade rebels would then be targeted by the Unified World Force military branch of UWC for execution. But this was a daunting and arduous task for those who refused the TM chip would elude capture and hide in places that made it seem as if they had disappeared from the earth, yet would rear up frequently to add to their numbers. This was a constant irritation to Abram and his conferences with the governors of the Four Regions were strategy sessions to rid the world of this threat.

The governors of the Four Regions, known as the Quad were appointed by Abram to oversee the four main areas of the world. The man that governed the South Region, which included the African continent and South America was someone by the name of Abrafo Uwamba, an Ethiopian who had an arresting manner that inspired almost slavish devotion from the people. So any rebellion was like a personal affront to him and he promised swift punishment to those who were part.

The governor of the East Region was a man named Jiang Tao-Wei, a former labor organizer from the Shanghai area of China and his territories included the nations of China, Taiwan, Korea, Vietnam, and the islands of Japan. He also oversaw the country of Australia, including the various tiny islands scattered in the South Pacific as well as India and Mongolia. As a former member of the powerful Labor Party in China, Jiang was experienced in leadership for the masses and because of his charisma he was admired even by the Japanese, who were more capitalist in their society in comparison to the communism of China. He was charming and yet there was an almost ruthless coldness in him that was underlying and acted as a deterrent to any uprisings. So the rebels that managed to defy him infuriated him so that the unfortunate ones who were caught were dealt with brutally and as an example, publicly.

The region to the North was governed by Sergei Rodrinka, a man that came from an obscure Siberian village and became a force in the political realm of the cluster of countries that had once been the Soviet Union. He, like his colleagues, all had arresting and magnetic personalities that drew the masses to them. But Sergei had one thing above the others and that was the strict belief that order was necessary for the abolition of confusion and chaos. Like the former leaders of the USSR such as Stalin and Khrushchev, he kept the peace through the use of the military as an intimidation device. He also espoused a strong force to crush the rebellions that were rising up which were to literally spy on each citizen as a justified right and mete out retribution through immediate elimination.

The Western region, the most populated area and the central command of the UWC was under the stewardship of a woman by the name of Maria Elizabeth Rondalle, a direct descendant of Marie Antoinette and like the others a brilliant orator that inspired unwavering trust in the people. She had the power and charm of Eva Peron while possessing the quick mind of a true politician and the fact that she was the only woman in the ruling circle of UWC, she enjoyed the admiration of all women worldwide. She took her role very much to heart and was determined as the lone female to show herself worthy to be on the same level as the men so she was ruthless as she dealt with rebels. Because of this, she had the dubious honor of having the nickname "Bloody Mary" for the many that had died as a result of her command.

These four individuals were waiting in the Main Conference Room as Abram entered followed by Divine High Priest Ichabod, who walked with head bowed, as if in deep meditation. The others all bowed their heads in deference as Abram and Ichabod passed and went to the head of the table to take their seats. The others then followed suit as they went to their places around the conference table and stood to wait as the leader brought the meeting to order.

Abram strode forward, stood at the head of the table and gestured for everyone to be seated. He waited as Thora brought a mildly thick manila folder and placed it before him, then discreetly exited. The UWC leader then cleared his throat to begin.

"Before I hear your individual reports, I have here the daily record of works done across the world for the benefit of mankind and our Unified World Community. Just this morning a potential natural disaster of epic proportions was thwarted as an especially severe bout of weather was calmed at its peak." He rifled through the fax the office received on behalf of a grateful President of the USA. "…and we of the United States humbly offer our thanks to the benevolent move on the part of our dear UWC leader, Isaac Abram. We know that his timely intervention saved countless lives here and we acknowledge his divine Will to keep us safe."

Murmurs of approval issued forth from the leaders of the Four Regions, as Abram continued, reading excerpts from other reports of miraculous events spanning the entire globe. The recitation of the events was everything from calming EF-5 tornadoes to rescuing a bus of children from certain death when their vehicle stalled in the path of an oncoming train. Healings at critical care hospitals where those considered at death's door were recovering were included along with reports of breakthroughs in the treatment of chronic conditions which, until now had no hope for cures. As he read the reports, the background screens were flashing these very events as covered by the newly formed UWCPI public information bureau. As the reports were read and viewed each governor of the Four Regions made notes of each event taking place in their respective area. However, underlying the positives, there was a continuing problem that remained persistent, like the proverbial fly in the ointment: the Rebel Faction, those individuals who were refusing taking the TM chip. They were becoming a nuisance as their numbers were growing, as evidenced by the reports of insurgencies arising throughout.

Abram addressed the leadership grimly, "The Rebel Faction is getting larger, encouraging more to join their ranks by refusing to take the TM chip. This is troublesome, as it could cause the same unrest that occurred after the disappearances of the Great Vanishing. It is a threat to the order I am trying to establish."

"But Your Excellency, we are doing our best to—," Jiang began but his statement was cut off by the cold and piercing glare of the Supreme Leader as he refuted the claim.

"Your so-called best is not good enough!" Abram snapped as he gestured to the monitors. "Fools, open your eyes and see. That there is a growing population of rebels is proof that you are not, as you say, doing your best. So what are you planning to do to alleviate that?"

The room was thick with silence as the four governors had no pat answer or easy explanation, which caused different levels of anxiety in each. After all, nobody wanted to incur the wrath of the Mighty leader as his powers were evident in the supernatural acts he was performing daily.

As he observed the non-response of his subordinates, Abram sighed and brought the discussion to the simplest terms. "Let me ask you all now. What is the basis for most of the uprisings taking place?"

Sergei was bold enough this time to reply, "I don't know, Your Excellency. It appears to be that the rebels are being fanned by some archaic teachings from the Bible. At least that is what it seems to be in my jurisdiction."

"Well?" Abram addressed the others. "Is that also true for the rest of you?"

Uwamba scoffed as he replied, "It's not as simple as that for me. Some of the people under me are naturally rebellious as they balk at any kind of rule, living like savages in the jungle." He chuckled as he said confidently, "All it takes is some strong discipline to make examples of the troublemakers and they will come around."

"Well, strong-arming and brow-beating may work for your so-called 'savages' but the people under me are much more sophisticated and as the former governments of the countries were democracies, are used to the freedoms of such, "Maria Rondalle reasoned coolly as she took a sip of water. "They are more likely to question authority that is thrust upon them with little explanation and will rebel at overt shows of force."

Abram saw the potential for endless debate so he nipped it in the bud by raising his hand in dismissal. "It doesn't matter what tactics you use to quell the uprisings. Just do it. And I will use what I can to discover the whereabouts of the source of this latest instigation." He rose and informed the group, "I am headed to Israel to talk to Prime Minister Elias personally to try to convince him to join the Community…although it has been reported to me that he has taken ill."

"Humph!" snorted Sergei. "I think you're wasting your valuable time, sir. Those Zionists have always been an obstinate lot and refusing to unite with the rest of the world is just proof of that fact. Force, I believe is the only way to bring them to their senses and see reason."

Abram closed his eyes and looked almost serene. The response was typical of a former KGB hardliner like Rodrinka. "I believe that once the good Prime Minister is approached with the proper invocation, he will do what is best for his people. The old saying 'you can catch more flies with honey than with vinegar' comes to mind. Especially since Lazerai Elias is a popular leader and has been known to be uncompromising, a traditional Zionist." He then gave a sage glint as he added, "Not entirely unlike you, my friend."

Rodrinka sniffed in disdain, "I am not a Zionist."

"True, but you follow the same rigid conformity in your viewpoint." Abram then continued, "In that respect, you could be brothers." He addressed the rest. "Enough then, you all know what to do. This meeting is adjourned." The Supreme Leader then exited the side door, leaving the four subordinates staring after him…

About forty-five minutes later, Abram was on a private jet, heading to Tel Aviv to meet with Lazerai Elias, settling in for the flight as the craft was ascending into the sky. The captain's voice came over the speaker.

"All clear, Your Excellency. We should arrive in Tel Aviv in two hours."

"Thank you, Captain. Please let me know when we are about to land, I'm going to be resting."

"As you wish, sir."

The speaker went silent and Abram closed his eyes as he laid back against the headrest, intending to take a quick nap to pass the time. But something bade him to open his eyes and when he did, a figure glowing in a crimson aura sat in the swivel chair in front of his own, with a smile that did not reach his smoldering eyes. Abram sat up, fully awake.

"Lord Baal."

"Hello, Isaac," the spirit being known as Baal greeted him. For this visitation he was in tangible human form clad in a gray suit, very dapper with a neatly cut raven coif. He appeared to be a trendy business associate save for one thing, his eyes which appeared as twin flames and were as mesmerizing.

Abram's own eyes were pinned as he asked, "What do you require of me, my lord?"

Baal replied, “You are on your way to Israel to meet with Elias, are you not?”

“Yes I am, as you directed,” Abram responded. “We should be there in about an hour.”

Baal wasted no time but got right to business. “When you arrive there, you will discover that Elias…is dead.”

Abram blinked as he echoed, “I was aware that he had taken ill. But dead?”

Baal nodded and said, “Indeed, and will be so for three days. In which time you will offer comfort to the grieving masses and then…” He smiled as he delivered the coup de gras. “You will bring him back from the dead.”

“I will bring him back from the dead?” Abram was incredulous.

Baal laughed, “Don’t be so obtuse. You are the Chosen One of Lucifer our Great Master and as such you will be infused with his mighty power. It is how you will be seen as the Messiah.” He added, “The children of Abraham, Isaac and Jacob are still waiting for the Messiah. When you bring back their beloved Lazerai Elias from the dead, you will, through that miracle become their Messiah.”

Abram’s mind reflected on the demonic spirit’s declaration and a sense of growing awe and pride filled him. I will become Messiah by returning Elias from the dead. I will have the power of Christ himself he exalted silently.

Baal, who could see Abram's emotions by studying his eyes, inwardly laughed in glee as he saw the meaning of his words take root…

Because Abram was a dignitary and the recognized Supreme Leader of UWC his jet was cleared to land on an airstrip that was designated strictly for government aircraft. The plane soon landed in Tel Aviv, and as it taxied to a stop, the Deputy Minister of the Israeli Cabinet, Chiam Blum, met Abram as he descended down the stairs. He bowed as the Leader came forth.

"Your Excellency Leader Abram, we are honored to have you interrupt your busy schedule and come to us. However, we had no idea that it was to be such a tragic time." He was a man in his mid fifties, with salt and pepper hair and a full beard; wearing a yarmulke signifying that he was a member of the United Torah political party, whose foundation had arisen from orthodox Judaism. "You were informed en route here, I take it?"

Abram acknowledged the greeting and offered his hand saying warmly, "As soon as I heard, I was deeply saddened as I was looking forward to the meeting with Prime Minister Elias. Even though Israel has chosen to remain separate from the UWC, I still consider the children of Israel a part of us. After all, we are a worldwide family."

"Yes, I can see that," Blum remarked as he returned the handshake. "Please come with me, the car is this way."

They headed to a waiting limousine the chauffeur standing at attention, along with some Israeli soldiers who surrounded the vehicle. Both entered the back seat and the chauffeur closed the door then got in to drive them away as the soldiers saluted.

In the back seat, Blum filled Abram in on what had actually happened. Lazerai Elias was reporting to the Knesset his outline for maintaining Israel's lone sovereignty when he suddenly and mysteriously collapsed, of a seeming heart attack as he had clutched his chest before he went down. He had been rushed to Hadassah Medical Center and had the best heart specialists flown in from all over the world to work on him. But all was for naught as Lazerai Elias was officially declared DOA after a feverish attempt to save his life. His body was now lying in state at the capitol assembly in the Matcal Tower as the public was allowed to mourn the passing of their much beloved leader…

At the same time all over the world people were glued to their media sources as they watched the proceedings, having known of Elias' hard-lined stance to keep Israel a sovereign state some were actually glad that the final stumbling block to true world unity would be removed. And the arrival of the UWC leader to honor his passing was just another way to show Isaac Abram's benevolent manner dealing with someone who had aggressively opposed him in his quest for world unity following what was now called The Great Vanishing…

However, not everyone was as enamored of the UWC leader…and six who were in that particular camp were the inhabitants of an underground bunker that was the abandoned

Y2K base for the para-military and now defunct group American Patriots League or APL, now the new base fore these Holy Spirit summoned warriors…

The APL, like all covert vigilante groups had equipped themselves for anticipated disasters with state of the art technological media such as an independent satellite dish and computer to monitor events and news in the event of a nuclear holocaust with a solar powered generator as a power source. In the room where all the telecommunications equipment and computer were installed four young adults, three men and a young woman were grouped around a monitor that was showing the somber proceedings from Tel Aviv. The boys were standing around the girl, who was sitting before the monitor…

Leah Pax said in hushed awe, "This is such a sad event." Her pale periwinkle eyes, partially blind could still make out the view of the procession of mourners.

"Yeah," her brother John affirmed. "Lazerai Elias was a man of strength and integrity who stood by his beliefs…even in the face of worldwide opposition."

"Right." Josh Nunn, a lanky but muscular youth with shoulder length mahogany hair agreed. "But he hadn't made many friends in the global community with his stand. He's been demonized by the press as an obstructionist to world unity." He snorted in derision as he added, "Especially by the Grand Poopah, Abram himself."

"Uh-huh."

The siblings nodded but the third of the boys, Peter Roccque was watching without comment periodically glancing at the closed door directly across from the room that had the electronics, a worried expression on his fine features. Josh, the most perceptive and outspoken of the group took note of his reticence and sidled over to him.

"She's okay you know…so don't worry." He laid a hand on Peter's shoulder and continued, "She's been called special…like we all have. But her role is different as is her burden…remember what happened just a month ago?"

Peter sighed, "Yeah." He frowned thoughtfully as he recalled the event…

Who could forget how the five of them, strangers thrown together by circumstance; bound by their faith in the living Savior had been divinely called to supernatural service in this dangerous time after the sudden disappearance of one third of the world's population. And how he had been on the run after refusing to take the implanted ID chip that had been mandated and then stumbled upon this underground sanctuary where he met the Pax siblings, Josh, and the man known as Brother Danny. Then the group expanded to include Angelica Scales, a young woman whose former involvement in an occultist coven had uncovered a special gift for prophetic vision. A month ago the five youngsters had been visited by the Holy Spirit and given supernatural abilities that were represented by the Full Armor of God and since then Angelica had upon direction by Him sequestered herself away from the rest of the group, for hours on end, only coming out for meals. But for the last week she had been in near total isolation, taking few if any meals whatsoever causing concern to everyone and especially Peter…

I know she's in good hands…the best of the best…but I can't help worrying for all of us actually. What's coming down the road for all of us…and if we can handle it.

As if in answer a voice in his head of quiet authority spoke, do not fear…for I am with you always.

Immediately confidence and a sense of peace flowed over Peter as he responded yes Lord…

In the room behind the closed door Angelica Scales was sitting on the floor, leaning on her altar; a wooden bench with a candle and the notebook waiting…just as she had been for the last three days. She had isolated herself after blacking out following the visitation where the Holy Spirit spoke specific instruction just for her, telling her what she was to do. So she followed His directions and now was waiting for the group's marching orders.

I've been in here for three days and haven't heard or seen anything…but Jesus was in the wilderness forty days and forty nights so by that standard I've barely scratched the surface…

You won't have to wait that long…so just endure…and tarry a while longer…

Her heart pounding in anticipation, Angelica said, "Yes, Lord…"

The next day over at the Matcal Tower in Tel Aviv Unified World Leader Isaac Abram sat in the office of the Deputy Minister and bided his time. Elias' body had been lying in state for the past three days and his visit had been as a comforting presence to the citizens of Israel and the entire world. It was because of this, the usual Jewish traditions connected with someone passing were set aside and his body was not immediately interred. Also a unique point was that although Elias' was mostly demonized as the prime obstacle to total world unity, his sudden death had been something that nobody, in the now universal spirit of peace and harmony wished. Abram's visit as world leader had not only helped solidify his role in that capacity but gave the extra added bonus of showing him to be benevolent and all loving.

Abram sighed as he sat contemplating his next move. The official funeral service was scheduled to begin in half an hour, with the service being conducted by the chief rabbi from the Great Synagogue of Tel Aviv and all media from around the world were covering it because of his appearance. So he had requested to pay his respects just following the rabbi's prayer for the dead, as directed by Baal.

A knock on the door admitted Ichabod, the UWC Spiritual Leader and chief advisor who had decided to accompany Abram to further promote the sense of unification, especially in the face of tragedy. He pulled up a chair and sat down, addressing the world leader in intimate terms as he often did when they were alone.

"Are you ready, Isaac? Because the time is nearly upon us."

"I know."

"Then let us prepare." Ichabod raised his arms and rose, his eyes closed as he called upon the top of the demonic hierarchy to infuse them with his power.

"Lord Beelzebub we invoke your holy name and ask your blessing on your servant Isaac whose one purpose is to serve you. Fill him to overflowing so he may carry out your will and glorify you…"

At those words the room went dark save for a reddish gold glow like a flame that hovered above Abram, then slowly descended down and entered him, like a searing heat. However all he felt was warmth and the unmistakable feeling of surging power. It filled him with exhilaration and when he saw the flame slide into his hands; a triumphal glee.

"Yes! Oh yes!" Abram cried his elation out, accepting Satan's gift. And then the room grew bright again. He rose with intention.

"Let's go."

Ichabod also rose. "As you wish, sir."

The service was being held in the Hechal Yehuda Synagogue because of its symbolic significance to Elias due to the fact that his grandmother had been a Holocaust survivor and he had immigrated back to Israel in his twenties to honor her last wish as she passed away. And the interior was packed with leaders and potentates from every nation with jumbotron screens installed outside to accommodate the millions of mourners, some who had made the pilgrimage from afar to pay their last respects. The service was a reflection of Elias' life and went on, saying how after having made Israel his home he enrolled in classes at the Hebrew University of Jerusalem, earned a Masters degree in political science and then became involved in the ultra-conservative United Torah Judaism party which gained national support due to escalating threats from Arab countries. His outspokenness on Israel's rights as a sovereign nation was embraced by the people of Israel, banding together to almost unanimously elect him prime minister. His leadership in keeping Israel separate of the world especially after the Great Vanishing, which had decreased world population by a third and their country by nearly a fourth was seen as courageous; an "Us vs. Them" attitude against mounting criticism…the portrait of a true patriot.

And as the accolades continued to be listed by various officials who had known Elias and worked closely with him, in the vestibule Leader Abram met with Marthe Elias, the wife of Lazerai and his daughter Meri to offer his support for their loss. He stepped over to the grieving widow, clasping her hand…

"Mrs. Elias, I cannot adequately express my shock and sorrow at this sudden tragedy…I was looking forward to working with your husband and helping Israel to join with the rest of the Unified World Community."

Mrs. Elias, a vivacious woman in her late forties with bright hazel eyes and chestnut hair was outspokenly supportive of her husband; a helpmeet in every sense of the word. She had been his sounding board and advisor though his taking on the duties of Prime Minister and his determination to do what was best to protect their homeland. Her determination was to aid him in his endeavor, even in the face of all the opposition. So when the Supreme Leader; who had been Elias' main opponent in the political battle approached her she was coolly cordial and distrustful, blaming Abram directly for the increased stress that his pressing and the media's endless badgering had brought her husband, certain that they both had caused his death. However, she covered her resentment with a veil of courtesy.

"Thank you for coming, sir."

Abram continued, "He was a man I respected and admired… someone who had drive and was steadfast in his beliefs."

Marthe Elias heard words that to her were hollow and the veil over her animosity rend in two. She remarked with more than a tinge of bitterness, "Even though you did everything in your power to break him…threatening to impose sanctions on him and using the media to harass and degrade him? All because he refused to surrender Israel's sovereignty to you like the rest of the world? Forgive me, Supreme Leader but with all due respect the reason and cause for my husband's death…rests entirely upon you."

And with those words she and Meri turned and strode away, leaving Abram and an outraged Ichabod who snapped, "How dare she speak to you like that when you took the time to come and pay your respects!"

Abram sighed with a resigned frown. "It can't be helped… Mrs. Elias just lost her husband and her reaction is understood, even expected considering the acrimonious relationship between Israel and the UWC."

Like any fawning lackey Ichabod grunted, "Still she should show you the respect due you as UWC Supreme Leader."

Abram patted the disgruntled ally on the back. "Never mind now. It's nearly time for me to go and I need a moment to collect my thoughts so if you don't mind—, " He made a dismissive gesture.

Ichabod bowed and obediently responded, "As you wish, my lord." He quickly exited and Abram headed for the closed area by the altar in the synagogue to prepare for his appearance.

Once alone, the Supreme Leader took a deep breath and closed his eyes, concentrating on the force that was surging like lava flows through his veins and then opened his eyes wide as a red-gold glow radiated in an aura around his hands. He again felt euphoria as sense of the enormous power at his fingertips took hold.

A knock sounded on the door and Ichabod stuck his head in. "The time has come, my lord."

Abram nodded regally and exited to head into the synagogue…

The Hechal Yehuda Synagogue was built in 1980 in memory of those who perished during the Holocaust in the Jewish community of Thessaloniki. With its shell-like architecture the interior was designed to hold 600, with acoustics that enabled any seat to hear as well as see equally. The seating was divided into floor seating for 400 for the men and 200 balcony seats for women in the congregation for regular services but for Lazerai Elias' funeral service the seating was divided as the floor seats for family, friends, dignitaries and officials; both foreign and domestic. The balcony was designated for the media; reporters, cameramen, and photographers, including the closed circuit cameras that were broadcasting the proceedings to the huge throng outside via jumbotron and worldwide via satellite.

The rabbi, Aaron Chaikin, stood at the lectern to recite the blessing of the dead ("El Maleh Rachamim") and the 23rd Psalm as Elias' body lay clad in a white tachrichim with a tallits behind a veil. He then recited "Baruch dayan emet" (Blessed is the one true Judge) as he tore swaths of black linen, a symbolic gesture of grief and handed them to Marthe and Meri Elias as cameras flashed and there was a soft murmur as the crowd watched UWC Leader Abram come forward. In the balcony, commentators from media outlets throughout the world gave their reports…

"Our exalted Leader is making his way down to the body of deceased Israeli Prime Minister Elias…a very magnanimous gesture considering the acrimonious atmosphere the prime minister had promulgated as Israel shunned the global community…"

Back in the hidden bunker the newly formed Full Armor team, as they now called themselves four of the five members were still gathered about the HD monitor, watching the event, provided by their own private satellite link. Along with their mentor, known as Brother Danny the four youths watched the somber proceedings with varying, emotions and differing responses…

Josh cynically snorted, "The media's its usual sycophantic self…the Israeli PM's dead and all this is about Abram. I may lose my lunch."

"Me too," Peter agreed. "It makes you sick when you think of how up to now the two of them were battling on the diplomatic front. It looks like an act played for the cameras."

"You got that right…phony…and nauseating." Josh said in the perfect mimic of an infomercial pitch man.

Leah giggled at his sarcasm and Brother Danny raised a brow as he admonished, "Nauseating or not it's prophecy fulfilled. He is the antichrist and his position is supposed to be as Savior to the world…and the media reaches the world. But we know the truth from the Word."

"Right," John chipped in. "It's to be expected really." He and the others continued watching…

The UWC Leader made his way to the raised altar and after embracing Elias' widow and daughter he went to the platform on which the body of Lazerai Elias lay in state in an open elaborate wooden coffin. The veil was extended from the ceiling and surrounded the platform and Abram pulled it aside gazing at his fallen adversary…

Well my friend it looks like you battled me to the death, literally…yet you're being given a second chance…so use it well and serve me…

He reached out his hands and closing his eyes concentrated his thoughts. As he did, a golden glow surrounded him and supernatural power resonated as Abram spoke with authority…

"Arise…and come forward…"

At those words Lazarai Elias instantly opened his eyes and sat up invoking a collective gasp of utter amazement from the crowd in the synagogue. He then rose up from the coffin and, with Abram's assistance stepped out as a worldwide stunned silent crowd greeted him. Even the media throng was dumbstruck.

Rabbi Chaikin was the first to speak as he came forward trembling. "Prime Minister Elias?"

Marthe and Meri also rushed forward as Marthe said in awe, "Lazarai…is that really you?"

Lazerai looked at the rabbi then his family and nodded, "Yes, it is me." He seemed to have an otherworld-like detachment, like he had been on another spiritual plain and was making a return to the human realm…which he was.

Leader Abram came forward and addressed Elias, "Lazerai… how are you feeling?"

The prime minister of Israel…the lone opposing voice in the total unification of the world following the global catastrophe now known far and wide as the Great Vanishing…previously as impenetrable as a granite wall…fell prostrate before him.

"I-I am...alive...breathing. My heart is beating again," Elias replied, incredulous.

He raised his shaking hand and covered his breast where his heartbeat was steady and strong. He then lifted his head and gazed up into Abram's concerned visage and before the still rolling cameras broadcasting to the ends of the earth Lazerai Elias; steadfast adversary to the UWC rose to his feet and proclaimed to all with no shadow of doubt...

"All see and believe in Ha'Mashiach Abram...our Messiah Abram!"

The synagogue erupted in an excited murmur then cheers as everyone simultaneously found their voices and responded to the miracle that they had been privy to. And the media reporters were completely caught up in the oracle, reporting in worshipful tones...

"We have just witnessed the impossible...Israeli Prime Minister Lazerai Elias who was tragically cut down three days ago by a massive heart attack...has been brought back from the dead by the benevolent hand of our Leader Abram...our Messiah..."

In their bunker the Full Armor Team stood in amazement as they too bore witness to the miracle. Even Josh, who was never at a loss for words, especially when it concerned UWC Leader Abram was tongue-tied as they all watched Elias walk toward Abram and shake hands...

John, whose eyes were round amber saucers spoke first. "Wow."

Leah shook her auburn head and asked in quiet awe, "Did… we all see that? I'm not seeing things?"

"No." Josh shook his head and affirmed, "We did, little bird…we did. Abram brought Prime Minister Elias back to life. If I hadn't seen it myself I'd never have believed it."

"Me either," Peter added as he studied the HD screen and saw Abram and Elias both standing together as various leaders from the nations came forward to offer respect and confirm what they had witnessed. He immediately saw the parallel between the scriptural account of one of the miracles of Christ *it's just like when Lazarus was brought back from the dead…the only difference being that there is no tomb…*

Brother Danny, who had remained silent up to now remarked, "The stage is set…the last barrier to Abram is now removed. A covenant with Israel is what will follow. It's almost curtain call for the first act." The foursome all gazed at him and nodded in acquiescence, their faces tense with anticipation.

"Right." Peter agreed as he turned and looked at the closed door across the way *all we need to do is wait…*

Behind that closed door the fifth member was deep in reflection, knelt down before the yet to be opened notebook, the lantern that lit the room affording the only light. Angelica sat quietly as she reflected on the various prophets in the Bible but especially the verse in the book of the prophet Joel...with nearly the same words in the book of Acts in her favorite verse:

And it shall come to pass afterward, that I will pour out my spirit upon all flesh; and your sons and your daughters shall prophesy, your old men shall dream dreams, your young men shall see visions...

See visions...that's something I've always managed to do...since I was small I could remember seeing things that came to pass...like that time I saw that man attack my mother then it happened...and what happened to Cassandra when I was in the Spirit Circle. But can I really be that...a prophet or heavenly messenger?

At that moment a soft light filled the room and a gentle voice answered her...

Do you still doubt Me, My daughter?

Angelica's heart lurched as she lowered her head and replied, "Never You, my Lord...only myself. My abilities from my life before are a burden to me since they were used for evil."

Are you not a new creation? Bought by My Blood on the Cross?

She meekly replied, "Yes Lord."

Then trust Me...I will now show you what will come to pass for this mission...bear up under the strain until you see it all...then write down everything you saw.

Angelica raised her head and the room was filled with a scene that appeared to be from Africa. The plain was flat and grassy with animals…gazelles, giraffes, elephants, leopards, lions, and the like roaming about. And the people…dark and beautiful; men, women, boys, and girls were busy doing daily activities, living their lives. She was shown a darker side as well…famine and suffering used to manipulate the masses into submitting to accepting the TM chip. She then saw the UWF forces armed with high powered AK-47 rifles, lining the people up to inject the TM chip…nobody, even babies were exempt. And those who refused were gathered into groups to be led to a large holding tent to be killed with a bullet to the heart and beheaded in a mass execution.

Vicious…so cruel…the world is no longer a free place Angelica lamented as she continued to watch…

Then the scene changed, hours of the day passing like time stop photography and it was night. It was different…hundreds of people from all over were moving; by vehicle, vessel, animal, and by foot to a special camp, guided by her comrades in Full Armor and others clad in shirts that bore Hebrew ילדי שם—**Children of Shem** where they were welcomed with joy. Worship was taking place as a group sang and led them and Angelica could feel in her own heart that they were praising and worshiping Christ. She then saw her friends…Peter leading them in prayer, John playing his guitar, Leah singing with her beautiful voice, herself and Josh all working in the village and being accepted by all. Then there were others who came forward to receive the ultimate Gift. Seeing this and how she and the others were about to be used Angelica was filled with elation until…

A huge force…an army of hundreds in all terrain trucks swarmed the premises…and a systematic and methodical slaughter began. Soldiers, wearing UWF Force bands shot semi-automatic machine guns, threw grenades, and used machetes to kill each and every person gathered. Adults of every age, children, and infants were slain; decapitated with cold precision and in some cases sadistic means were employed as pregnant women were not only beheaded, but cut open so that the unborn child was as well. And as the screams of the dying pierced the air, their blood, limbs, heads and corpses congealed, created a gruesome lake that turned the grass and soil into a sticky crimson morass…

Angelica gasped and trembled, her chest tightened as she felt suffocated and sickened by the hideous tableau. The brutality continued while she sought escape by covering her eyes but the gory scene was implanted in her mind's eye and she stifled a scream as she broke down weeping.

"Oh dear Lord," she sobbed. "I-is t-this t-true? W-will this actually happen? Is this really what we've been called to do? H-how c-can I t-tell the others w-when it will be us bringing these people to this place…t-to die?" She shook her head numbly as the scene continued unfolding around her.

The gentle voice that spoke before said, **"Keep watching, Daughter."**

Hearing that Angelica looked up dully, her eyes half lidded as she prepared herself for even more horror when the scene changed. She then watched in rapt amazement as from the seeming mountain of mutilated bodies, and dismembered heads bright orbs of light rose out of the slain saints that once again became bodies; whole in heaven. From a revolting spectacle there emerged the thousands, clothed in radiant robes of white that ascended to a place bathed in light, before a crystal throne. Then the scene vanished as the room was also flooded with light with the appearance of a figure; with hair white and eyes like flames of fire bearing the scars of the Crucifixion. Seeing this Angelica fell prostrate before Him…

He spoke in a voice of assurance, **"Are you sure now, Daughter."**

Her head still on the ground she replied in quavering voice, "Oh, yes, Lord…please forgive me for doubting."

"I have not erred in choosing you to receive the message. Now write everything down as you have seen but when you tell the others do not reveal all…just what you have seen that will be your tasks. Keep the other things unknown for the human heart is fickle and sways easily. Bear the burden well."

The light then disappeared and Angelica slowly raised her head, glancing about as she sighed and calmed her pounding heart. She then leaned over the crate and opening the notebook, picked up the pen to write…

Outside in the common area the others were still in a state of amazement over having witnessed the miracle that had been broadcast to the world. And the comments ranged from stunned awe to guarded cynicism…this from Josh. He was over the initial wonder and now back into his usual skeptical mode he began to criticize the event, displaying his innate suspicion of the UWC Leader.

"Well that was unexpected…everything that's happened up to now's been easily explained…the aversion of disasters, sick people healed, and all that. But this…has no explanation."

Still astounded by what he saw John said, "Yeah but we all saw what we saw, dude. Elias was dead…and Abram brought him back. Spin it any way you want it's still a miracle."

"Miracle or not, I still don't trust him." Josh's gunmetal orbs were narrowed and he scowled as he leaned against the wall, staring.

Leah gazed at him and although she said nothing understood his attitude. She knew the true root of his ongoing animosity and kept the promise they made when he told her about its source by keeping silent. But her eyes met his in empathy and he sent her a slight wink in grateful acknowledgement.

Peter sighed and reasoned, "Yeah, well there's no other way to see it. Elias and Abram weren't exactly buddies so there's no way they could have staged this. Face it guys, Abram's got real deal supernatural powers…he is the Antichrist."

Brother Danny affirmed, "That he is…and now that a covenant with Israel is imminent, our mission is about to start." He then exited and headed into the computer room.

And then the door to the room where Angelica had been isolated these past days opened, drawing everybody's attention. She stepped out and they all rushed to her, Peter getting there first.

Eyeing her in concern he asked, "Hey…are you okay?"

Josh said, "Long time, no see."

John added, "Yeah, we wondered if you'd ever join us in the land of the living."

Leah nodded and said, "You didn't even come out to eat… you must be starving."

As the others waited with worried expressions Angelica looked at all of them with a strangely guarded expression of her own…almost as if she felt guilty about something and owed them an apology. But she quickly covered it with a smile…

"I'm fine, everyone…and it's time for us to move." She held up the notebook and gestured for everyone to take a seat but as she went to join them Peter detained her by grasping her arm.

"You're sure you're alright?" he asked dubiously, his cerulean eyes probing.

Gazing back at his scrutiny Angelica felt pinned as she asked, "What makes you think I'm not?"

Ever observant Peter reached over and brushed his index finger gently down her cheek, tracing the wet trail from her eye…the track of her tears. He then gazed at her, waiting.

She met his eyes with hers as if to plead please don't ask… then assured him, "It's all good…so let's not keep the others waiting."

Angelica went over to where the others were and with no other choice left to him Peter followed…

CHAPTER 2—
TRIMMING THE LAMPS

In the computer room Brother Danny sat at the keyboard, using the secret messaging software developed by him and Josh to communicate with a certain ally. He did this by tapping into a basic online IM then used an encryption code that rendered the chats nonexistent to anybody but the two communicating, using the software to send messages to a man by the name Mordachi Malensky, alias Michael Malachi…the leader and organizer of a group of insurgents that have refused to take the TM chip and eluded capture and execution. Malachi was actually Daniel Roccque's former seminary roommate; a Messianic Jew who converted from his conservative roots. He typed in a generic greeting and immediately a window popped up…

Preparations for UR2K are proceeding…migratory routes planned throughout the South Kingdom in four locations…to meet Disciples. Mission status needed…

Daniel typed back: *Mission to commence…about to receive marching orders from Angel…deployment of Full Armor to commence in 24…tell Disciples to expect arrival then…Shalom.*

The window then closed and Daniel logged off. He reached for a manila file and then headed out to the common area…

Over there in the area the party of five sat as Angelica was perched in a subdued position with head bowed while the others were circled around her. She eschewed offers of food or urging of rest from a worried Leah while the men all stared at her, waiting…

John spoke first. "I take it that you have where we're to go and what we're to do for our first mission."

She nodded and replied, "Yes," but ventured nothing more.

Josh, fighting his innate impatience asked, "So…can we at least know where we're heading?"

Angelica looked up at him just as Brother Danny stepped up to the group to answer for her, "I have the particulars of information concerning a place that needs our assistance…the continent of Africa to be exact…now known in the UWC as the South Kingdom." He looked at her for confirmation…

She nodded and opened her notebook as he continued, "There is to be four mass executions or 'disposals' as the UWC Leader calls them of those refusing to take the TM chip."

Peter nodded as he affirmed cryptically, "I hear that was decided as the most efficient…and humane way to dispose of the rebels."

"Yeah right," Josh snorted. "That's a load of bull…they still slaughter innocent people…adults, children, babies…it doesn't matter. And the fact that they're poor and starving makes it even worse."

At that Angelica bit her lip, clenched her hands on the notebook and cast her eyes to Brother Danny who went on…

"The insurgent group known as COS or Children of Shem is planning an operation…code named UR2K…Underground Railroad 2000 to move these people to a secret place for them to gather to be ushered into the presence of the Savior."

"So when are these…executions supposed to take place?" Leah wanted to know.

Brother Danny replied, "In approximately two weeks." He opened his manila folder and added ruefully, "Governor Uwamba of the South Kingdom likes to make a statement and since his UWF forces have combed the continent and completed distributing the TM chip…and have gathered those refusing in four locations for simultaneous executions, wiping everyone out in one fell swoop." His disgust was evident as he finished, "According to my source, he plans on making it a holiday, with arranged worldwide media coverage."

Josh snapped, "That sick son of a—,"

"Josh!" Leah admonished.

Duly chastised he apologized with a sheepish expression. "Sorry."

Peter smirked and John snickered as Brother Danny said, "That's okay, Josh…believe me a few choice words came to mind when my source first sent me the report and I read it. But inherent evil is in this world and is looked at as right…so things like this are to be expected…but not accepted…by the Lord or us."

Peter asked, "So who exactly is this source?"

"A man called Mordecai Malensky…real name Michael Mordecai. He's a former commander in the Mossad…the Israeli Special Forces. He resigned his post just after the Great Vanishing and through the Web has recruited and amassed a force worldwide through covert means. And I've been assisting him as we've used an encoded and encrypted program that enables us to communicate hope through the Word to those awaiting the injection of the TM chip and plan on refusing without being tracked along with directions to escape to designated safe houses or harbors. The program was designed by our own resident computer expert, Joshua."

Josh smirked as he said, "It was easy to create…and a pleasure when Brother Dan told me that he wanted to go undercover on the Web to send encouragement and prayers in a way that couldn't be traced."

Everyone was visibly impressed with John saying, "Sweet deal, dude…I had no idea you had that kind of talent."

Josh shrugged as he responded, "It was nothing…anyone who knows basic encrypting can create a way to operate without detection to the average person. But a BH can figure it out."

"A BH?" Leah asked. "What's that?"

"A Black Hat, little bird. That's a hacker term for a cyber criminal...someone who steals identities and such. But he can also figure out any back door of any program. Which is why I made this program with very intricate encryptions...very hard to break into."

Peter smirked as he said archly, "Sounds like you've done this before."

"I plead the fifth, man...if the Constitution is still even recognized." Josh's tone was dubious as the atmosphere became subdued, everyone thinking about the world in which they now lived.

Brother Danny broke in. "So now we need to know—,"

He eyed Angelica meaningfully who up until then had been silent with her head bowed. However, she raised her head and opened her notebook to speak...

"The place for this gathering is a village in Tanzania...south of the southern coast of Lake Victoria in the wilderness that is known as the Central Zambezian Miombo woodlands... because of its locality it is perfect for migration...since the lake is the source of the Nile and the border of Rwanda is near. Also, because it's a thickly wooded area close to the mountains, the place is hard to find...the perfect refuge." She pulled out a perfectly drawn map of Africa with four different locations; north, south, east and west...

"Uwamba has designated four areas as disposal camps...one in the Sudan...one in South Africa...one in Nigeria and one in

Ethiopia. These areas have been chosen because they have shown the least resistance to the mandatory ID plantings. Ironically, these locations are also significant because they were all areas which had been places of either great freedom or oppression before the Rapture. And Ethiopia had ancient significance going back to the days of Noah when his son Ham settled there after the Flood. We'll be rescuing those in the camps."

Without skipping a beat she turned a page in her notebook and pointed to the map. "The best time to perform the rescues will be at night. John will be sent to the Sudan, Peter to South Africa, Josh to Ethiopia and Leah and I are to go to Nigeria. But first, we are to go to the village named 'Adanech' which means 'she has rescued them' and meet the two disciples that we're helping. Their names are Hasani and Disa. They, like us are new Christians on a mission to direct the rescues by encrypted online messages with secret cell groups that are also rebels that have refused the mark and eluded capture."

Brother Danny broke in, "As I told you before I have had constant contact with the leader of a worldwide group of Messianic believers numbering 144,000…they're known as COS or Children of Shem who have also eluded capture for refusing the TM implant. They're using the same encryption program that we developed to communicate where and when the mass disposals are taking place. And they're also helping those who wish to refuse to hide until we can get them to designated harbors where they can be brought to Christ. Under the cover of night the ones resisting have been migrating to the village but they are under constant peril doing so because of the seeding raids."

"Seeding raids?" John asked, confused.

"Yes…the UWC has recently completed a global census after the Great Vanishing to keep track of the remaining population. But even with the latest technology the rolls are being done by region to ensure that everyone has the TM chip implant with the most advanced nations…like here in North America, Europe, Asia, having the most people with the chip. But less advanced and more remote areas are being systematically sifted through with so-called 'seeding raids' to accomplish this. With the ongoing famine in these poorer parts they are easily convinced by the promise of food."

Leah asked Daniel, "I never heard of this. How did you find out about all of this?"

"Through Malensky…his abilities as a former Mossad commander comprised of covert activities that included gathering information undetected…he's a BH level hacker and can get through any firewall to obtain secret files."

"My kind of guy," Josh remarked. A born tactician and already visualizing the mission he then asked, "So we're to assist these Children of Shem to bring those who want to refuse taking the TM chip to a designated place to be led to Christ. Then what?"

His question hung in the air like thick smoke and the other three…John, Leah, and Peter gazed at both Angelica and Daniel…the messengers for all intents and purposes. The older man remained silent but the young woman whose name described her role calmly met the curious eyes trained upon her…

"It will be revealed…in all good time," she replied with quiet authority that rendered everyone, even Josh…silent.

Brother Danny then rose and said, "I think we should eat… then after a time of study and prayer we should all get some rest. Tomorrow we will prepare for departure." Almost as if he knew her burden he placed a fatherly hand on Angelica's shoulder then turned and headed back into the computer room…

After supper they all gathered again…a somber group that seemed to be restless and poised for combat as Brother Danny shared several scriptures about battle…starting with Joshua in Exodus, Numbers, the book of Joshua and finishing up with Jehoshaphat in 2 Chronicles. Through these passages, he pointed out the faith that sustained the warriors even in the face of imminent defeat, pointing out that the outcome belongs to the Lord. He finished with a reminder before they adjourned…

"Just remember, people…whatever happens as the outcome of this mission your steps are ordered by the Lord…like David said in Psalm 37:23…please keep that in mind…Good night."

The bearded mentor then rose and headed into the room that Angelica had been in as she was isolated, waiting for God's order the past days. And as he withdrew the atmosphere was tense between the Full Armor Team while each one contemplated about what lay ahead, still seated in a circle…each silent; pensive.

After an undetermined time John spoke softly, "Well I guess we'd better grab some sack 'cause it looks like we're heading to Africa."

Both Peter and Josh grunted in agreement and Leah nodded but Angelica just sat there, her eyes downcast as if she was again distancing herself from everyone. However, Leah even with her limited vision saw the strain in the pretty blonde member of the group and laid a gentle hand upon her shoulder…

"Angie…are you alright?" Leah's soft inquiry garnered the men's attention as well as the three all stared at her with looks that were concerned and from Peter's direction downright worried.

Angelica sighed. The entire evening her mind had been filled with the constant replays of the visions shown her by the Spirit and try as she might she could not shake the myriad of emotions roiling inside from the experience. Yet the admonition from the Lord was clear and her desire to be obedient strong. So she took a deep breath and drew from her Savior's strength and the promises of the Word. She raised her head and met them with a genuine smile…

"I'm fine, guys…just tired. So don't worry, okay?" She got up and went to where the bedrolls were and taking hers began to unfurl it and spread it out to prepare for bed.

The other four all exchanged glances, shrugged and followed suit…

It was just past midnight when asleep Peter found himself immersed within a dream…

He was standing engulfed by a gray mist…not dark or light but a region just between; a place that was formless and vague, like a dense

fog that left one disoriented and unsure where to move. However, this was not how Peter felt as he tried to decipher his whereabouts amidst the drifting wisps. It was a strange place but what was stranger still was his state of emotion…he was neither fearful nor confused but instead held a feeling of calm expectancy. And he stood there a light emerged and became steadily brighter, driving him to become prone face down…

A voice that spoke with authority called to him. **"Peter…"**

He knew the voice and answered without hesitation, "Yes Lord."

"You are named after the Rock on which I built My Church…the cornerstone and as the leader of the gleaners you too are a cornerstone as well as a sheath. You are to protect them all but most importantly you must protect My chosen herald."

"Your herald, Lord?" Again immediately knowing he stated, "Angelica."

"Yes…for she has been shown the path…and will be shown to the others leading to the harvest fields…along with the things that will come to pass. The burden is hers to bear and it is a heavy one so you must help her by being the Rock that supports her and the sheath that protects her."

Understanding everything with amazing clarity Peter answered, "Yes Lord." Feeling compelled to raise his head he did and saw the face of his mother as she stood before him. Tears began welling up as his mother's verdant eyes broadcast her love to him…

"Mom? I-is that really you?"

Ruthanne Baines Roccque smiled at her only child. "Hello Peter… how have you been?"

He wiped the tears from his eyes. "I-I'm okay…I've been safe, hidden in a place with friends."

"I'm glad…I wondered how you were, left behind. But I knew that you would be alright if you turned to our loving Savior for guidance and strength. And you have."

Peter nodded then asked, "Mom…you knew, right? That I'd be left behind?"

Ruthanne nodded. "I knew that bitterness had festered inside you…anger toward your father's actions; his affair, leaving us made you bitter. All of that you held away from me, hiding it behind your hard work and smile…but I knew. Your unforgiveness had become the tie that bound you to earth and blocked your way, Peter. But you're a man and made your own choices."

Feeling chastisement even with those gracious words Peter lowered his head and apologized, "I'm sorry, Mom…for ignoring you all those times you tried to get me to prepare for the day." He brightened and raised his head with determination lighting his cerulean eyes as he finished, "But I'm where the Lord wants me to be…and I'm ready to do anything He wants me to do."

"I see." Ruthanne smiled serenely as she stepped back, slowly receding into the mists. "Then all I'll say is…do your best…and I'll be waiting at the Banquet Table for you at the Marriage Supper. Farewell for now, my son."

"Mom." Peter spoke her name as she vanished then he heard the muted strains of a piano…playing Chopin's Etude Opus 10 Number 3, named Tristesse…Parting Song in French. The song she played endlessly on her piano after his father's betrayal and departure…

"Huh?" Peter woke up and sat bolt upright as he continued to hear the song then glanced around at the others in the dark area, the only light from a lantern. He saw that John and Josh were both asleep, with John snoring softly and then over at the girls' sleeping area he saw just Leah. But Angelica's bedroll was empty. Disturbed, he scanned the common area to search for her but she was nowhere to be seen.

Where can she be? Uneasy from his dream and the melancholy music that seemed to be coming from one of the two other rooms in the bunker Peter got up carefully to not wake the others and made his way around to the closed door of the computer room. Spying a light from underneath, he quietly turned the knob and opened the door…

He was relieved to see the one that he was seeking. Angelica was there, listening to the Chopin piece…a beautiful orchestration with piano and violin on the computer with her eyes closed, having fallen asleep. Enthralled by picture she made and suppressing the urge to reach for her Peter silently gazed at her and then his heart caught when he saw a tear trickle past her lashes and down her cheek.

She's crying…just like before when she came out of the prayer room… she tried to hide it but I knew. I saw the tears on her face. What did she see? And why won't she tell us? The Lord's words, spoken in his dream then echoed inside…

The burden is hers to bear and it is a heavy one so you must help her by being the Rock that supports her and the sheath that protects her."

T*he rock that supports her and the sheath that protects her...*Peter leaned down and gently scooped Angelica up into his arms. In a deep sleep she stirred slightly and curled in to him, causing his heart to quicken. He then softly crept into the common area, past the guys and Leah and knelt down, cradling her head as he lay her down on the bedroll. He gently reached and covered her up then this time following his desires caressed her cheek with the back of his hand. Leaning back watching her until the finale of the etude faded away into silence Peter then made his vow...

*No matter what happens...I swear I'll protect you...*He rose and returned to his own bedroll to finally fall sleep.

Tomorrow...the mission begins...

Several thousand miles and four time zones to the east in the wilderness jungle of Tanzania the sun was shining over the mirror surface of Lake Victoria in the distance of the village of Adanech...appearing like a red disk immerging from the water, laced with purple clouds as dawn broke revealing a lone figure knelt at the lake's south shore. Hasani Kelile Okoro...a tall man of dark and muscular appearance was in deep reflection and prayer as daylight began, like every day since the day of the Great Vanishing when he gave his life to Jesus. But this day was different for this day he knew his real mission was about to begin...

That day he and his wife Disa Chiuke Okoro both witnessed the way friends and family all vanished right before their eyes, fulfilling the foretelling they had heard countless times but considered nonsense. However, after seeing the truth they both cried out for salvation from the Savior. From then on, they purposed to serve Him by helping others open their eyes, creating a refuge for those who shunned the TM chip. Word of mouth spread from city to town to village to village and more people were arriving every day after traveling all night under the cover of night to Adanech, which was hidden within the deepest part of the Central Zambezian Miombo wilderness but the UWF was managing to herd most rebels in four separate holding places for the mass execution South Kingdom Supreme Governor Uwamba was planning. Hasani had been taught prophecy in Sunday services and had listened with a then unbelieving ear but now saw everything eerily falling into place.

As the sun rose so did Hasani with mixed emotions…great anticipation with great sadness as he knew what lay ahead; getting into and driving a jeep back into the wilderness and to the village as daylight chased night's shadows away. But the impending darkness that he knew was coming lay across his shoulders; like a yoke of almost unbearable weight…

Lord, this must be how You felt on the way to the Skull…as You bore Your Cross. But I am not bruised and bleeding, I haven't been beaten…yet the day draws close and I am filled with unspeakable joy, knowing that You have chosen me for this appointed time…

As he pulled out of the wilderness and into the clearing the village stood before Hasani and he saw the stirrings of early morning…everyone preparing for breakfast, men tending goats…sleepy children wandering out of huts yawning and wiping their eyes. Then behind the traditional primitive setup was a former secret military base with barrack like dormitories in rows, a storehouse, a former mess hall known as the meeting house, and a platform that resembled an outdoor stage, like for concerts He drove into the square and spotted the trim form of his wife, preparing the daily lessons for the village…

Disa looked up from the bible she was using to create word fill-ins for the middle school age children she was teaching saw her husband's tall form exit the vehicle and rose to greet him as he came over to her. They exchanged a kiss then she spoke…

"Is the time drawing near?"

"Yes…the executions will be in a over a fortnight so we must move now." Hasani glanced at the hut behind her and asked, "Did you see anything on the laptop…any messages?"

"I haven't checked it…you should."

"Yah." He went over to the communication shed; right behind the meeting house and sat before the computer.

The village was actually a blend of modern mixed with primitive. The home huts had no electricity but the dorms and the largest structure…the meeting and worship house were powered by a generator…one large gasoline one that powered the lights and the high tech communications equipment all provided by the covert and powerful secret organization known as COS…and Hasani was a free-lance operative working in conjunction with them…

He sat on a folding chair and opened the laptop, booting it up then logging into a popular social networking site then entering an encrypted code watched as a private message window popped up with the following…

"Armor" is ready for deployment…will be arriving in 24H at the airfield in Mwanza…Transport Armor to village for strategizing URY2K. Further communications with COS when final strategy complete…

Hasani logged out *Well Lord…as You said the mission begins…*

Back in the States the five youths known now collectively as Full Armor or FA were making last preparations for their journey, packing carry on bags for two weeks with just clothing, footwear and toothbrushes…barebones necessities to allow for no delays during pre-flight bag and body searches. With the beefed up almost paranoiac travel regulations from the UWF toiletries were considered contraband and could be purchased at the airport when they landed. So keeping everything in mind they were gathering the few belongings they were to bring.

The two girls, Leah and Angelica were finishing the packing while they and the boys were huddled with Brother Danny getting the itinerary for their trip. He handed out the plane tickets…

"Here are your tickets…the five of you are anthropology majors from Harvard on a sabbatical for a class on Third World cultures. The tickets were actually obtained from a faculty member of the anthropology department who happens to be a

COS operative so your roles are legitimate should there be any question at airport security checks."

John gave a long low whistle. "Wow…these guys are everywhere, aren't they?"

Daniel nodded. "As I said there's 144,000 worldwide…all Messianic Jews and recruited in secret by Michael Mordecai and dedicated to the cause of our mission…code named 'The Gleaning' or gathering after the harvest…which was the Great Vanishing or the Rapture."

Peter nodded in understanding as he remarked, "Like in Revelation."

"Precisely."

Josh, always the practical one pointed out, "But what about the TM chip? We can't go anywhere without it for ID and none of us have it."

Daniel smiled and directed, "Place your right hands over the brooch you received when you had the visitation."

All five glanced down at the brooch and then did as he asked. As their hands touched, they glowed golden then the appearance of the symbol of the TM chip…a stylized graphic of the demonic numeral "666" was on the front of their right hand. It was the exact mark that everyone was taking globally…except for themselves and those they were to rescue…

"The mark will stay with you as long as the brooch is on you as will your powers," Daniel pointed out. "However, if it's removed all of your powers…and the mark…will vanish. So keep it on at all times during the mission…it will guard your lives."

All five nodded solemnly as they continued to finish packing… except for Josh, who was in the computer room gathering together a laptop, compact high capacity portable hard drive, and several flash drives along with a broadband 4G modem with Wi-Fi and satellite capability. As he was packing the plug and play peripherals Daniel joined him.

"You all set, Josh? That portable HD ought to provide enough memory to continue to infiltrate and monitor the UWC databases and information sites without detection or glitches from the OS…COS and Malensky will need daily status updates."

"Yeah, I think so." He zipped up the case and asked, "Hey BD…are we gonna be okay carrying all this with us? I mean, I know it's typical now to have all this but with the UWF at airport security checkpoints making it tight will bringing the extra drives raise any suspicions?"

Daniel shook his head. "It shouldn't. In the event that you do run into a problem the computer, hard and flash drives serial numbers are registered with the anthropology department thanks to the COS faculty member who'll vouch for you. And the modem is universal."

"Covered all the bases, huh?" Josh was impressed.

Daniel's visage…and response was grave. "To complete the Lord's work now…we have to."

About two hours later the five FA members were on a MTA shuttle bus for Logan International and headed into Boston. They were able to test out the faux TM chip when they caught the bus in Concord at the depot as they passed through with no difficulty. So any anxiety about being exposed was dispelled as they melted into the groups of other travelers heading to the busy airport. Sitting inside the close confines of the bus the five kept the conversation light; all in line with their roles as college students...they even had textbooks with them to promote the appearance. So when the bus arrived at the drop off terminal for their flight the portal for the pre-flight body and baggage inspection stood as their next test. They split up...girls with the women, boys with the men. The first one to go through was John, who waited as he was patted down and had his pockets checked. He had brought along his guitar in a case and the airport inspection officer for the UWF had checked his fake TM chip for ID and information, scanning his body...

Shining the special inferred detector on his right hand the officer recited, "Pax, John, 21...anthropology major at Harvard." He gestured to the case. "So why are you bringing the guitar with you?"

"Why do you think?"

"Just answer the question."

John rolled his eyes *is he for real?* "I just like to bring music wherever I go."

"Is that a fact?" The officer, a burly, drill sergeant type with glacial eyes ordered, "Put it up here…now."

Complying John, eyeing the dour officer grinned as he inquired, "Hey man what's the big deal? It's just a guitar…I'm not carrying a bomb or machine gun like Al Capone."

"Uh-huh." The man opened the case and saw the contents as such…an acoustic guitar, some picks in a plastic bag and a folder of sheet music. He even reached his hand into the instrument as if to search for something. However, finding nothing the officer said, "Looks okay," then went through John's duffel bag and after rifling through his clothes he signaled that he had passed.

As he went through the portal the joker in John could not resist. He turned toward the others and gave a mock "Seig heil!" which although it garnered some snickers from Josh and Peter earned him a glare from the officer.

"What're you…a comedian? Get going," he snapped then turned to Peter and said sharply, "You a funny guy like your buddy over there?"

He swallowed his mirth and answered promptly, "No sir."

The officer grunted and ran the scanner on Peter's body first then on his right hand for identification. "Roccque, Peter…20, anthropology major, Harvard." He patted him down, checked his pockets then bade, "Put your bag up here."

Peter did as he was told and waited as his duffle bag was searched thoroughly. Finding his cell phone the officer ran the

X-ray scanner over with no problem and then after waving him through gestured to Josh…

"You with those two?"

"Yeah."

The officer repeated the pat down and body search, then ran the scanner on him stopping at his right hand. "Nunn, Joshua…20, anthropology major, Harvard." He remarked snidely, "So you three are Harvard brats, huh?"

Josh did not bat an eye. "So what?"

"Where are you guys going anyway?"

Josh replied archly, "What business is it of yours?"

With a scowl the officer snapped, "Don't smart mouth me, kid…I can make sure that the three of you don't go anywhere." He gestured to a group of travelers being held in a detention room where UWF soldiers were running further investigations and searches.

Taking note of the strongly implied threat Josh grunted then answered woodenly, "We're heading to Africa to study different former Third World cultures to research material for our Masters theses…*sir*."

The sarcastic emphasis on the address of respect was not lost on the officer as he made a sound that was a cross between a snicker and a snort and said, "Is that so? Well, put your bags up here, Professor."

This guy's a real tool Irked Josh did what the officer told him and as he watched him go through his bag suppressed the urge to make a cutting remark or two about how it felt going through people's underwear for a living. But considering the way the guy was acting he decided to keep his witticisms to himself.

The officer finished inspecting the duffle bag with his clothes and then turned to the computer case. "Empty it."

Josh unzipped the case and took out the laptop, external HD, flash drives, and modem. The officer, getting ready to scan the electronics grunted and remarked, "You got a lot of hardware there, Poindexter…why so much?"

His temper rising along with his anxiety Josh snapped, "Look, I can bring these…they aren't against regulations so what's with the interrogation, man?"

The officer got right into his face. "Because of the law, genius. Suppose you're one of those lowlife Rebel scum and you're planning a terrorist act. It's *my* job to make sure you don't succeed, got it? And for your information, these items although you're allowed to carry them aboard the aircraft must be scanned individually for possible concealed contraband explosive detonators. Understand?"

"Yeah," he replied, his expression sullen.

"So answer me…why do you need so much data storage?" His lupine eyes pinned the FA youth.

Thinking quickly Josh met him unflinchingly. "Because we will be using the video cam in the computer to shoot interviews with villagers for our theses, *sir*. And I don't want to max out my hard drive on the laptop by saving them there. Does that answer your question?"

The officer growled, "Don't use that tone of voice with me…I thought I told you to watch that smart mouth…now step aside."

They met eye to eye and man to man for a moment…then Josh made a gesture as if to say "Be my guest" and stepped back as the officer scanned the laptop and the drives. Finding nothing he grunted and pointed at the computer case…

"Pack it up and move along," the officer said gruffly then watched with a thoughtful frown as Josh did and left to join Peter and John, waiting for him. However, Josh using his peripheral vision saw the officer's glare and turned to his comrades.

"Let's go find the girls and bounce."

Curious, Peter asked, "Problems?"

"Nope…just premonitions…so let's find them and get to the plane."

"Yeah, I hear ya," John agreed. "That's one creepy dude."

They headed off into the airport to search for the girls…

Meanwhile, Angelica and Leah having gone through the security check with nothing more than some inconvenience and a few indignities were seated in the waiting area for their overseas flight. And so they chatted as they both watched for the three young men…

Leah, heaving a deep sigh remarked, "That was awkward and unpleasant."

"Uh-huh," Angelica nodded and said, "Especially the full body search…I swear the officer doing it was deliberately taking her time. She reminded me of half the gym teachers in school… definitely same-sex oriented. The way she was smiling as she searched us I'm sure she was enjoying herself…ehhhh!" She shuddered in revulsion.

"I'll take your word for it 'cause you can see more than I can." Leah giggled and added more somberly, "But really at this time there's such an…immorality, even worse than before the Great Vanishing. So much is given a blind eye and deaf ear now."

The bearer of the Breastplate of Righteousness nodded, "The scriptures are clear…in the last days there was a falling away and now that the Bride's been removed evil and immoral behavior is accepted as normal." She sighed and added, "So to keep a low profile we have to just endure."

"True…we have to blend into the crowd…to get the mission done. And that reminds me…I hope the guys are okay. Doesn't it seem like they're taking a bit longer to get through then we did?"

Angelica glanced at the clock near the flight board. "Yeah…I wonder if they ran into problems. Josh has the computer and other equipment with him; I hope he hasn't been detained like the girl in front of us was, remember how they took her into the detention room and confiscated her computer? As you just said we need to keep a low profile and we both know Josh speaks his mind, no matter what…or who. John and Peter I'm not so worried about…but Josh?" She looked right at Leah and asked, "Am I wrong?"

"No, I agree," the redhead said reluctantly. "Peter doesn't seem to be the belligerent type…and my brother, well he's more of a joker than anything…and that might get him into trouble. But you're kind of right about Josh. If he feels that he's being looked down upon or threatened he reacts…strongly." Her expression became pensive as she added, "But he has his reasons for being that way."

Angelica heard her companion's defense of the sometimes cantankerous youth, saw her lost in thought and feeling a bit guilty about her observation admitted, "Well, you've known him longer then I have. Knowing him in the short time I have I've noticed he can be…uh, difficult."

Leah nodded with a smile. "Yeah, he can be…but he doesn't go out of his way to pick fights. He's just not afraid to stand up for what he believes, even if he bucks authority to do it. His principles are very firm."

Angelica smiled back as she remarked, "You seem to understand him."

Leah gazed down and said softly, "I do. He's just like all of us, Angie. Trying to find our ways as the Lord directs us in a world that no longer welcomes us."

"Uh-huh." The conversation ended on that note as they both had nothing more to say…

However, Leah's profound statement brought Angelica into deep thought about what she knew lay ahead. And she wondered how they all would react to the tragedy that would take place on the heels of the gathering of those refusing the mark when they all believed that they were only being used by the Lord to bring them to salvation…

She spoke to herself dismally *I wonder just what the reaction will be from all of them…I know what to expect from Josh but what about John, Leah, and Peter? Will they hate me for not telling them everything? Or change their minds when they see that we are being used to literally lead people to their deaths while we survive? We're so new at being Christians, will firm principles and a desire to serve God be enough to keep us focused?* Her mind teeming with questions she barely noticed as Josh, John, and Peter emerged from the crowd and approached her and Leah…

"Hey ladies," John said with a wave.

They took seats in the chairs facing Angelica and Leah who said, "Finally! We were getting worried about you."

Josh put his computer case down and apologized, "Sorry about that little bird, but we just went through the Great

Inquisition." He then eyed her and asked grimly, "How about you...did they do anything to you...anything at all?"

His meaning clear she shook her head and replied, "No... it was strange and somewhat intrusive but I survived. So relax, Josh."

He grunted, dubious but accepting of her statement. And Peter, noticing Angelica's reticence studied her faraway expression and asked, "What about you...everything okay?"

Shaken from her reverie she looked up at the three men... John had a questioning look, Peter was gently concerned but Josh was intense as he urged, "Tell us, Angie...did they do anything to you girls?"

"You think I lied to you?" Leah inquired of Josh with a raised brow.

"Not at all," he hastened to answer. "It's just that I saw what an idiot the guy who we had was and I want to see if he was the exception...not the rule. So talk to us, Angelica."

Angelica saw that he was not going to give up...probably based on his own experience. So she gave him a smile and shrugged as she replied, "It's just as Leah said...not a great experience but we got through it." Then she pointed out, "But we both agreed that it's to be expected in the world the way it is now."

Peter agreed, "That's right...if we're to blend in we need to relax and to realize that this is the way things are now. And that goes especially for you, Josh. You were a little too mouthy to the airport officer before and I thought you were gonna be pulled into the detention room."

"Hey Pete, the guy was a jerk, man," Josh said defensively.

"Yeah…but he was baiting you, dude…and if you got into it any more and ended up in the detention room to get interrogated they'd have called the school and even though the COS man there would have vouched for us our cover would have been compromised. You know how the UWF works pal; it would've been hell to pay and no way to start our work. So just dial it down."

Chastened Josh grunted and nodded.

Peter continued, "The larger picture is our mission and what we have to accomplish…no matter what. What we have to go through to get there is insignificant." His cerulean eyes, filled with calm authority met the entire group but came to rest especially on Angelica.

Everyone nodded at the wielder of the Sword of the Spirit as Josh conceded, "Yeah, I hear ya."

Peter's right…and he will understand when the time comes…I can feel it at that thought Angelica saw his eyes meet hers in affirmation… and then knew instinctually that he would be an ally, her ally… always.

The PA system then announced their flight so the five young people gathered their things…and headed to board the plane; their first step of a very long journey. The trip was to be about sixteen hours…five hours to London…then ten hours on a redeye to Dar Es Salaam…with the final leg to Mwanza on a private plane then after meeting with a member of the village about a two hour and a half drive taking them to the final destination; the gathering place called Adanech…

The flight to London was smooth and uneventful…even getting through airport security went without a hitch as all five were in game mode as their mission stood topmost in their minds. But the British Airways flight to the large Tanzanian airport Dar Es Salaam was delayed for a few hours because of an occurrence of the infamous London fog. So when they finally were able to board and were airborne it was nearly midnight. Stowing their gear and taking their seats…John and Josh flanking Leah in the middle aisle and Peter sitting beside Angelica at the right window, the FA members settled themselves in and tried to get some sleep as the craft reached cruising altitude…

Fighting restlessness Angelica, as she entered a REM cycle saw in her dream the same vision she had seen when the Holy Spirit first gave her the mission…with the same outcome. It had been a constant thought; daily with her and as such engraved on the walls of her subconscious…unforgettable. However, now that they actually were en route to the mission the vision was even more vivid; her sight of the vicious extermination of people they would soon meet face to face in startling clarity. So perhaps that was the reason why her heart constricted sharply and she awoke with a gasp; as from a horrific nightmare.

Immediately, a warm baritone spoke her name softly calling her into full wakefulness…

"Angelica…Angelica? Are you alright?" Peter's even features showed concern as he leaned in, taking her hand.

She gazed back at her teammate, still upset from the vision and nodded. "Yeah…just a bad dream I guess." She then gave him a shaky smile and said, "Must be nerves about the first mission."

Peter eyed her askance and responded, "I guess." He then added, "You know, you can tell me about it if you want…why you're nervous." His gaze was direct yet empathetic; as if he knew that she would refuse and even why as he finished, "But it's okay if you don't want to."

Angelica lowered her head to avoid his stare. "It's not that I don't want to Peter, it's just that I—,"

"Can't." He completed her statement with the same look of perception and instantly she thought *he knows…and even if he doesn't, he understands…like before in the airport I can feel it.* Her conclusion was affirmed when he leaned closer, his expression earnest…

"I want you to know something, Angel. Whatever happens down the road, I've got your back. You don't have to worry because I will support and protect you, no matter what…I promise." His statement was steadfast and frank, leaving no doubt.

Drawn to the warmth and sincerity of his eyes Angelica felt a release. However she met him with the same level of intensity. "No questions asked?"

He nodded solemnly and replied without hesitation. "No questions asked."

No questions asked…it became their pact; between the two of them exclusively so with Peter's candid answer Angelica was filled with assurance and she entwined her fingers with his. Their bond established they both laid back and like their comrades, closed their eyes to sleep. So while the Full Armor team sought much needed repose the plane carried them to where the Lord's great work was waiting for them.

CHAPTER 3—COUNTERFEIT LIGHT

While the FA team had been traveling to their first mission the news about the Israeli prime minister's resurrection from the dead was trumpeted everywhere as a post-modern day miracle… performed by the man now presented as the shining light of hope to a world that was in chaos following the Great Vanishing… Isaac Abram. In fact, the entire world was now under the control of the UWC Leader and his Chief Administrative and Spiritual Advisor…Ichabod. The global media UWCPI potent media propaganda machine was using all of its power to deify Abram…even going so far as to actually call him "messiah" or "savior" of the world; accepted now by everyone. What was the one obstacle to complete world unity was now removed as thanks to his miraculous return from the netherworld Lazerai Elias gladly joined the rest of the world. His affirmation of that was solidified with the covenant struck between himself and Abram. The announcement came as a special report, broadcast throughout the world.

In the front of the Metcal Tower, where just three days ago he had lain in state dead, Elias stood with the UWC Supreme Leader amid the television cameras, print and internet media as the historic event took place…

"As leader of the Jewish State of Israel I am here to greet you all…and to thank all of you for the support and love you have shown me and my family during my ordeal. The cards and messages sent to us from all around the world touched us deeply…"

He went on. "Until now, returning from the dead was unthinkable unless performed by God…a miracle. And we, the Jewish nation have waited eagerly for thousands of years for His promise to be fulfilled with the coming of the Messiah. Without any further doubt I can attest to the fact that the day we have waited almost 6000 years for…has arrived."

He then turned towards Leader Abram and spoke once more…

"His Excellency, our great UWC Leader has shown himself to be the epitome of the role…stepping in when the world as we once knew it was plunged into turmoil when almost 3 billion people mysteriously disappeared and being the lone voice of reason during the Great Vanishing. He has performed miracle after miracle as proof of supernatural abilities for the last couple of weeks and as a man who experienced one of the miracles first hand I see no further reason to isolate Israel from the rest of the world. As our father Abraham had a covenant with God 6000 years ago so we are here to announce the new covenant with His servant…Ha'Mashiach Abram!"

The crowd roared and all hands were raised in adulation. "HA'MASHIACH ABRAM!"

The Leader and Elias both then sat at a ceremonial desk and amidst flashes and glares of the cameras, signed the document that stated the covenant struck. Then Abram rose and faced the throng…

"My dear friends…I am pleased and excited that the great nation of Israel and her leadership…Prime Minister Lazerai Elias have joined our worldwide family; like the prodigal son returning home…and we welcome him. We are now truly a community; united…and united we will remain strong!"

As he was whisked off to his waiting jet Abram used his satellite cell to contact the Governor of the South Kingdom, Abrafo Uwamba in his palace to address the ongoing problem of what he and his referred to as the Rebel Faction…

The special phone on the elaborate oak desk in Uwamba's office rang and the former militia leader and fighter, who had been going over daily seeding tallies knowing who was calling immediately picked up the receiver…

"Yes, my lord."

"How are the seeding rolls coming?" Abram wanted to know.

Uwamba replied, "I'm working on them now."

"Well? Do you have the ratios of those seeded and those not?"

Abram's voice was pleasant enough but the underlying steel was evident as Uwamba felt a chill skitter up his spine. He took a deep breath and replied, "There are areas we have not touched yet, sir. As you know there are many remote towns and villages that are being affected by famine that we are having some difficulty. As a matter of fact certain dwellings are entered and the troops find evidence of fleeing…clothes scattered and other signs of abandonment."

"I see." Abram was thoughtful as he pointed out, "There are similar reports of the same happenings elsewhere…and usually when the seedings are announced. The Rebel Faction is hard at work. That's why you must make an example of those refusing. We have to keep the world in unity by banding together. I'm counting on all of you Supreme Governors."

Uwamba heard the Leader's words and felt the sacred duty of the office he held weighing heavily. He responded with no hesitation. "As you wish, my lord."

Abram cut the connection and Ichabod leaned forward. "It appears that we have a problem here…something I've been monitoring for a while…along with a sensation."

"And?"

"I've noticed stubbornness in the Rebel Faction to still cling to the archaic rule from the Bible, sir. In mission reports I've read from seedings those rounded up for execution after refusing often have bibles or other types of literature related…and they are either Christian or Jew."

"Hmmm." Abram scowled as he heard the voice of Baal inside ***the falsehoods of a dead belief system*** "Well, it seems to me that due to the residual fear of the Great Vanishing the people of the world are seeking spiritual leadership…leadership that offers hope in a time of fear. So you must unify them as the enlightened one you are…drawing everyone into one accord. So I leave it to you and the Spirit Circle to eradicate the old, outmoded religions."

Ichabod nodded as he too heard the voice of Baal ***you are the new voice of the Holy One***. So gather your Flock for him "Yes… so leave it to me."

Meanwhile back in his office Uwambo was getting increasingly more disturbed by the seeding reports. Indications were clear that there were incidences of those without the TM chip that were managing to bolt before the UWF could get them seeded. Following the census taken after the Great Vanishing the troops were finding in some cases, empty houses and apartments where there should be people; only this time unlike the first disappearance there were also empty closets, drawers, and food cabinets meaning the inhabitants had left on their own… not vanished. And along with that further investigations were showing some patterns of organization…like someone behind the scene was guiding them…

He picked up his phone and summoned his adjutant. The office door opened and a burnished cocoa colored man of average height with a bald head and too-easy smile entered. He stopped before the desk with a sharp salute…

"Governor Uwambo Sir."

Uwambo returned the salute. "Moses Konkosani…I have gone over the last report…and I have a special job for you…"

At the same time all this was happening it was about 8 AM when the plane carrying the FA team was approaching to land at Dar Es Salaam in Tanzania with flight attendants having awakened the passengers twenty-five minutes before to prepare for arrival. The five posing as anthropology students all having slept lightly were now fully awake and getting ready to disembark…

In the middle aisle seats Leah, Josh, and John having retrieved their belongings had belted themselves in for touchdown. The same with Peter and Angelica, both were wide awake and girding themselves for the last leg of the journey. Shaking the last bit of drowsiness from his head Peter yawned, stretched, and ran his hands through his hair. He glanced over at his seatmate, remembering the exchange from last night and noticed her staring out of the window with a preoccupied look on her face. Lightly, he touched her arm…

"Hey—,"

"Huh?"

Angelica was so into her thoughts that she jumped reflectively; accidently bumping her elbow sharply into Peter's side, eliciting a grunt from him.

"Whoa!" He rubbed his offended person with a wary smirk. "Remind me to never sneak up on you…any harder and you'd have knocked the wind right out of me."

She looked sheepish as she apologized, "Sorry…I was startled. I guess I was just…thinking about the mission."

He shrugged and said, "No sweat," then leaned closer and asked, "Is it what you were thinking last night?"

"Uh-huh." Angelica sighed and continued, "The closer we get to our destination, the more vivid the picture becomes… faces, places, what we'll be doing. Like a movie marathon in my head and I'm sitting in the front row."

"Yeah…must be pretty weird." Peter nodded and said quietly, "I meant what I said to you last night, Angelica. No matter what happens, I've got your back."

"I know." She reached over and squeezed his hand in gratitude. "Thanks, Pete."

With her gesture warmth filled him and he linked his fingers with hers as the pilot announced that they had landed…

The airport at Dar Es Salaam was one of the largest international airports on the continent and as such teeming with travelers…rushing to and fro throughout the concourse as they hurried to board departing flights or disembark from arrivals. The five encountered this when they exited the turnstile and stepped to the side to avoid the milling crowd…

"Well, here we are," Josh remarked as they surveyed their surroundings then addressed Peter, "Now what, chief?"

Taking a folded document from his jacket pocket Peter consulted it and replied, "According to the itinerary BD gave me we head over to the area where private planes are chartered. There someone will hook up with us and they'll fly us out to Mwanza where someone from Adanech will meet us and drive us out there. So let's head over there…and stick together in this crowd so we don't lose each other."

"Yeah everybody," John said in a jovial manner. "Let's buddy up. Here, sis." He took Leah's hand as Josh rolled his eyes and took her other elbow.

Peter took hold of Angelica's and the five then threaded their way through the crowd. Holding on to each other and their belongings they got past security first then after asking directions to the chartered area continued their trek which became easier as the crowd was thinning, seemingly drawn to a rest area with a large screen TV.

Noticing this Leah commented, "I wonder what's so interesting."

"Yeah," Peter agreed. "Let's check it out."

Pushing their way to see for themselves the screen showed a news report, coming out of Israel which was being broadcast. A UWCPI reporter was describing the happening…

"Here at the Metcal Tower we are waiting for the first appearance of Prime Minister Lazerai Elias since his miraculous return from

the dead. And we are also awaiting the appearance of His Eminence, our Unified World Community Leader Isaac Abram, who since performing the miracle in his typical kind and magnanimous manner has remained, ignoring his many duties to offer support to the Israeli prime minister."

Turning toward the entrance he saw the two men exit and approach the dais set up. *"Here they are so let's listen…"*

Elias came on screen. "As leader of the Jewish State of Israel I am here to greet you all…and to thank all of you for the support and love you have shown me and my family during my ordeal. The cards and messages sent to us from all around the world touched us deeply…"

He went on. "Until now, returning from the dead was unthinkable unless performed by God…a miracle. And we, the Jewish nation have waited eagerly for thousands of years for His promise to be fulfilled with the coming of the Messiah. Without any further doubt I can attest to the fact that the day we have waited almost 6000 years for…has arrived."

He then turned towards Leader Abram and continued…

"His Excellency, our great UWC Leader has shown himself to be the epitome of the role…stepping in when the world as we once knew it was plunged into turmoil when almost 3 billion people mysteriously disappeared and being the lone voice of reason during the Great Vanishing. He has performed miracle after miracle as proof of supernatural abilities for the last couple of weeks and as a man who experienced one of the miracles first hand I see no further reason to isolate Israel from the rest of the world. As our father Abraham had a covenant with God 6000 years ago so we are here to announce the new covenant with His servant…Ha'Mashiach Abram!"

In fascination the five continued to watch as they heard the gathered throng chanting "Ha'Mashiach Abram!" Then Elias and Abram sat down at a desk and signed a document after which Abram rose and addressed the world…

"My dear friends…I am pleased and excited that the great nation of Israel and her leadership…Prime Minister Lazerai Elias have joined our worldwide family; like the prodigal son returning home… and we welcome him. We are now truly a community; united…and united we will remain strong!"

As the crowd cheered the reporter came back on and gushed, ***"Finally we are a world truly united as the final obstacle has been removed. The nation of Israel has relented in its stalemate to join the rest of the world as a community…"***

He blathered on as the group at the airport screen broke up and walked away, murmuring about the report…along with a sprinkling of anti-Semitic remarks…

"What good news!"

"Leader Abram is a great man!"

"It's about time…those Zionists are a stubborn lot."

"Elias was brought back from hell where he belonged…he should be grateful…"

"The Jews always expect to be treated special…the Chosen…"

Ignoring the comments buzzing about them the FA team huddled together to discuss what they just saw with Josh as usual giving the most vituperative remark…

"Well, that was the typical brown-nose reporting from Abram's propaganda machine we've all had shoved down our throats 24/7."

John said, "Yeah, but you know we expected it. After the miracle of Elias the covenant with Israel was a given. Everything's going down…fast."

Angelica said cryptically, "The beginning…of the end."

Leah, Josh, and John all looked at her with inquiring eyes but before they could voice any questions Peter nodded and said briskly, "And we're here right now. It's battle time so let's get moving to the front line."

With that the five headed down the concourse for the area near the air freight loading bay where private planes were chartered. They approached a counter where a cinnamon colored young woman was in lively discussion with a tall, taciturn black man in a suit…

"You gotta be kidding me, man! I've been flying here now for the last month and now you're givin' me grief for usin' your runway. What's with that, huh?"

The man replied in a rather wooden manner, "As I told you before, freight planes have first priority. Smaller courier planes like yours need to allow for that and make sure you move to the side to make room when you come in."

"Yeah well how'm I supposed to move it now that I'm boxed in?" She was petite but feisty; unafraid as she got up right into his face.

Sighing he replied, "I'm sorry but you'll just have to wait until the other plane leaves." He consulted his watch. "In about thirty minutes."

The girl glared at him, opened her mouth then with a "humph" of exasperation went and sat in a chair in a huff.

He bore a pained expression, like someone dealing with one who did not understand…or did not want to. Heaving another sigh and shaking his head he turned and addressed the FA team, who had been watching the exchange with varied measures of puzzlement, "Can I help you?"

Glancing at the disgruntled young woman Peter replied, "Uh, yes. Can we get a private flight to Mwanza here?"

Before the man could open his mouth to respond the girl jumped to her feet and came before the group boldly addressing Peter, "Hey…are you the group from Harvard?"

He nodded. "Yeah, we are."

She grinned widely and announced, "Well, I'm your girl… name's Merci Fofana and I'll be flyin' you all to Mwanza. That is—," she cast a withering glance at the tall man at the counter, "if his highness there will let us, don't ya know."

The man snapped back in exasperation, "I said you can leave in thirty minutes!" He then gentled his tone. "Look Merci, I keep tellin' ya…you need to follow the rules when you pick up here. Your father understood that and followed them so why can't you?"

Merci met him eye to eye then her obsidian ones shadowed as she replied in a subdued tone, "Because my father was a saint… in many ways. And I'm not…in any way." She abruptly turned away and stood apart as the underlying meaning was clear.

The atmosphere became thick with melancholy tension and sensing the purveying sense of sadness Angelica went over to where Merci stood. She addressed the reticent girl with a soft voice…

"Merci…your father…he was taken in the Great Vanishing… right?"

She nodded, the cataclysmic event foretold by biblical prophecy still fresh in the minds of those left behind. "Him, my mother, my brother, his wife and children…they're all gone." Her eyes wore the bleak mantle of many who had witnessed their lives altered in the twinkling of an eye by watching as over a third of the world's population disappeared.

Angelica looped an arm around her and spoke words of comfort sotto voce, "And now you're alone. We were too," she gestured to the rest, "until we were brought together…in

Christ." She introduced herself, "I'm Angelica and those are my friends…Peter, John, Leah, and Josh," then spoke even softer as she added, "We're all new believers…do you believe?"

Merci gazed at the group and whispered, "No…but I want to. Brother Hasani and Sister Disa speak of hope in Christ. My family did too…but I thought they were crazy. Now I know they spoke the truth."

Angelica nodded and said, "There's a lot of people who now know that what the Bible said was true…refusing to take the TM chip because they want to be on the right…not the left. How about you?"

The girl nodded again when the clerk interrupted, addressing her, "The runway should definitely be clear in another thirty minutes so you can leave then, Merci." He looked at Peter and apologized, "Sorry to keep you waiting but it's the best I can do."

"No problem, sir…we're not really in a hurry." Peter offered him an assuring smile as he and the other FA members sat on the side while filled with nervous energy the girl named Merci paced, drawing his attention.

Taking a seat next to Angelica he asked in a whisper, "So what's going on with her?"

Sighing she replied, "She's like a lot of people now. Having lost her family in the Great Vanishing, she's alone, unsure…and feeling regrets that she didn't listen to the truth when she had the chance. I'm sure we're going to meet many just like her."

"Yeah," Peter agreed, pondering about the task before them…

Exactly half an hour later the clerk gave the okay for their departure and the FA team followed Merci as she led them out through the cargo bay and onto the tarmac to her aircraft, a Cessna Caravan Amphibian…not new but in excellent condition. John, who had an affinity for any kind of conveyance, was especially impressed. As everybody else climbed aboard he went to the front of the craft, gazing at the engine…

"A Pratt & Whitney PT6A-114A turboprop, huh? This Cessna land/sea bird has a pretty impressive range versus payload."

Merci regarded him with surprise. "You know planes?"

"Kinda." Rubbing the back of his head John grinned while as she deftly climbed into the plane Leah answered for him, "The two great loves of my brother's life are music and motors…cars, planes, motorcycles. It doesn't matter which he's obsessed."

"C'mon sis…stop exaggerating. I'm not obsessed, just interested." Ignoring his embarrassment he asked Merci, "Do you do all the maintenance on it all by yourself?"

Checking the propeller she replied, "Yeah. I watched my father take this thing apart and put it back together so many times I can do it in half the time he did. And it always passes safety inspections so I must be doin' something right." She gestured impatiently to the hatch. "Go ahead and climb on so we can get goin'."

"Yes ma'am."

John did as he was told, heading to take a seat behind Josh and Leah. At the same time, Merci jumped into the pilot's seat and after belting herself in switched on the engine. The smooth whine of the turboprop sounded and then she contacted the tower for clearance.

"Rallidae-1 to Tower…cleared for take off."

A few minutes later the radio squawked to life…

"Rallidae-1 you're clear for runway 22."

"Roger."

Letting up the brake she backed from the bay then turned to the runway. Accelerating down the runway for take off, she called back…

"Everybody hang on 'cause we're off!"

The FA team did just that as the Cessna lifted off and ascended through the clouds and into the blue expanse of sky. The plane climbed until it reached a cruising altitude of 15,000 feet and banking east to turn headed northwest to Mwanza…a three and a half hour flight. During the flight it was quiet as all had their minds on what awaited them; pre-mission nerves for all but Josh, who was focused like a soldier…and Angelica, who actually knowing what was to come was trying to keep her mind clear.

Staring out the window she gazed at the tops of clouds catching the sunlight like foam on the crests of ocean waves and wondered *is heaven like that…all blue sky and light? Looking at the sky makes me feel free…like I have no worries. Such a nice feeling. When I was a kid, I loved sitting on the grass at the neighborhood park watching the clouds until dark…*

She continued musing *yeah I stayed out as long as I could while my mother…"entertained" men…and when I was older and got away from her staring at the clouds was still a way to escape the pictures that were stuck in my mind of the things she did with them…and what they tried to do with me when I got older. It always worked and it's working now, blocking out the pictures of the vision. I'm getting more used to seeing them but they still disturb me…so much tragedy ahead…*

Feeling herself becoming burdened again Angelica turned her attention to a particular cloud that caught her eye…and was amazed to see a shining white dove breaking though the top to hover above; made in brilliant contrast to the blue sky by the back light of the sun. To her it was a sign from the Lord, especially for her and she heard the words of hope echoing in her ear and resonating in her heart…

Yea, I am always with you…even to the ends of the age…

"Wow!" Angelica said aloud, drawing Peter's immediate attention.

"What's wow?" he wanted to know.

She pointed out the window. "That."

Leaning over he peered out and said, "It's a great view."

"Don't you see it?"

Peter leaned back in his seat. "See what?"

Curious Angelica turned to look out again…and saw that the dove was gone strange…*but I guess that was only for me to see, huh Lord.* Feeling a renewal of focus and a sense of peace as her answer she sighed softly as she settled back in her seat.

"Hey, are you okay?" Peter asked quietly, his eyes soft yet probing. The other three, their own concern evident all looked over as well.

"What's going on?" Josh asked, wary. "Something come to you that we need to know?"

Peter threw him a look but Angelica shook her head facing her teammates with a genuine placid smile and assured them, "Hey guys…it's okay. I was watching the clouds and saw one with an unusual shape. I just thought it was it was kind of cool so it's all good."

They all relaxed and Leah admitted, "We're all tired and jumpy so forgive us, Angie."

"It's okay…forget about it," Angelica said, dismissing the matter as they all remained uncommunicative; wrapped in their individual thoughts for the rest of the flight.

CHAPTER 4— SHE WHO HAS RESCUED

It was late afternoon when the aircraft carrying Full Armor entered Mwanza airspace, the sun westering as the Cessna made its approach to the airport. However, instead of making preparations to land at the airport Merci flew past 75 kilometers to the west and then approaching what was a private airfield with Lake Victoria in the distance to the north began her descent…

"Everyone hang on because we're headin' down," she announced as she banked to align the craft to land.

The five passengers all braced themselves as the small craft bounced and the landing gear made contact with the ground, decreasing speed. The Cessna then slowed as it came to the opening of a hangar and stopped right before its portal. Merci shut down the engine and released her belt, getting out of the pilot's seat.

"Okay we're here. This is my family's airfield and hangar… it's a lot closer to the village." She hit the lever that opened the hatch, the steps lowering. She continued, "There should be someone from Adanech to pick you up soon."

Full Armor got up slowly from their seats, the long and arduous traveling with nothing but fitful rest taking its toll; evident in their haggard and tense expressions. Gathering their belongings the quintet disembarked. As the others scanned the surroundings Peter addressed Merci…

"Thank you for getting us this far," he said gratefully.

"No problem."

Angelica, who was near him asked, "Won't you be coming to the village with us, Merci?"

She shook her head and replied, "Not this time, I have to refuel and head out on another job. But don't worry; I'll be seein' ya there."

Just as Merci said that a gray Range Rover emerged from the rear edge of the airfield, from a makeshift road coming from a wooded area. It rumbled up to the hangar, just behind the Cessna and parked. A cocoa colored man of medium height exited the driver's side and flashed an easy gold-toothed smile as he approached FA.

He bowed and stated in stilted English, "Group from Harvard I am Moses Konkosani…I'm here to take you to Adanech so please come this way."

Peter heaved a travel weary sigh and announced to his colleagues, "Okay guys we're off once more." He said to Merci, "Thanks again."

She responded with a grin and repeated, "No problem."

Everybody else also thanked the petite pilot and they entered the waiting vehicle as the driver Moses stood by. When all were inside he headed to the driver's side and tossed a thumbs up and a wink to Merci, who rolled her eyes in return. She watched as he started the Rover then turned the car and headed back down the air strip toward the road leading back into the wooded area. Shaking her head she then turned and strode over to the fuel pump in her hangar, grasping the hose.

There's something about that guy that I don't like. Ever since he showed up at the village he just acts…weird. He gives me the creeps Merci mused as she attended to her task…

The trip to the village known as Adanech took over two hours, first riding through grassy flatlands, past the occasional isolated baobab tree and stopping now and then for wandering fauna; zebras, gazelles, giraffes that meandered into the Rover's path. And often along the way, the FA team was treated to eyewitness scenes that that could only be seen before in books, *National Geographic*, the internet or *Animal Planet.* Even as exhausted they were, all five watched raptly as the abundant wildlife was displayed in perfect unison to the beautiful landscape. However for the final leg of the journey Moses drove into a thick tropical forest; wending his way down a path through various brush and bush, sending smaller creatures skittering in and out of the shadows. The vegetation was so lush in some parts the daylight was almost completely blotted out, requiring the use of headlights to navigate the path.

All along the way Moses was congenial and chatty; acting the part of a tour guide while trying to figure out what five college students from Harvard were really doing heading to a village; this village in particular with the state of the world the way it was. With over a third of the world population inexplicably gone and the panic that had ensued, ordinary activities for everybody like attending classes at a university had been if not totally forgotten then strongly curtailed. *So why were these five here?* As he drove along presenting a benign mask to his passengers inside he was silently pondering; brooding…and calculating as he remembered how he had ended up there himself…

Supreme Governor Uwamba called on me to investigate the way more people were vanishing before seedings. I planted myself in a place where a seeding was to take place and noticed that when night fell people were leaving. So I endeavored to follow them by stowing away in a vehicle and eventually ended up at Adanech…

He then mused about the unique setting at the village…

Adanech…She Who Has Rescued…very interesting…the village itself hidden in a protected wildlife reserve is like a refuge; with dormitories and huts, a store room and generator…almost like a military headquarters. As soon as I arrived there I knew so I made myself useful, gaining trust. The head of the village Hasani appears to be a strong leader, almost like a general of a secret army so I've tried to get close to him but it isn't easy…it's like he's set himself apart. And now these five students from America are coming. Although they appear to look like ordinary college students there is something about them…

With his thoughts probing Moses surreptitiously glanced at the five. First John, who seated beside him was dozing; his head resting on his arm propped against the door. Then Moses glanced in the mirror, back at the other four, also napping. He dismissed the girls and sized up the men, starting with Peter…

He seems capable…built bigger than me but all of them are taller than me, typical Americans…he appears to be the group leader, everyone follows his direction. The one sitting up front with me seems harmless and genial…but the third one…he may pose a problem…

As a soldier he studied Josh with an experienced eye and noticed the same state of readiness in his posture and apparent light sleep he himself had learned for use in the battlefield. He had also noticed how earlier when introductions were made Josh had covertly examined him with an underlying wariness, immediately raising a caution flag in his mind. However, unknown to Moses, awake and feigning sleep Josh was doing the same as he…watching and drawing his own conclusions…

This guy Moses…seems funny. He's got military training for sure, based on his posture and build…there's no fat on him just muscle. He's not tall but he's got a build like a commando, like a lot of guys that were with me in the APL. I wonder what's really his deal…he's got something that stinks under that phony smile. I think I'm gonna be watching him, just to make sure…

Through his peripheral vision Josh noticed that beside him Peter was also awake, studying Moses so he lightly nudged him. The two men exchanged a furtive glance loaded with meaning indicating that they shared mutual unease regarding their chauffeur…

Twenty minutes later the Range Rover slowed as it broke into a clearing that led to the village Adanech, pulling into a paradox to what was supposed to be a primitive African village. As the vehicle entered the main path going through and heading to the village square the FA, now awake gazed around them in amazement…

"Wow," John expostulated. "I've seen pictures of African villages before…but I never expected something like this."

"It is unique," Leah said as she took in the sturdy row buildings, built along beside conventional simple huts. "Almost like a makeshift town."

"Almost," Josh said with subtle emphasis as he spotted what seemed to be a large generator and power transformer *looks more like a secret base to me…very impressive…makes me real eager to meet the guy in charge.*

"Uh-huh," Peter responded as he too noticed the unusual layout. He spotted a tall man with the demeanor of quiet strength over by a large building that looked like a gymnasium, near what appeared to be a stage in conference with three other men. There were also vehicles like military transport trucks parked nearby. "This is quite a setup, Moses."

"Ah yes…I will take you to meet the village chief, Hasani. He will direct you to where you can eat and rest." The man known as Hasani dismissed the three men and stood as if waiting for them, his eyes focused on the approaching vehicle.

Moses pulled the Rover to where the man was standing and parked, turning off the engine. He and the FA got out and with a smile the tall man came over to greet them as Moses announced the guests.

"This is the group of students from Harvard in America, Chifu. I brought them as you requested."

"Thank you, Moses," Hasani said firmly dismissing him. "You may go and assist Elimu with maintenance and inventory of supplies."

"As you wish, Chifu." He obsequiously bowed and left, heading for the supply depot. Always suspicious Josh watched him with a thoughtful frown.

Peter stepped forward with his hand extended. "Hello… my name's Peter Roccque…and these are my classmates and friends…Josh Nunn, Angelica Scales, John and Leah Pax. But just using our first names is fine."

Taking his hand Hasani bowed and responded in accented but superb English. "Welcome to Adanech…I hope your stay here with us will be of help to your endeavor. I am Hasani, the leader of the village and am at your service."

Peter replied, "Likewise…we'd like to assist you in all ways." He sent a subtle but significant look with the statement.

Immediately understanding Hasani nodded then changing the conversation briskly stated, "I'm sure you are all hungry and quite tired from your long journey." He called into the building. "Disa! Our guests have arrived."

A slender woman with a smooth bronze complexion stepped out and came over to join Hasani. Wrapping an arm around her waist he made the introduction…

"This is my wife Disa…she will show you where to go to get something to eat. But first she will assist the girls to the women's dormitory and I will assist you three to the men's…so if you would come with us, please?"

"Sure…let's go, guys," Peter said and then addressed the girls. "We'll see you later."
Hasani then led the three men over to a building to the left… one of the men's dormitories.

Disa then went over to Angelica and Leah addressing them with a warm smile. "I'll take you to the women's dormitory where we have a prepared a place for you to rest. You can leave your things there and then I will take you over to get something to eat." She eyed the two and asked, "You are hungry, no?"

Leah replied, "Yes, I am…we haven't eaten in a while right, Angie? Angie?" She glanced at her companion and became alarmed when she saw her pallor. She grabbed her arm. "Are you okay?"

Pale and Wordless, Angelica was looking about her with an eerie sense of déjà-vu. For all around her she saw faces that she had seen continuously in complete clarity…as if she had been here before and more than once. Smiling, beautiful faces belonging to people full of life that she saw in her vision; who visited her nightly in her dreams and daily in her thoughts…they were never far from her…

"Angie? Angie!"

Leah's shaking brought Angelica back to the here and now. She blinked her eyes and gazed back at her friend and Disa blankly as if she had just returned from a time trip. Shaking both her head and the wraithlike haze that had enveloped her mind she offered a tremulous smile.

"I'm okay…just really tired. I'm not hungry so if I could just go and get some sleep I'm sure I'll feel better." However she still looked wan and distressed.

"Of course," Disa said in understanding. "I will take you to the dormitory right away so you can rest." She took Angelica's arm to guide her to the women's dorm while a worried Leah followed…

Over at the men's dormitory Hasani led Peter, John, and Josh to a first floor room. The dormitories were two story buildings with flat roofs and in this one was capacity for 32 single men in six rooms of double occupancy with a room on each floor holding four beds, with a window in each room with slated light wooden shutters. There was a shower and toilet on each floor and a storage closet with sheets and towels for a total occupancy of 64. The village chief led the trio to the end room where one of the three men he had been conversing with before was seated on one of the cots, studying some documents…

When they were in the room Hasani closed the door and announced, "Chiaga, these men are with the group from Harvard."

Chiaga, a leanly muscled man of 5'11 with an easy smile rose and said, "We've been waiting eagerly for you…Full Armor."

"So you do know all about us," Josh stated.

Hasani nodded and said, "Mordecai Malensky and COS helped to organize and create this village called Adanech…'She Who Rescues'. They assisted us in not only building and supplying the village but arranged for the location during the initial chaos after the Great Vanishing. Now we are a secret haven for those fleeing the seedings and we lead them to salvation."

"Amazing," Peter said as he glanced at the documents Chiaga had been perusing. He reached for them asking, "Do you mind if I take a look?"

"Please."

Chiaga handed them to him and with John and Josh flanking they all examined the documents. They included a census of the village, reports highlighting various locations and a detailed map of the continent of Africa which outlined road, water and air routes with four main lines drawn in red…east, west, north and south…with Adanech as the center. The map commanded the most attention from the three FA men…

"Hey guys," Josh murmured, "Doesn't this look like the map Angelica showed us before?"

"Yeah it is," Peter affirmed grimly.

"Thought so," John remarked.

With an eagle eye on FA Hasani continued the intel…

"For the past weeks we have been assisting those resisting the seedings by being a haven. They travel here from four routes… east, west north and south all night, from land, water and with sister Merci's help, air."

"So Merci assists you by transporting resistors to the village?" John inquired.

"Yah…she flies a different route every night, rotating directions…doing about two, sometimes three round trips to help bring many to us. We begin every night, as soon as the sun sets to go to pick up those who have risked their lives to get to us, many by foot, avoiding main roads where UWF troops or mercenaries can stop them. We use those transport vehicles that were former military transports and pass for official UWF vehicles."

"Mercenaries?" Josh was piqued. "Why would the mighty UWF need any help from mercenaries? They're usually freelancers that play by their own rules."

"True…however former Islamic extremists have now offered their services to assist the UWF as mercenaries. You know that since Abram's miraculous feat of bringing Prime Minister Elias from the dead he's been deified by everyone who doesn't believe in Christ. And sadly, many trying to continue to believe have resisted seeding and have lost their lives fleeing, being slain by the UWF and these mercenaries. But there is much wilderness throughout Africa and at night the dangers increase, with animal attacks even thwarting the UWF diminishing their ability so we move under the cover of night. Which is why we call our mission Kuitwa Usiku…Midnight Call. We work from sunset to dawn to bring resistors to the safety of Adanech."

"It's a well organized op…I'm impressed you have a setup like this, like a military base," Josh said. "Though I kinda wonder why the South Supreme Governor and UWF haven't recognized it and found you out."

Hasani smirked and replied, "You remember the global economic crash that happened just before the Great Vanishing? At that time all governments around the world closed military installations to cut spending and even sold them. This particular base was forgotten but not by COS…a wealthy member purchased this as is, along with six transport vehicles from the Tanzanian government to help bail them out. It was ideal; hidden in a protected wildlife reserve, which made it practically invisible. When the disappearances happened I accepted Christ and met with COS as Disa and I fled. They harbored us and then shared the plan for this place as we saw Uwambo's scheme unfold. So we have been guiding those fleeing the tyranny of accepting the TM chip to safety here for all this time. COS continues to send food, water, clothes, fuel, and other supplies to us and we provide for those who come to us."

"It's amazing," Peter stated. "So how many can be harbored here?"

"We can hold a total of 64 in each the twenty dormitory buildings…and the huts have individual families so throughout the area we are about 800 now but can harbor about 2000." He sighed heavily and added, "However, there are many problems… mostly getting the word out. Communicating is difficult now that the UWCPI is not only the lone media source but the UWCPI—Unified World Commission of Press and Information has taken control of every communications outlet…telephone, television, online…they even took control of the online networking sites."

Josh, who had sat on his bed and unpacked his computer and said eagerly, "Not for long, my friend…not for long." With an evil chuckle like a mad scientist he booted up the laptop, attached a 24G flash drive to one of the USB ports and began tapping away at the keyboard.

"Oh…is that so?" Hasani said as he glanced with interest at what Josh was doing.

"Yep."

Smirking Peter said, "Rest assured, Hasani…if Josh is doing what I think he is communication won't be a problem for long."

"Yeah…just trust me. I've been working on a program that'll break open the comm lines for us rebels. The UWC will never know what's under their own noses. I'll show you everything when it's ready to roll."

"Mmmm…I look forward to it," the village chief said with an intrigued expression. He reached in his pocket and pulled out what looked to be gold laser pens. He handed them out to the men.

"The communication shed, storehouse, and a few other buildings have electronic locks with scanner pads." He turned a silver ring into position on the pen and continued, "When you when you turn this ring it activates the combination for each of the high security buildings and the doors will open for you."

"Impressive," Josh remarked as he fiddled around with the device.

Hasani turned and headed to the door and finished, "When you're settled I'll see you all at the meeting house…it is where we eat our meals." He let himself out.

After Hasani left Peter and John began settling into the room, unpacking their gear. As they did this Chiaga noticed John's guitar case and asked, "So you are a musician?"

John shrugged and said, "I play…but since I haven't written any of my own music I'm not a true musician…at least to me."

"Don't be so modest, dude…you can really shred." Josh said while working on the computer, his fingers still flying over the keyboard.

Trying to take the attention off of himself John remarked, "I just play for fun…but Pete here is a piano virtuoso."

Chiaga smiled as he turned to the now blushing FA leader. "Is that so?"

Running a hand through his unruly curls he admitted, "My mom taught me from when I was five as she gave piano lessons to other kids in my dad's church so I couldn't help but pick it up. But John can really play different styles…classical, jazz, folk, and rock…he does it all. So you *are* a musician," Peter affirmed as he continued to finish unpacking.

Chiaga smiled and said, "Me too…I play guitar, one of two of us in the worship band. We play during Sunday service and Wednesday night worship and practice Saturday evening, Tuesday evening and Wednesday afternoon. So please come and join us."

"Sure," John said. "If I can, I will." He looked at Peter who nodded imperceptibly.

However Chiaga knew the reason for his hesitation and sagely said, "We in the worship band are all part of Kuitwa Usiku… so practices are held later in the day. Also, we rotate and go on missions when we don't have to play."

"Is that so?" John commented.

"Yah…we all believe in doing the main work for God first… to rescue those lost and bring them to Adanech…She Who Rescues."

He met the eyes of FA in silent but unshakable understanding…

About twenty minutes later the three FA men headed to the large gym like building known as the meeting house. It was set up with four rows of 15 long tables and folding chairs with a cafeteria serving line where food was distributed. Since it was time for the evening meal the building was bustling and noisy with children scampering about. They entered, and as they scanned the crowd they spotted Leah alone sitting at a table eating so they went up to join her. Her plate had what appeared to be rice, greens, and an odd colored mashed vegetable with some meat.

"Hey sis," John greeted as he took the seat to her right while Josh straddled a chair at her left.

"What's up?" He glanced over at her plate and added, "And what is that?"

She finished swallowing her mouthful. "It's the meal they're serving tonight and it's really quite good."

"Oh yeah?" Leaning closer Josh peered at the food and remarked, "It looks like—OOF!" He rubbed his side where Leah's elbow made sharp contact and protested, "What was that for?"

"To make sure you remember your manners," she replied evenly as she took another bite.

"All I was going to say was that it looked like something that could've come from a can of Alpo—owww!" This time he rubbed the upside of his head because that was where she slapped him. "C'mon knock it off, Leah!"

"You knock it off," she retorted. "I'm trying to eat and can do without your color commentary. Besides, we're guests here and you're being rude."

"Sorry," Josh apologized then added gruffly, "but that really hurt…did you have to be so harsh?"

"Sometimes with you I have to be harsh."

Having watched the exchange between his usually placid and soft spoken sister and the irascible often times FA problem child John smirked and snickered, nudging Peter who also smirked shaking his head.

"Hey Pete let's head over and grab some for ourselves."

"Yeah."

He then gave Leah a thumb up and said, "Good one, sis… keep him in line."

"No problem," she said as Josh threw him a glare…

Both boys headed to the front hot table where the food was and got in line to get theirs. As they made their way to the front they were still laughing at the debate between their two comrades…

"Boy, Leah keeps Josh on a short leash," Peter pointed out. "I just noticed that they seem kinda close, he's always with her."

John smirked, "Yeah…even more so lately."

"I've noticed…you think something major happened between them?"

"Oh yeah…Josh has changed even more."

"How'd you figure?"

"When we met Josh he was the ice man, the original Mr. Freeze. He didn't get too close and trusted nobody but he respected us, and with all of us being new Christians led us to the former APL bunker to hide, acting like he was the leader between us. Then when we met Brother Danny he was different…he acted like a soldier and BD was his commanding officer. But as far as me and Leah were concerned we were still like followers that he felt responsible for. Especially her, he took it upon himself to protect her when he found out that she was partially blind. But something between them happened a month ago, just before the visitation. Since then they both seem pretty into each other."

"Uh-huh," Peter responded. "So what do you think happened?"

John shrugged, "Dunno…they haven't said anything to me which is strange 'cause Leah tells me everything. But she's not talking and I'm not pushing. And I'm not gonna pump Josh 'cause he won't say anything anyway." John grinned and added, "You guys are a lot alike."

Surprised by his comment Peter scoffed, "Oh yeah…ya think?"

"Well…it's kinda the same with you and Angie…right?"

"Hmmm." Peter made what sounded like a noncommittal grunt but his face gave him away as a slow blush crept up from his neck. *He's right though…ever since I met Angelica starting from when we rescued her I've wanted to stay by her. She's in my thoughts constantly and I'm always worried about her so I guess I'm into her…but does she feel the same way about me? I'd like to spend more time with her, just the two of us.* He then shook his head and reprimanded himself *Get a grip, Roccque…now's not the time to think about all this…we're on our first mission sent by the Lord to help bring the lost to salvation and safety… all that other stuff I'm feeling can wait, we gotta get to work…but still…*

Surreptitiously watching him wrestle with his dilemma John turned away smirking and the conversation ended as they got to the serving area. Picking up plates they waited as the food was served and when they walked off to the side Peter looked closely at the contents…

He sniffed at his plate. "You know I don't usually agree with Josh's take on most things but I gotta go with him here. This looks like—,"

"Is everything alright, gentlemen?" A soft alto interrupted him as Hasani and Disa came to them. She smiled cordially while Peter, who realized that he was about to insult his hosts blushed and scrambled for an answer…

"Uhhhh…s-sure everything's just fine. We were just about go and eat…right John?"

"Uhh...yeah," he answered. "My sister Leah was really enjoying it and she's our gourmet so I'm looking forward to it."

"Good." Hasani and Disa then accompanied John and Peter back to the table where Leah and Josh were still sitting; she was just finishing her meal.

As John and Peter sat down to dig in Disa addressed Leah, "How are you liking the food?"

She smiled and said, "Oh very much...the spices and flavoring are very unique."

Josh, looking at the food again asked, "What exactly is it?"

Hasani replied, "It is called ndizi ni nyama...plantains and meat. The greens are mchicha and wali...rice. It is a basic meal served in the region. You should try it."

"Well...uhhh—," He caught Leah's subtle warning glint and let it hang with a sheepish expression on his face.

However, catching Josh's dilemma and wanting to ease his discomfort Disa smiled and offered, "We also have chapatti flat bread...and mkate wa kumimna...bread made with spices and rice. And we have fruit."

"Okay."

Tasting the food on his plate Peter commented, "This has a bite to it...I like it. You should try it, you like spicy food."

"Yeah it's really good," John stated. He needled Josh, "C'mon dude don't be such a wuss…take a walk on the wild side."

Having been pushed into a corner Josh had no choice but to surrender. "Okay, okay! I guess I'll try some…so just chill about it." *I'll just wait and see if anyone passes out or gets the runs before I do.*

"You'll like it…trust me it's very good." Placating him with a pat on the back Leah then said to Disa appreciatively, "I love to cook and always like to experience new tastes."

The lady of the village said enthusiastically, "You can come into the kitchen tomorrow. The cooks can share their recipes, we have been blessed to have several ladies and men who have fled here who are excellent cooks…and we can always use extra help."

Leah smiled but remembering the real roles FA had being at Adanech her pretty face became sober and echoing her brother's earlier words to Chiaga she said softly, "When I can…I will."

Knowing exactly what she meant Disa nodded. Changing the subject she asked, "How is your friend feeling? I was worried about her, she appeared so pale."

At that statement Peter, who had been eating stopped and asked brusquely, "What are you talking about…and where is Angelica, Leah? Why isn't she here with you?"

Biting her lip in consternation the petite redhead replied, "Uhh…she said she was too tired and not hungry so she stayed in our room. She fell asleep as soon as we got there."

His expression was wary. "Okay." He stared at his plate for a moment, a thoughtful frown on his face then looking up he asked quietly, "Did anything weird happen to her?"

At Peter's question the other two men also pinned their eyes on Leah which made her feel cornered but she knew that they all were as concerned about Angelica as she. However she hesitated, searching for the right words…

"Little bird?"

Josh tapped her hand gently to get her to respond but Peter; leaning forward, his cerulean eyes burning and intense pleaded, "Please Leah…if something happened we need to know…so talk to me."

Heaving a sigh she answered, "You guys had just left…I was chatting with Disa and I looked over at Angie and she had totally spaced out. It scared me…I had never seen her do that before."

Both Peter and Josh were scowling fiercely while John probed, "So what happened next, sis?"

Sighing again Leah replied, "I called out to her and she finally came out of it, saying she was fine but she didn't look fine…she was pale and she looked like she wasn't there…like she had been gone and come back."

After she had shared that observation the atmosphere was tense and everybody was silent while Peter immediately got to his feet, abandoning his half eaten meal.

"I'm gonna go check on her." He demanded of Leah, "Where's your room?"

"First floor, fourth door on the right as you come in."

"Thanks."

He whirled around and strode out of the meeting house while Hasani watched him leave. He then addressed the others collectively…

"The other girl…Angelica. She's the Messenger…correct?"

They all nodded and said in unison, "Uh-huh."

"I see."

Hasani exchanged a significant glance with his wife while the other three sat in quiet contemplation…

The women's dormitory was identical to the men's in appearance and setup so it was easy to find after Peter asked where it was. He then sprinted over entered the dorm and immediately felt wariness if not hostility aimed his way…making him feel like an intruder as the women; especially the older ones made their disapproval of a man entering their domicile clear. Undaunted to achieve his objective he nodded politely their way and ignored their attitude, heading for the fourth door on his right…

He rapped lightly on the door. "Angelica?"

No answer so he tried again…

"It's me, Peter…can I come in?"

Still there was no answer so he quietly turned the knob and let himself in. Once inside, he headed over to the bed where Angelica was curled up, deep in what appeared to be a rare and untroubled slumber. Peter heaved a sigh of relief as he knelt beside the bed and gazed at her, studying her delicate features for signs of distress. He was glad to see that for once she was at peace; maybe for the first time since they had the Visitation…

As he continued to gaze at her the verse of an old song came to mind…

And a sorrow no one hears still rings in midnight silence in her ears…

Angel…I wish I could see what you've been shown, what you see every day in your thoughts and every night in your dreams. I know that you were chosen by God for us as the Messenger, like your name but I can't help but worry…the way you acted on the plane and now when Leah told me about you seeming to black out has me bugged about what is ahead for us. And what kind of pain you're experiencing as you carry this burden…

Peter then spotted Angelica's knapsack and tote bag, leaning against the small chest of drawers at the foot of her bed. He got up and picked up the tote, rummaging through it until he found the leather bound notebook from which she read when she briefed them back at the bunker. Leafing through it he found pages of narratives, notes and her meticulously drawn map; the same map she showed them back home and he saw with Chiaga. Fascinated by the contents of the notebook, he thumbed through further and was amazed at what he saw on the next pages…drawings of animals, scenery…things that they all saw during the journey to Adanech.

I had no idea Angelica was such an artist he flipped the next page and his eyes widened. *My God…this is…*

On the pages were sketches of people…detailed portraits of men, women, children that all appeared to be like those he saw earlier in the meeting house. But what really amazed him most were that the drawings appeared identical to both Hasani and Disa; so detailed that they could have sat for them.

"Oh wow," Peter murmured as he returned the notebook back to her bag.

He went back and kneeling once again beside Angelica he was again speculating about what exactly she had seen. Based on the sketches he saw depicting places and people they have now seen it appeared that she was eyewitness to what might be true prophetic visions of things that will come to pass. He had been told by the Holy Spirit that she was the Messenger…the herald but now he had some idea of the breadth and depth of the burden of having been shown places and faces that had now become real and a future that had materialized and become the present. And again he pondered about what was to come.

Trying to dispel his frustration Peter sighed softly and following a spontaneous urge he reached his hand to her face…

to brush a stray gold strand from her soft cheek…and cupped it as he leaned forward to plant a kiss on her forehead when the door cracked open to allow Leah and Josh into the room, she holding onto his arm. Startled, he jumped to his feet, feeling like the proverbial kid caught at the cookie jar as he met their eye. Both gave him a smile of understanding.

"Hey," Josh said softly as he guided Leah into the room and to the vacant bed.

"Hey," Peter murmured as the two came over to where he was standing.

Josh gestured to their blonde comrade. "Is Angie okay?"

"She's out…hasn't moved…didn't even answer when I knocked so I just came in," Peter whispered back as he continued gazing at Angelica's sleeping form.

Her own eyes also on Angelica Leah whispered, "She collapsed when we got here. Whatever happened before really took a lot out of her. Do you know what's going on, Peter?"

"Pete?" Josh probed.

But he said nothing just replied cryptically, "Let me know if anything else happens."
Heading for the door he asked, "You coming, Josh?"

"Uhh, yeah." Josh turned to Leah and murmured, "Sweet dreams, little bird."

She smiled and said, "You too…thanks for helping me get back."

"No prob…see you in the morning."

He followed Peter out, closing the door and sighing Leah sat on her bed watched her friend sleep and wondered *what is going on?*

Once they were outside Josh wasted no time. "So talk Pete… what's goin' down?"

"Goin' down?" he echoed, not turning.

Josh grabbed his arm to turn him around. "Don't play dumb with me…Angelica saw something, another vision, right? She saw something on the plane too. So tell me, man." His eyes were pewter daggers, aimed and sharp.

Wrenching his arm free Peter glared back; eye to eye and man to man…then sighed and said tonelessly, "I know as much as you do…nothing." Then he added, "But we'll all know soon enough."

Josh opened his mouth…then scowled and acquiesced, "Yeah, I guess we will."

With no further comments they wearily headed to the men's dorm to get some much needed rest…

The dawn sun sent a ray through the window to tease at Peter, who opened his eyes and saw that day was breaking. He leaned over to open the slats to peer outside and saw that early morning activity at the village was beginning, with a group of men gathered at the meeting house with Hasani.

I wonder what's up he wondered, still a bit disoriented as he came to awareness. He also noticed that the transport vehicles that were parked near the meeting house were gone and then spotted Disa with a group of women joining those already gathered; some carrying light blankets. Now awake and aware that a Kuitwa Usiku mission was probably returning Peter decided to get a closer look so he got dressed and leaving his still sleeping comrades went out of the dormitory and over to the meeting house. Feeling awkward like the newbie he was he glanced about, not knowing anyone…just stood there to quietly observe with a sense of anticipation growing within.

I'll check this out to see just how everything works…then tonight FA will join the party. From the first look it appears really organized…obviously these people are waiting for new arrivals…

And as if on cue a rumbling sound that became louder came from the northern part of the village, announcing the arrival of a convoy of vehicles…

Whoa…look at that…

As they pulled over to park at the meeting house Peter was engrossed; watching while the men in the previously gathered group got into position behind each of the transports, whose job appeared to be to open the truck gate and assist the mass of passengers out of the vehicle. Out came men and women; some with sleepy children, elderly people and youths, single and married some carrying bags and bundles of belongings… refugees all seeking safety from the uncertainties of an ominous new world order and in search of a better life. He saw the tense expressions on their faces, reflecting fear and worry on those of the very young but mostly he saw relief…as if everyone had reached the end of a long journey and was thankful to have finally arrived. Then he watched as Disa and the other women wrapped the blankets around the weary shoulders of the elderly and pregnant women when Hasani addressed the crowd.

"Good morning brothers and sisters…welcome. There is food waiting in the meeting house but first let me bless you with these verses…

O Lord, you have searched me and known me. You know when I sit down and when I rise up; you discern my thoughts from far away. You search out my path and my lying down, and are acquainted with all my ways. Even before a word is on my tongue, O Lord, you know it completely. You hem me in, behind and before, and lay your hand upon me. Such knowledge is too wonderful for me; it is so high that I cannot attain it. Where can I go from your spirit? Or where can I flee from your presence? If I ascend to heaven, you are there; if I make my bed in Sheol, you are there. If I take the wings of the morning and settle at the farthest limits of the sea, even there your hand shall lead me, and your right hand shall hold me fast. If I say, "Surely the darkness shall cover me, and the light around me become night," even the darkness is not dark to you; the night is as bright as the day, for darkness is as light to you. Amen. Now please go in and eat. After that we will show you where you will be staying."

Hasani dismissed the crowd; then with guidance from the Kuitwa Usiku group from the village who greeted them they headed into the meeting house. As the crowd dispersed he met with several men, including Chiaga and the other two he had been with when FA first arrived. From his vantage point Peter watched as the three appeared to be briefing Hasani and turning to head back to the dorm his thoughts were full of a sense of awe at what he had witnessed…

Amazing…just watching this operation for the first time…so methodical and structured, like a well oiled machine. Hasani has this place in God's perfect order for sure. And to give them a greeting with that particular passage from Psalms was the perfect welcome…Psalm 139…I remember how Mom read that to me after Dad bailed on us and how it gave me comfort. But my anger toward him took over, and I turned my back on God, got left behind…so here I am.

"Good morning, Peter." Disa's soft alto shook him from his reverie and he met her gentle smile with one of his own.

"Morning, Disa." He gestured to the remainder of people filing into the meeting house and said, "I was just watching Kuitwa Usiku at work…and thinking about Psalm 139."

"Ah yes…Hasani chose that verse as a welcome benediction. It was given to him one morning in his devotion and prayer time by the Holy Spirit and he felt it was perfect to offer comfort to these coming here who are seeking safety."

Peter nodded and recognizing the symbolism mused, "Coming to 'She Who Has Rescued', huh…God's perfect order."

Disa nodded and following with a fitting metaphor she responded sagely, "And now He has sent His Full Armor to assist us…we are so grateful." She offered her hand.

Her almond eyes met his cerulean ones and he was immediately filled with a feeling that pieces were falling into place *I guess this is what's called 'divine purpose'.*

"We'll do everything we can to help," Peter promised taking her hand.

CHAPTER 5— VISION BECOMES REALITY

When he had become the global ruler UWC Supreme Leader Abram had partitioned the world according to the four hemispheres and appointed the four supreme governors; the Quad, giving them complete autonomy in carrying out his wishes and overseeing the chain of command. He told them to choose their own headquarters; only suggesting that they be as central to their territories as possible so they would be a visible presence to the people as the authority so Supreme Governor of the South Kingdom Abrafo Uwambo followed that edict. The office and residential mansion were located southwest of Cairo in Giza right in the center of the Giza Governorate; the center of the South. He had chosen that location because it was close to the famed ruins of Ancient Egypt…the Sphinx and the Great Pyramid of Giza, where the fourth dynasties of pharaoh have been entombed for millennia. This had special significance to Uwambo because he had a longtime fixation on the reigns of the pharaoh, and had, in his appointed position fancied himself a modern day ruler in that vein. Therefore, his residence was palatial and his office was like a throne room; with burnished oak, leather and fine marble furniture and pure gold fixtures. He sat before a large glass topped marble desk, studying the computer screen showing him digital reports sent of the most recent seedings with a perturbed scowl across his face…

I do not understand this…despite the increased efforts by the UWF to patrol scheduled areas for seeding, they are still discovering disappearances, the incidences increasing more in the last five days…evidence of people having fled before and right under their noses. This is not good…

Uwambo clicked to another screen and saw something even more disturbing. In the midst of seeding raids taking place in those hit hardest by the ongoing drought and famine; taking its toll on the poorest and most remote villages…the UWF troops were discovering that the villages were completely deserted. This was a disaster in that those villages…away from the more metropolitan centers where access to Rebel Faction information was readily available…were assumed to be pretty much easily seeded. However…

It's impossible…how can those ignorant, simple sheep be able to escape so easily? It's inconceivable! How is this happening? And then theses bizarre reports of soldiers being thwarted while apprehending rebels fleeing by some invisible 'force?!' Preposterous! If His Excellency Leader Abram—

As if on cue the phone buzzed and Uwambo's secretary announced that the UWC leader was on his special line. An uneasy chill skittered up his spine as he picked up the receiver to answer his master's voice…

"Good day, my lord," Uwambo said with respect.

Abram answered warmly enough…like the spider welcoming the fly, "Good day to you too, Abrafo…how are you?"

"I-I am fine, my lord…never better."

"And the seeding operations?"

Feeling a noose dangling above his head the supreme governor tried subterfuge. "Everything is progressing along well, my lord…in spite of average the small issues that arise."

"Is that so? And you are able to handle them adequately with the UWF troops assigned to serve under you? Because if not I will send more to assist you."

Relieved by the offer of support he replied, "Absolutely, my lord." Trying to sound sincere Uwambo's tone was unwavering… thinking that his ruse was working, his mind eased into a sense of false security.

"I am glad to hear that." The tone of his voice now several degrees cooler Abram asked, "Then Abrafo…can you be kind enough to enlighten me about the discrepancy in the seeding reports?"

Uwambo felt his belly twist and echoed, "Discrepancy?"

"Yes…to be frank there is a vast difference between your progress reports and the seeding reports."

The noose lowered so he tried the route of feigning ignorance. "Is there, my lord?"

Abram sighed, "Abrafo…you have the same report on your computer as I have on mine. Compared to the most recent census rolls the number of citizens seeded does not match…in fact it is considerably lower then before, disputing your reports. Surely you can see that based on the reports from UWF seeding missions the problem persists still. Rebels are eluding capture and the disappearances prior to seedings are increasing, correct?"

Now around his neck the noose tightened…so with his heart pounding and left with no other choice but to agree Uwambo stammered, "Y-yes my lord…a-and I assure you, I am addressing the problem."

"You said that before…however," Abram bade, "go on."

Taking a deep breath to calm himself Uwambo continued, his mind working as he spoke, "I have someone within investigating something suspicious happening in Tanzania…I expect a detailed account from him soon." Silence met his statement so he went on with his pitch. "My lord, he is our top expert in covert operations with exceptional skills. Trust me, he will uncover the facts for us."

More silence…then, "Indeed? Then I can believe everything will go smoothly by the time I arrive in ten days for…what are you calling it?"

"Hukumu…it means 'administration of justice'…as an example to all rebels…including those that my esteemed colleagues from the other four kingdoms are dealing with. And yes my lord…everything will be perfect."

"Good," Abram approved. "My visit will be to show the citizens of the South that to belong to the UWC is to be under the protection of my vast power…and to be an enemy and threat by refusing to accept the TM chip means total annihilation."

Uwambo felt the weight of an ancient iron cudgel behind the supreme leader's proclamation and a chill gripped him. "Yes, my lord."

"My executive secretary will send my itinerary through your e-mail…when you receive it contact her to make sure the details concerning my public appearances are clear."

"Yes, my lord."

Abram made a final statement. "Abrafo, you were chosen for your post with great care…which means I have the utmost confidence in your ability to lead and to eliminate those who oppose me, as I do with my other Supreme Governors. Take care of this rebel problem…don't fail me."

As the line went dead Uwambo simultaneously went limp with relief. He had picked up the subtle threat in the vein of ice and warning in the UWF Leader's last sentence and his instincts, honed sharp by his military background and training whispered caution in his head. However benign and pleasant Abram appeared, he knew that the power mentioned was immense and that the world's ruler would not hesitate to wield it…against anyone.

What is this force…this power that is literally blowing UWF forces away? If His Excellency knew everything…about THAT…I would be dead…but before MY head rolls…

Uwambo sighed and with a fierce scowl snatched up his satellite cell phone and punched a number…Moses Konkosani's. He wanted answers…now…

In a corner in the goods storage house at Adanech Moses was finishing stacking some barrels of rice when his cell vibrated. Glancing down he saw that it was from the Supreme Governor and quickly scanning the area to make sure nobody could overhear him in a hushed voice he then answered the call…

"Yes sir?"

"Major Konkosani…I am waiting for an explanation."

Moses swallowed hard. "Explanation sir?"

"Yes, explanation. Your reports every night are quite thorough…but tell me nothing. Yet not only do I hear from the UWF command that rebels of the UWC are eluding capture continuously but that for the past five nights soldiers who are in pursuit have reported that just as they are about to get them a great, powerful force has rendered them helpless…as if a great wind blows them away, literally. So I ask you again…can you explain this?"

Stumbling for an answer Moses stammered, "I-I really don't know what you are talking about."

Having lost all patience Uwambo barked, "Stop stalling! You were specifically chosen for your skills as a spy. I've been waiting for you to explain these reports of this so-called 'invisible force' that is allowing rebels to escape since the first report about it. I want answers…now!"

Feeling the heat and filled with a vermin's innate sense of self-preservation Moses was genuinely nonplussed yet tried to make his excuses plausible. "W-well sir I have not seen this firsthand—,"

"And why is that?"

Moses replied, "Well sir…there is, as the previous reports tell a village hidden here where rebels against being seeded come. And as I have also reported, many arrive here all night and members of the village leave in empty transport trucks then come back with them full of rebels. They leave at sunset and return before dawn."

"Yes, yes," Uwambo said testily. "I can read…now tell me. Where do they go to pick up these rebels? Who is leading them? And how are they finding out where to go?"

Moses heaved a sigh of frustration. "I have no idea."

Uwambo was incredulous. "You have no idea? Is that all you can tell me?"

Now cornered Moses had no choice but to defend himself. "Sir, since I arrived here a week ago I have tried to get close to the chifu, Hasani. But he is a very difficult man to get close to. He has a few trusted men who he confers with regularly but they too keep very quiet about the night missions. But those belonging to the group known as Kuitwa Usiku are closest to him and they are the ones who go every night. During the day they operate like an ordinary group of Christians, attending bible classes, having worship, and counseling the new arrivers."

"Humph," Uwambo scoffed. "It's pathetic how there are still many fools in the world that believe in the myths of that tired belief. Especially when his Excellency has proven what I knew all along…that the true power is within you and the ultimate power is in him…his power is absolute." He sighed, "Well, you can become one of these Kuitwa Usiku and then report where they go."

Moses hesitated, "That is easier said then done, sir. I've tried since arriving here to do that but they are very tight with each other…every time I try to get in with them they close themselves off completely."

Uwambo's voice was full of disgust. "Your job was simple enough for one of your level of expertise and training… to infiltrate and report of actions in what appears to be a rebel stronghold so you can guide UWF troops to them for apprehending. But you cannot even accomplish this… unbelievable."

"I'm sorry, sir," Moses said feebly…then a thought just came to him. "However…,"

"However…what?"

Moses thoughts then about the five youths from America… and how they had been absorbed into the work of Kuitwa Usiku immediately upon their arrival *strange how those five were just accepted into Kuitwa Usiku and are now one of the few closest to Hasani...especially that one named Josh...he spends a lot of time with the chifu...and so does the one called Peter* "There are five American college students who have been at the village for the last five days."

"College students from America? What about them? Why are they at the village?"

"I was told that they were anthropology majors from Harvard studying the village."

Uwambo snorted, "And why have you not told me about these college students until now?"

"They did not seem suspicious at first...but now thinking about it they are very close to Hasani...and they do go every night with the Kuitwa Usiku group."

"Is that so?" Uwambo intoned. "And yet you, a top expert in undercover operations with the UWF cannot break through? Unacceptable!"

"But sir they are—."

"Silence!" Uwambo roared. "I will listen to no more excuses...you will find a way to go with them tonight and guide the UWF troops to them to capture them...or you will face *dire* consequences."

The line went dead so with a nervous sigh Moses tried dispel the ominous chill Supreme Governor Uwambo's last statement left to him. So he abandoned his task at the storehouse and headed over to the rear of the meeting house where he knew Hasani was meeting to plan this night's mission with Kuitwa Usiku…

After hanging up with Uwambo Isaac Abram had sat at his desk in the UWC command center in his executive suite and stared at the computer screen before him, his calm being battling with dismay morphing into frustration. The call to Uwambo was disconcerting but affirmed what he had been hearing from the other supreme governors…that there was a problem brewing that threatened the very foundation of the throne upon which he sat.

Based on reports from all four regions there were increasing accounts of people mysteriously disappearing like the Great Vanishing…only unlike the Great Vanishing this time there was conventional evidence of fleeing…abandoned dwellings left with furnishings intact but clothes and food missing. This was all happening before scheduled mandatory seedings and all as if planned with an organized force working behind it flying right into the face of his platform of the citizens seeking safety in trusting his protection. That was the premise and promise he gave to the masses and was how he had gained his position so even with the supernatural miracles he had performed to solidify his role as savior the basic policy behind him was to bring a solid sense of safety to a world suddenly plunged in chaos. But the truly jarring account was from UWF troops who had been subject to an unseen but vast power that rendered them helpless while trying to thwart the rebels…it was this news in particular that made Abram's blood boil.

Abram pressed a button on a panel on his desk and a side door slid open to admit him into a dimly lit chamber where Ichabod, the Supreme Spiritual Guide, who dressed in a flowing robe of deep purple was kneeling before an altar. Eyes closed he was in another state of conscious; an altered state, with an otherworldly sense like he was firmly within the spirit realm. On the other hand Abram, although he had his encounters with Baal and was more absorbed with handling his own power… counted on Ichabod's vast spirit energy to inform and enlighten; further enhancing and strengthening that power. So he stood in silent veneration as Ichobod began to chant a mantra and was coming back to consciousness. With raised brows and his features twisted and distorted the seer made a cryptic, guttural sound, like a beast…then opened his eyes…

Immediately sensing Abram's presence Ichabod rose and bowed. "My lord."

Abram nodded in acknowledgement and inquired, "Do you have anything to tell me?"

Frowning thoughtfully Ichabod replied, "I feel stirrings… and vibrations I haven't felt in—," he left the statement hanging then said, "All I can tell you is the spirit realm is quite active… which means they are at work."

"Hmmm." The UWC Supreme Leader then asked, "And you can't tell me exactly how…just that vague statement."

"Forgive me, lord…when I know more I can tell you." Ichabod was contrite.

"Hmmm…well then I'll have to rely on more conventional information channels to dig into as to why citizens are disappearing before getting seeded."

Abram turned and left Ichabod, who began speculating about the spiritual vibrations he had been feeling…and his mind presented a picture of a young, pretty blonde whose powers of divination were vast and formidable when she first entered the Spirit Circle…

Angelica Scales…

Yes indeed…her ability to see future events was unparalleled. I was even a bit envious at first but then I knew I could use her…the incident with Cassandra had impressed me and I made her my Prime Clairvoyant. Then she foolishly filled her head with fables from the Bible and turned against my teachings. She betrayed me and I had intended to make her pay…and she would have…if not for those two young thugs that came out of nowhere…

His sherry eyes became black like onyx and narrowed *Angelica Scales…although I could never equal you in spiritual abilities my powers were enough to sense yours…I could always pick up your vibrations; I'm doing that right now. So don't think you've escaped me, my dear…because it's only a matter of time, I WILL find you…*

Ichabod smiled an oily, determined smile…

Over in the well-hidden village of Adanach in Tanzania the hazy sun was dimming as a dark bank of clouds was heading in from the west accompanied by steady wind…a storm seemed to be brewing as evening approached. However, Angelica paid no mind as she sought to clear her head and calm her heart by heading out to a secret place she had found exploring just outside of the village…a small enclosed place with two trees flanking a flat rock and surrounded by bush and shrubbery. She had discovered this haven, led there by the Holy Spirit as if it had been prepared especially for her to meet with Him. It was secret; known only to her…and to Peter, who she had told when he saw her leaving the village a few days ago, showing him the place and trusting him to keep it private. So she instantly escaped here to her sanctuary…

Earlier…

She had been assisting Disa and a soft-spoken lady by the name of Annakiya or Anna as she asked to be called…a recent arrival who had migrated to Adanech all the way from Guiana and prior to the Great Vanishing had been a schoolteacher. They were having a bible study session for the K-7 grade children…

Disa recited, "1 John 3:16-18…We know love by this, that he laid down his life for us—and we ought to lay down our lives for one another. How does God's love abide in anyone who has the world's goods and sees a brother or sister in need and yet refuses help? Little children, let us love, not in word or speech, but in truth and action…"

Angelica suddenly found herself suspended above a field where she saw the Kuitwa Usiku transports being loaded with refugees. Everything appeared to be going smoothly when she saw UWF soldiers and machine gun toting mercenaries rush from nowhere on jeeps attacking in an ambush. Shots were fired as the Kuitwa

Usiku workers continued their tasks moving everyone and she was horrified while she watched as one of the main members, a man named Elimu was shot and killed before John, Peter and Josh used the Full Armor power to blow back the attackers.

As with every vision she had Angelica had seemed as if she had lost consciousness and came out of it with everyone clustered around her in concern. Disa, Anna, and several of the children were all alarmed and asking if she was all right, which was a cause for her to be concerned as her visions were to remain unknown to all but her. After the incident Disa assisted her by escorting her to her room and had offered to call the other FA members to alert them but Angelica begged her not to…so she promised that she would get some rest. However rest of any kind was elusive as all she could see when she closed her eyes was guns going off and one of the mission warriors…was dead. And what made it even more eerie was that as she just left the dorm she ran right into the man Elimu; the man whose death she foresaw…who knowing she was part of FA and having seen them use the Full Armor power as they went with Kuitwa Usiku greeted her with reverent respect. Her response was to nod and then flee like a frightened rabbit…

Wiping tears from her eyes Angelica began lambasting herself *Coward…you have been shown the future and instead of heading to warn them…you're here hiding and afraid. That's not what you as the Messenger are called to do. You HAVE to warn them…*

She closed her eyes and prayed for courage *Oh Lord please help me to have strength to do what You have called me to do…*

Keeping an eye to the sky, the members of Kuitwa Usiku filed into a classroom that was located in the rear of the meeting house along with the three male FA members. Peter, Josh, and John were seated in the room, near the head of a table where Hasani was standing as plans for tonight's mission were discussed. With a map unfurled and spread out before the group Hasani pointed to three areas of interest south of Tanzania… Mozambique, Zambia, and Angola…all countries bordering to the south…

"Since we've been concentrating efforts lately to assist refugees from the north we have now been asked by COS to transport 150 men, women, and children to safety up here to Adanech from the south, now harbored at three locations… Songea, Mbeya, and Sumbawanga and we will be picking them up and bringing them here from where they are now waiting in hiding at the Rungwa Game Reserve. Up to now they have been harbored by COS in secret places in those three countries, knowing where to go thanks to the computer genius of Josh and his program." He acknowledged the FA master hacker with a significant look and a gleam in his eye…

With a self-depreciating shrug Josh answered, "Awww, don't mention it…anytime I get a chance to throw a monkey wrench into Abram's plans it totally makes my day."

"So…can you tell us what exactly you did, Mr. Josh?" An earnest looking young man by the name of Abasi inquired with great interest.

"Sure…and just call me Josh, okay?" He pulled out his laptop and brought up a browser window…then clicked over to a newly popular social networking site…

"Here…" He right-clicked on an icon and a floating window popped up…he then keyed in a sequence for a password. Josh then turned the computer around so the others could see…

"Whoa…"

A collective murmur of awe arose as the Kuitwa Usiku group of warriors gathered around to see…on screen was a list of all the countries in Africa. Josh clicked on Angola and a map of the country appeared with road routes and gold starbursts on several areas. He then ran the cursor over the starburst and a popup showed the location for each.

As the group watched the screen Hasani explained, "Josh and Malachi Malensky of COS worked together to create this as a way to communicate to citizens who do not want to be seeded to help guide them to COS harbors. They log on to the social networking site using the screen name 'beloved' in their own language and the password 'child70X7' after which they are redirected to what looks like an online atlas…and then you see here the locations of COS harbors and safe houses."

One man asked, "Why use that screen name and password?"

Josh replied, "Because we want them to know three things. First, that God still loves them…that as His children they're not alone…and the number stands for the amount of times Christ directed the disciples to forgive because of God's own forgiveness to them." He added ruefully, "It's really my own personal struggle to believe and follow those things at times so I registered it that way."

Touched John commented, "That's deep, bro…I never knew you to have those kind of struggles…I mean, you never say anything."

Usually silent Elimu spoke to Josh with the wisdom of a respected elder, "A strong man is always aware of his weakest area." They eyed each other with the brotherhood bond of soldiers. It was an unspoken affection only true men of war shared.

Embarrassed Josh grunted and Peter hastened to support him. "Some things we can't tell anyone *except* God."

Several of the men nodded in agreement and Hasani acknowledged, "Amen. Getting back to business he said, "This system is in place for use all over the world. However, there are signs that the UWF have become more aggressive in their search for rebels. It seems that they feel that their pride is stung each time they find that people have fled so they are doubling their efforts to find these hiding places. In the three countries mentioned the UWF has become more of a problem of late, having captured numbers of rebels that failed to seek the safe places and finding the locations of the safe places. That's why we're being called to help tonight. These refugees have been moved from threatened areas where safe houses have been if not discovered then compromised. The game preserve is safe due to the fact that it is government protected land and above reproach." With a smile the Kuitwa Usiku leader then added, "However, we can be thankful we have the Lord's Full Armor to protect us."

Peter, Josh, and John sat quietly in genuine humility. The members of Kuitwa Usiku and in fact the entire village had been made aware of Full Armor's true purpose almost as soon as they had arrived. They had been introduced to the entire village in a special service the very next day where Hasani had announced how God had foretold of the coming of His armor to assist them in rescuing those fleeing from the tyrannical new world order under the UWC. Then he enlisted the five in not only the nightly rescue missions but also the daily activities of the village where they also assisted in specific roles, suited to their individual talents. Josh helped with electronics, technology and basic military training those assigned to Kuitwa Usiku and another squad named Ngao…Shield…designated to guarding and alerting the village of independent refugees arriving. John joined the praise band and lent his ability with engines to the mechanics keeping the transport and other vehicles running smoothly. Leah was putting her culinary talent to work in the kitchen while Angelica, always drawn to children worked closely with Disa in the school. Peter, as the recognized leader of FA spent his days with Hasani monitoring communiqués with COS and planning rescue missions based on the intel and sometimes played piano with the praise band during worship. So the five were not only recognized but respected and accepted as a part of Adanech as if they had always been there. In addition, there was daily worship, Bible classes, and independent prayer groups where the refugees were encouraged to seek the comfort found in knowing Christ. And because of the uncertainties of the new world, all embraced the opportunity so the five relatively new believers of FA were able to build upon and strengthen understanding of their own paths. All of the youths were affected greatly, but Josh especially had bonded with Elimu as he participated in the military exercises with Kuitwa Usiku. From the time he began with them both men had begun to spend a lot of time together…working side-by-side during missions, eating together, and just talking together, with Josh listening raptly to every word the slightly older man said…looking up to him like an older brother.

Everyone murmured somber gratitude and recognition when Chiaga asked respectfully, "Will you be using your powers again tonight?"

The trio exchanged guarded glances…then Peter answered, "If the need arises…and the Lord wills…we'll do whatever He asks."

Hasani nodded, "We are indeed blessed with His weapon at our disposal…so let us go into the dining hall, eat and head out."

Meeting adjourned, everyone rose and headed through the door down a hall leading to the door that opened into the dining hall. When the door closed a figure carefully climbed into the now empty room from an open window. Creeping stealthily to the table, Moses picked up and skimmed through the notes then looked at the map…

So they are heading to the south tonight…to the Rungwa Game Reserve from harbors in Songea, Mbeya and Sumbawanga with rebels advancing from Mozambique, Zambia, and Angola. There must be rebel strongholds there so I can communicate their positions to the captains of the UWF troops in those areas and alert them to the movements from here…however, I MUST find out just what is this great power is that Governor Uwambo spoke about…

Turning from the table Moses went back to the window and peered out where the transport trucks were parked, ready to leave as sunset approached. His next objective clear he climbed out of the window and looking around to make sure nobody was around made his way over to the vehicles. He crept into the storage area beneath the truck bed, deep within the chassis where he then used his cell to send the information for tonight's mission to the UWF region command…

As the three FA men followed the Kuitwa Usiku group they discussed the use of the Holy Spirit powers that they had been given among themselves…

Always the pragmatist John stated, "You know it's kinda weird…knowing that we have the literal power to protect these people."

"Uh-huh." Peter nodded remembering…

Five nights ago…

It was the first mission that FA was included…after arriving and getting about nine hours of sleep four of the members…Peter, John, Josh, and Leah (Angelica remained behind to protect the village and monitor other refugee arrivals with Disa) prepared to join Kuitwa Usiku. At the final glow of the setting sun they headed north to Merci Fofana's airfield near Lake Victoria, where the transport trucks parked on its southernmost shore. There they waited as motorized longboats carrying approximately 20 to 25 people apiece arrived from the lake, and with the other workers helped unload them into the transports. Josh and Leah did that while Peter and John accompanied Merci as she flew her Cessna to a field the southern tip of South Sudan to pick up refugees that had been held in a COS safe house. Through the night they flew four sorties to transport about 15 people each trip and it was at 3:30 AM the final trip where two UWF jeeps came racing out of nowhere with guns blazing…

The people screamed in terror as Merci cried in Swahili, "Get down! And don't stop, keep moving to the plane!"

"Keep going!" Peter barked to her then to John, "You ready?"

"Just say the word, boss!"

"Let's do it!"

Without hesitating Merci urged everyone onto the aircraft while Peter and John, their broaches glowing used the supernatural power that flowed from the Sword of the Spirit and Shoes of the Gospel of Peace. At that moment Peter's hands and John's feet glowed bright blue-white and a mighty beam of light shot at the approaching vehicles, upending them and completely immobilizing the UWF soldiers. And as they made their getaway the glowing light enveloped the Cessna, shielding it from other UWF forces trying to shoot it down.

When they returned to the airfield Josh and Leah told them that they too had to employ their own Full Armor powers to keep the refugees from being attacked by mercenary gunboats on the lake as they headed towards shore. It was a similar occurrence…the same blue-white glow was around Josh's hips and above Leah's head as another beam of energy burst forth…this time in a huge orb that pushed with the force of an invisible wave, causing the gunboats to capsize. After the danger had passed the refugees and other Kuitwa Usiku workers had gazed at them in amazement…as well as fear, embarrassing them. Even Merci, who was a true skeptic; unflappable, was stunned by the display of Holy Spirit power. So when they all arrived at Adanech at dawn the refugees regarded FA as gods, even going so far as to bow to them…much to the chagrin of the five until Hasani set them straight using the scriptures to direct their gratitude and worship to the true source of the power they saw…the Almighty God…

Peter came out of his reverie just to hear the tail end of the conversation between his colleagues with Josh saying with typical aplomb, "Yeah…I told her it was like shooting fish in a barrel."

To which John quipped, "I'm sure sis *loved* your allegory… with some of her love shown in the form of knuckles on your head…enemies are still human beings, dude. As Christians we're supposed to be peaceful…wise as serpents but gentle as doves."

"Yeah, I know," Josh conceded grudgingly. "But as a former neo-military man I can't help but feel satisfaction when we have the power at our fingertips to obliterate the enemy…old habits die hard."

I hate to admit it but I feel just like Josh…but…"It felt great laying out those mercenaries, huh?" Peter looped an arm around him and piped in, "Yes, but we're new creatures in Christ, my man… old things are that are made new. Besides you know that's not our job…those things are decided by Him. We're just His tools… which is why we need to lay low about these powers."

"I hear ya." Josh then wrenched himself away from Peter scoffing, "And what's with getting so touchy-feely all of a sudden? Hate to tell you Fearless Leader, but I don't swing that way."

John began snickering and with a smirk Peter retorted, "In case you haven't noticed bud, neither do I."

All three laughing they entered the dining hall and headed for the chow line…

In the dining hall the late serving of the evening meal was in full swing. Because the Kuitwa Usiku missions took place all night the kitchen was open 24/7 with three eight hour shifts to provide meals for the refugees coming in. So Leah, when she was rested enough from her night missions helped the cooks. Tonight she was at the serving counter as the boys came to get supper…

Josh was the first to be served. "So little bird…what's on the menu for us tonight?"

"Well let's see," she replied, peering at the serving trays. "We have nyama choma…grilled meat with curry sauce for dipping and I showed them today how to make my special honey barbecue sauce so we have that for dipping too, ugali, chapatti, coconut bean soup, and pineapple slices and bananas with honey."

"Sounds good," he approved as he accepted a plate from her. "Pile it on."

John gaped at him in amazement as he waited for his. "Dude, am I hearing right? Are you actually saying what I think you're saying?"

"Whattya mean?"

Gesturing to the laden plate in Josh's hand John stated, "You're finally admitting that this is real food…wow…a miracle." Peter, who had been standing next in line to get food and was watching the exchange between them grinned as if egging him on.

Leah shook her head as Josh heaved a pained sigh. "I know I'm gonna regret feeding into your comedic aspirations and making myself your straight man by saying this but I was a jerk, okay? I admit it. This food's great and besides have you ever heard the saying about when in Rome?"

"Sure I have," John replied with a deadpan expression. "But we're in Tanzania."

"I know that, idiot…but I had to get used to it," Josh retorted.

"Yeah." Chuckling John added, "But for three days you just ate bananas and coconuts…I thought you were gonna start climbing trees and scratching your pits."

Peter snickered and Leah pleaded, "Don't laugh, Pete…it only encourages him." She handed him a plate while always edgy before a mission Josh's expression showed that he had enough ribbing.

"Ha, ha, ha…you're killin' me…and I'm gonna kill you."

Josh made a motion as if he was about to chuck his plate at John, who was doing his best "I dare you" taunt like waving a red flag before a bull while Peter sighed and said, "Guess I'd better nip this before it becomes a reenactment of the cafeteria scene in Animal House."

Leah nodded with pursed lips. "Emotions are high and everyone's ready to leave on a mission…I don't think they want to deal with a bout of adolescent foolishness."

Putting his plate down Peter turned and placed his 6'2" frame between the two combatants. Shooting them both with a no-nonsense glare he snapped, "Alright you guys…knock it off! We've gotta eat and be ready to roll when everybody else is so John cut the comedy and Josh chill out. We're here to do a job and don't have time to mess around."

Both boys sported cowed expressions and John was contrite. "Sorry, man…I'm just trying to shake off the nerves. I don't know why but I've got a bad feeling about tonight."

"It's okay…yeah I do too," Josh admitted with a scowl. "And I had a weird feeling during the briefing that something was up…like we were being watched by someone. It left me feeling creepy."

"Uh-huh." Nodding Peter picked up his plate and said brusquely, "Let's hurry up and eat so we can leave with the others right after sunset." A low peal of thunder rumbled with the patter of raindrops falling and he mused *I'm with them…feeling creepy…sounds like it's going to be quite a night…*

He and the other two headed to the table where Hasani and the rest of Kuitwa Usiku sat taking their evening meal. They sat down to join them just as Disa came over to her husband to give him the usual report of readiness for the newcomers.

"The rooms are all set up for everyone coming in…the dormitories here are each set to receive about 150 people." She pointed to the chart of the village and the buildings to the left of the women's dorm made to hold families. "The kitchen's also ready and hot meals will be waiting when you return."

"Good work, wangummoja," Hasani approved. "We will be bringing about that number here from areas to the south."

"We will be waiting." Turning to Peter she said, "I hope Angelica is feeling better."

He immediately stopped eating. "What do you mean? What happened to her?"

Josh and John also stopped to listen as Disa replied, "Earlier she was helping us in the school with the children like she usually does when she seemed to black out and did not respond when we called out to her. It frightened us and when she finally did respond she looked pale and terrified."

"I see." Peter was pensive as he digested the news. He then asked, "Where is she now?"

Disa looked concerned. "After that I helped her to her room so she could rest…but—,"

"But what?" Peter demanded his expression fierce.

Disa sighed as she answered, "Before coming here I went to check on her…but she was gone."

"Gone?" John asked while Josh grunted and scowled darkly.

Peter, however got up and turned to leave, with Josh calling after him. "Hey…you know we're leaving soon."

But paying no mind he strode towards the main door, his intention clear. As he headed out he nearly collided and came face to face with the very one he sought…Angelica.

"Whoa." He grasped her by the shoulders and halted her progress. "Where've you been?" Examining her appearance he frowned and inquired, "Are you okay?"

She was damp from the rain, her hair wind-tossed and had a peculiar expression on her delicate features. "Y-yeah, I'm good," she replied in a shaky voice.

"Uh-huh." Peter eyed her critically his hands still on her shoulders. "Disa just told me what happened earlier and that she had checked up on you before she came here but you were gone. So where were you?"

Angelica met his direct gaze with a sense of both desperation and determination to get away from him but she knew he would not be deterred. "I went to…that place."

That place…the secret place she showed me a few days ago…the place she meets Him Immediately Peter understood. "Okay…so you saw something else when you were with Disa, right?"

"Uh-huh."

She looked over his shoulder at the table where the Kuitwa Usiku members were finishing their meal and especially at Elimu, who having finished was sitting there waiting for his comrades. Without taking her eyes away Angelica disentangled herself and stepped around Peter, who let her go then followed her to the table…

Stopping right before the taciturn man she drew a look of respectful curiosity from him as he asked, "Is there something you need from me?"

Angelica just took his hand. "Please…be prepared," she said with quiet authority.

Elimu's brows raised slightly but with understanding he met her steady gaze unflinching. "Yah," was all he said as he released her hand.

The simple exchange had a monumental effect on those witnessing it. A purveying feeling blanketed the table that something eerily uneasy had taken place…like they had been granted a glimpse into some unknown and imminent event that was looming large but unavoidable. A heavy silence fell over the table as another roll of thunder echoed in the meeting hall.

Rising up Hasani grimly addressed the group at the table. "We must go…now."

Everyone instantly rose regardless of whether or not their meal was finished and headed toward the rear door which led to the back of the meeting house where the transport vehicles waited. Josh and John also rose to follow while Peter addressed Angelica…

"Listen…you and Leah hold down the fort here. Put a barrier around the village if you sense enemy approaching." As she nodded in acknowledgement he took hold of her shoulders again and inquired softly, "You saw something about to happen in tonight's mission, right?"

Unable to help it her eyes were pinned on Elimu as he was conversing with Hasani by the open door as the Kuitwa Usiku members filed out. She nodded, her face registering a significant sadness. Peter glanced over at Elimu and he understood right away what Angelica had been shown. Gently he squeezed her shoulders as he spoke…

"I'm driving with Hasani and I'll prepare him. Josh, John and I will do what we can to protect Kuitwa Usiku but God's will is gonna be done and sometimes that means sacrifice. Hasani's been preparing them by teaching from the Bible so all of them are aware of that and especially Elimu."

"I know."

"Then trust in that…and trust in the Lord, Angel. He chose us to be His Armor and although we have been given powers by Him we aren't Him. He still calls all the shots whether we like the results or not."

Peter then turned to head out with Kuitwa Usiku leaving Angelica to watch them leave and reflect. She recalled the past five days how she saw when Elimu had assisted Hasani in teaching the youth of the village biblical principles and how he had worked diligently and with focus training Kuitwa Usiku like a soldier. He had impressed all of FA but Josh especially had seen his discipline and bonded with him as they worked together for a few of the missions so she knew that he definitely would not take Elimu dying well. I hope what I said was enough…I couldn't reveal everything but as Peter said the Lord is in control…

The three transport trucks left Adanech just as daylight faded and the storm threatening arrived, bringing flashes of lightning and roars of thunder accompanying them as they headed south. Once out of the village the convoy cut through the brush and bush into several miles of grassy flatlands and plains which were made all the more difficult to navigate due to the driving rain. However, the heavy duty 4WD trucks ran at a steady 50 kpm which enabled them to cut across the plain and get to the main road; Route B6 heading south through the towns of Nzaga, Tabora, and Sikonge. The three transport trucks were former military vehicles so they were above suspicion passing through more populated areas since UWF vehicles were unmarked as well. Then able to pick up speed they headed toward the westernmost part of the Rungwa Game Preserve where there were 150 refugees waiting in hiding.

Scowling while driving the lead truck with Hasani beside him Peter brooded about the conversation with Angelica before they left the village. Having grown up as the son of a prominent pastor he had spent much of his formative years' time at church; involved in children's church, Sunday school, bible study, VBS, and camps, absorbing the scriptures. So he knew how even despite being filled with Holy Spirit power, men like Moses, Elijah, and Daniel had to face sacrifice and even death to fulfill God's will. Nevertheless he also knew well the wavering of the human heart when someone close was lost…with the inclination to blame the circumstances on God or anyone even remotely connected with information or a way to avert the tragedy or disaster. One word screamed out…BETRAYAL…a word with which he had an intimate connection…

I have to tell Hasani…to prepare him…but how? And how will the others take Elimu's death?

It was a dilemma…a dilemma for which Full Armor and especially Angelica as the Messenger would bear the repercussions. The blame and anger they would undoubtedly experience from the villagers would be plentiful and harsh… they would feel betrayed thinking that they were safe; protected from all things and especially death. Thinking of that and feeling frustrated he heaved a sigh, drawing the attention of Hasani…

"Something wrong?" he asked, looking away from his notebook which had all the information for the mission.

Peter hesitated a bit then replied, "It's just the weather…it makes it extra hard to drive these roads when the visibility's so poor. I really miss our 'pillar of fire' tonight."

The 'pillar of fire' he had been referring to was Merci Fofana who not only transported refugees in her Cessna but also acted as a guide, flying at a low altitude with a high beam halogen floodlight to light their way on dark roads every night…like the guide God sent to Moses and the Israelites fleeing Egypt. "Yah…but it would not have been safe for Merci to fly low in this storm."

"Yeah I figured." Peter sighed again as Hasani persisted.

"Then are you troubled about something else, Peter?" the chief of the village named for rescuing inquired in a calm voice that had the resonant quality of quiet authority.

Glancing at his companion Peter saw Hasani's eyes reflecting the dim glimmer of the dashboard lights, lit with intensity and pinning him. Left with no means of escape he admitted, "I am… but not about the mission."

"I see." Hasani then asked, "Does your unease have anything to do with the Messenger and Elimu?"

H-how did he know? His scowl darkening Peter just nodded.

"Hmm." Hasani grunted then added, "I have known Elimu for a long time…he is a man whose one desire is to live for God. He knows his final reward is not here on Earth, he fears only Him and will gladly give his life in His service."

Humbled by those candid words Peter just nodded and continued to drive…

It was an hour before midnight when the three transports came to the edge of the game preserve. The land had signs posted…warnings to poachers but other than that there were no fences so the transports, once off of the main route were able to drive right into the preserve grounds. They were about three quarters of a kilometer in when a uniformed guard came before them halting their progress then came to the driver's side window and peered in. Leaning over Hasani spoke to him; saying something in Swahili to which the guard replied in kind, nodded and then went to the front of the truck pointing ahead.

"He wants us to go up 50 meters bear left and pull up to the drainage ditch," Hasani directed.

"Okay."

Picking up the radio to communicate with the other trucks Peter relayed that order to John and Josh. He complied as the guard went to the front of the truck and led the way, reflected in the headlight beams. He then followed him, creeping along slowly on the rain slicked wet plain all the while wondering why *I don't see any buildings or shelters of any sort…There isn't even any type of trailer so where are these people hiding?*

The guard stopped at a line of tall bushes and gestured to the right. "He wants you to park over there," Hasani stated.

Peter did as he was told and parked; shutting off the engine as did the other two transport trucks. As he and Hasani donned rain ponchos and exited the cab, they met up with Josh and Elimu, and John with Chiaga, congregating by the guard. Standing before the concrete drainage ditch in the driving rain they all watched as the guard pressed a button on a remote and the ditch itself retracted revealing a staircase heading below ground. Hasani stepped forward and called loudly in Swahili…

"Kuja nje…ni salama!"

At those words, there was a great rumble…the sound of many footsteps as men, women, and children climbed up the stairs and gathered in groups of 50…three groups altogether equaling 150 people. And then beneath intermittent flashes of lightning and the downpour guided by Hasani, Elimu, and Chiaga the groups quickly filed into the rear of the three transport trucks, as Full Armor observed, as always standing sentry. The trio discussed the happenings among themselves…

"I didn't figure they'd be hiding underground…and in all places under a drainage ditch," Peter stated as he watched everyone climb aboard.

"Yeah," John affirmed. "Usually when we go on missions the people come from shelters and harbors of some sort… abandoned buildings, warehouses, some kind of housing. This is a really new type of shelter."

Josh was smug. "I recognize this design. It seems like it's something that I had seen in some old APL blueprints and plans that I shared with BD. When I belonged to APL after 9/11 they had longstanding plans to implement for building subterranean shelters in the event of a rogue nuclear attack by terrorists. He must've shared this particular plan with Malensky and COS… It sure looks like something that they'd use since they go for all that high tech military stuff."

"Well, I guess you'd know all about that since you're our high tech guru," John remarked.

Meanwhile, Moses Konkosani the UWF spy who had hidden himself within the chassis of the transport truck that Josh was driving was waiting. All along the way he had used the GPS on his cell phone and had broadcast the coordinates to the UWF troops…leading them right into the game reserve…

The refugees were finished being loaded onto the transports and the very last were settled in. The transport gates were closed, locked, and secured for the trip home, with members of Kuitwa Usiku in each transport. The three men from Full Armor along with Hasani, Elimu, and Chiaga all headed to the cabs of the vehicles and were about to climb in when all of a sudden roaring in from the distance in the vicinity of the eastern part of the reserve came high beams splitting the night as several jeeps arrived with guns blazing. Bullets ricocheted as they hit the sides of the transports prompting frightened screams from the refugees huddled in the back…

"Get down!" Peter bellowed to everyone as the six men got down on the sodden ground, covering their heads.

Forgetting himself in the heat of the moment Josh swore, "Where the hell did they come from?"

"I don't know, but you know what we have to do…ready guys?"

"Oh yeah!" John yelled.

The FA trio jumped up reaching under their rain gear and touched their brooches…Peter's hands, John's feet, and Josh's waist glowed and they held their hands forward where bright blue-white waves of energy shot out like a powerful tsunami… literally blowing the advancing UWF ambush jeeps back and causing them to tumble end over end like toy cars kicked and scattered by a moody toddler having a temper tantrum. Seeing the incredible display of supernatural power the terrified screams and gasps of disoriented refugees in the transports joined the pained grunts and cries of fallen UWF troops echoing throughout the rain swept fields…

"Everyone get inside the trucks and let's get outta here!" Josh yelled turning to where Hasani, Chiaga, and Elimu had hit the ground when the shooting started.

"Yah," Chiaga responded, getting to his feet…however, Hasani and Elimu was slow getting up with the former holding up the latter.

"What's wrong?" John asked as Peter came over, kneeling beside them. His eyes widened in horror when he looked at Elimu.

"Oh, my God!" he exclaimed, drawing both Josh and John's immediate attention. They too leaned down to take a look…

It was a clean shot straight through the heart…a bloodless hole that pierced Elimu's poncho; the one in one million hit that even the most crack marksman could never make in a lifetime, eerily accurate. Elimu had died instantly, knowing no pain at all with hardly any blood shed. But what was more astonishing and maybe even numbing was his expression…It was completely and utterly peaceful almost as if he were expecting to die.

Hasani sighed softly and then asked, "Would you please go in back and get me a blanket? And please assure the people that everything is fine."

"Sure." John went back to get what he had asked for while both Peter and Josh remained in stunned silence, unsure of what to say.

When John returned with the blanket Hasani carefully wrapped his slain friend with gentle hands and no expression, his eyes downcast. When he had finished, he asked Peter to assist him in getting Elimu's body into the cab of the truck.

"I will drive with him back to the village…please do not say anything to anybody until we get back there."

"Of course." Peter was subdued and Josh nodded, both in saddened shock.

After making sure the body was secure in the passenger seat, Hasani slid over to the driver's side and behind the wheel while Peter and Josh got into the transport parked to the left. All three vehicles started their engines and pulled out to turn around and head out and away from the game reserve. Ironically, when they reached the main road the rain intensified almost as if the sky itself was crying; heaven mourning the loss.

On the drive through the downpour back home to Adanech Peter was silent…there were no words that he could say. He knew after speaking to Angelica before they left the village that something was going to happen to Elimu; he just had no idea what she had meant at the time was that he would die or that it would be so sudden…or so quick. *Maybe this is God's mercy* he reasoned *to leave this life in such a way, with no pain…no suffering. Just like the poet Dylan Thomas wrote going gently into that good night, to where I'm sure he has a reward waiting…*

However, while Peter was musing behind the wheel over in the passenger seat Josh was fuming. *I don't get it…we're the Full Armor…we're supposed to be the protectors; just like armor, with God-given power. So how can this happen?* He then remembered when Angelica came to the table and knelt before Elimu, telling him to be prepared…

So is that what Angie meant and she said that to Elimu? To be prepared to die? Then what's the point…what good is everything, having these powers if we can't prevent those we're supposed to protect from dying? She's the Messenger; she knew what was going to happen, God told her. So why didn't she tell us?

"Talk to me, Pete. You knew, didn't you…you knew this was going to happen. Angelica told you, didn't she?" Josh's accusation echoed in the small space of the cab.

Scowling Peter said nothing but just kept driving.

But Josh was relentless. "When she came over to the table while we were eating and she knelt beside Elimu telling him to be prepared this is what she meant, right? To be prepared to die tonight. And she told you right? She told you, didn't she?"

She didn't tell me…I just guessed still silent Peter just sighed; his mouth a taut, grim line.

Josh made a long, low whistle. "Oh wow…of course she did, she tells you everything. The two of you with your heads together all the time, I knew you weren't just chit-chatting. So tell me something, were the two of you ever gonna to tell the rest of us what was going on? Or were we just supposed to be surprised?" His tone was dripping with sarcasm.

Again, Peter gave no reply.

Josh heaved an exaggerated sigh. "Well, I guess that's it, huh. The so-called 'Messenger' only lets us know so much then leaves the rest for us to just find out on our own." He glanced over at Peter. "Still got nothing to say, huh Fearless Leader?"

Incensed, Peter took a deep breath to compose himself before finally answering, "Are you done?"

Glaring out of the windshield Josh nodded. "Yeah."

"You want me to talk?"

"Yeah, I do. I'm part of this, too…you owe me." Josh glowered at him, waiting.

"Okay, then listen up…first, the only one I owe is God, we all do…He chose us for this…and He especially chose Angelica as His messenger which means she does what He tells her. Next, God doesn't always spell everything all out for us, genius. He doesn't have to, He's Almighty God or did you forget? But I will tell you this…when we get back if you hassle her about what happened tonight in any way, shape, or form, I'll come down on you like a ton of bricks. You won't know what hit you, I promise. So chill out…understand?"

He shot Josh a look loaded with meaning with his eyes narrowed to slits and the volatile bearer of the Shield of Faith momentarily met the challenge with his own eyes, filled with defiance. But he was not stupid, and saw that Peter as the leader of Full Armor was in complete control; not giving an inch. It was a textbook Mexican standoff and Josh had no choice but to yield…

"Yeah, I understand," he said grudgingly.

"Good."

The drive back to the village continued with no further words between them.

It was nearly daybreak when the rains finally eased and the three transport trucks rumbled into the village complex, pulling up beside the meeting house where Disa, along with Ngao and Kuitwa Usiku members were waiting in front with extra blankets as they did with every load of new refugees arriving every night. Leah and Angelica were there as well to offer their assistance, also holding blankets as the trucks cut their engines. As Disa and the Kuitwa Usiku workers hurried to assist the tired and still frightened refugees to disembark from the transports, Leah and Angelica came over to the cab of the first truck just as Peter and Josh were getting out, both youths looking grim and tired. John joined them from the next truck over…

"So how'd the mission go, guys?" Leah asked, noticing the somber attitudes of the three.

Their reactions were similar but varied…John looked sad and disappointed, Josh appeared thunderous barely restraining his anger and Peter looked miserable; his eyes shadowed and bleak.

Leah examined each of their expressions and asked softly, "What happened?"

John opened his mouth to answer but was interrupted with a wail that erupted from the vicinity of the furthest truck. All five FA hurried over and watched as Hasani and Chiaga lifted the slain body of Elimu from the cab, and lowered him gently to the ground while Disa stood by sobbing. The blanket had separated on the ride back to the village plainly showing the wound on his chest; the cause of his death.

"Oh, sweet Jesus," Leah whispered while Angelica stood there biting her lip, her turquoise eyes wide and welling with tears she was fiercely holding back.

The party of five could only watch as Chiaga helped Hasani rewrap Elimu's body, then the two men carried their comrade around the side of the meeting house and in a rear door. Disa remained behind, wiping her eyes and trying to compose herself.

As the FA leader and feeling responsible Peter stepped forward and laid a soft hand on her shoulder. "Disa I am so, so sorry this happened…before we knew it we were being ambushed by the UWF. They came out of nowhere."

She sniffled softly. "It's all right…Elimu knew the dangers he would face with each mission, yet he knew he was serving God, and didn't mind. He's in Glory now and waiting for all of us."

Completely humbled by her response Peter just nodded and said, "We'll assist in any way we can…you can count on us, right guys?" Everyone nodded immediately offering their total support.

"Thank you all for everything. Now if you'll excuse me I must go and see what I can do to help prepare for his service and to tell everyone else what happened." Disa offered a shaky smile; turned and headed for the same direction her husband and Chiaga had gone, leaving the FA standing there, cloaked in heavy guilt.

The air was thick around the five; pregnant with a sense of failure when Leah's soft voice cut through. "So you were ambushed?"

"Yeah," Josh replied flatly, his head lowered. "We had just finished getting everybody into the trucks and were about to take off when they came out of nowhere…UWF Jeeps shooting at us from almost every direction. We told the guys to hit the dirt and then used our powers to blow them away. We blew 'em off and thought we got 'em but somebody managed to get a shot off and nailed Elimu." He raised his head eyeing Angelica and added in disgust. "We were completely caught off guard…and we didn't have to be."

Responding to his insinuation Peter snapped, "Back off, Josh!"

With tears flowing freely now Angelica murmured, "I-I'm s-sorry…I'm so sorry." Backing away slowly she then turned and fled, pushing herself through the crowd of refugees still coming off of the transport.

Furious, Peter lunged at Josh, grabbed him by the collar and slammed him against the side of the transport. "What did I tell you before about hassling her?"

Just as angry, Josh pushed him away. "Get off me…if she had told us what she saw, we could've stopped it and Elimu would still be alive."

Peter glared at him, shook his head with his hands raised and backed away. "If anything happens to her I'm gonna lay you out." He turned and ran after Angelica, leaving John and Leah there staring at Josh.

John sighed heavily, shaking his head…but Leah stood in front of him arms akimbo, her expression reproachful. "You're really something you know…do you even think before you speak? The Lord sends her His visions, and they really torment her."

"I know." Josh had the grace to look ashamed. "I'm sorry…I really am. I'm just so frustrated, we let Elimu die." His eyes then showed his misery as he went on. "I never had a brother and my father and I never were close…I kept my distance in the APL as well, never trusting anyone after everything at home blew up in my face. But since coming here and meeting Elimu for the first time I felt that I met someone who was just like me; a fighter who thinks like me, someone to look up to. And his own faith in God was rooted in his soldier's soul. A great man's dead and it's all our fault." He slammed his fist into the side of the transport in frustration.

"Just admit it, Josh…you really mean it's all Angelica's fault," John said quietly as Josh looked off to the side, scowling…

Leah came over to him and reached up to turn his head to face her. "I know how close you were to Elimu but playing the blame game does nothing…it won't bring Elimu back." Heaving a sigh she reasoned, "Let me ask you something, Josh…If Angie had in fact told you what was going to happen and you did everything you could to prevent it and Elimu still had gotten killed…How would you feel?"

He scowled darker and replied, "I'd wonder if she had really seen a vision from the Lord…And I'd wonder just what kind of powers we really had…if we could protect Elimu or anybody."

"So what you're saying is that you would doubt Him and His choosing us as gleaners…That in fact the Lord had made a mistake. The only one who is infallible, who makes no mistakes."

Leah's softly spoken sensible words hit Josh like the proverbial iron fist in a velvet glove. He sighed and running a hand through his hair, he admitted, "I really don't get being a Christian at times…what's our purpose anyway? Didn't God give these powers to us as weapons so we can protect those coming against the UWC?"

Laying a hand on his shoulder John replied, "Sure dude, that's part of it…but we're still human…flawed, but God still uses us. Even with our powers, which He gave us, we can still make bad decisions when we use 'em…poor choices…bad timing… whatever. And don't forget we're not Him. He makes all the final decisions about who lives and dies."

Leah added, "And at the end we'll all be together in heaven. Remember, Brother Danny taught that to us back when we first met him. So we'll see Elimu again."

Josh looked from one sibling to the other and heaved a sigh. Having spent most of his teen years in a neo-military organization he was well aware of the fact that lives were lost in battle. However, as a fairly new Christian, he did not expect that lives would be lost on the mission field. This was something that he knew he probably would have to get used to but thinking like an average new Christian he felt that if you should be able to trust anybody, you should be able to trust God to keep you safe…

*We have these supernatural powers…these unbelievable abilities that He gave us…the power comes from Him. Yet, people can still die while under our watch? I'm having a real hard time wrapping my head around this one…*Realizing that he had to agree in order to keep the peace, Josh simply nodded…

Meanwhile, Angelica had pushed her way through the crowd of refugees towards the back of the village and headed to her secret place, the tears pouring from her eyes nearly blinding her. As she ran through the thick brush Josh's accusation echoed in her ears and throughout the walls of her conscience, joining her own in self flagellation. When she came to the flat rock where she regularly communed with the Lord she collapsed, face in hands, sobbing in agony…

Oh dear Lord, I knew this was going to happen…You told me…no, You showed me. But what was I to do? As the Messenger, You need to make it clear to me, Lord…how much can I say, how much can someone know of their future? Your will always will be done, but we're all human Lord; like children our trust is fragile, we easily feel betrayed. I know when I go back to the village everyone will feel I've betrayed them, so how can I face them?

She was crying in earnest; deep, heart wrenching sobs wracking her slender body…oblivious to all but her own sorrow until she felt two firm hands and corded arms pull her into a safe harbor of warmth in the shape of Peter's broad, muscular chest. He enfolded her; cradling her head against his shoulder, all the while murmuring words of comfort. Her arms wrapped around him, his soft baritone enveloping her…

"Shhh…It's okay, Angel…just let it all out."

Clinging to him as if she were drowning Angelica surrendered in abject misery, allowing the pain flooding her heart to funnel out as she drew from Peter's strength. Like the Rock of the Church for which he was named, he was solid, steady…and just what she needed right now as she was feeling totally and completely shipwrecked by the storm of her emotions; slammed against the rocks of doubt and fear. However, his rhythmic caresses on her head acted as a calming influence on the choppy waves tossing about in the depths of her soul. Time seemed to stand still as they stood there holding each other; surrounded by the jungle brush and small animals chittering, welcoming the dawn. There was a glow on the eastern horizon and the night sky was brightening to cobalt blue when they finally pulled away, still holding on to each other loosely.

Cupping her face in his hands Peter asked Angelica, "Are you okay?"

She gazed up at him and nodded. "Uh-huh…I just wasn't sure how I would take everyone's reaction to Elimu's death. As the Messenger appointed by the Lord, I bear full responsibility. But I was a coward and when Josh pointed out to me what I had been feeling when I saw Elimu's body, I took the coward's route and ran." She lowered her head in shame.

Peter took hold of her chin and raised her head. "Stop beating yourself up over this…You've been bearing the burden of these visions every day since we all received these powers. Seeing what's to come and to keep it a secret takes a lot of strength…I don't know how I'd be able to do it. And Josh is a jerk."

Angelica shook her head. "He's just reacting as anybody else would if they've lost somebody they care about. You know how close he became with Elimu, they were kindred souls."

Peter nodded grudgingly. "Yeah, I guess you're right. As a former military nut he worked closely with Kuitwa Usiku and bonded with Elimu. So it's to be expected. But I told him not to come down on you and he did anyway…so he's a jerk."

Angelica giggled and asked jokingly, "Are you going to beat him up for me?"

"I already did."

"Peter, are you serious?" Her eyes were as wide as saucers.

"I just roughed him up a bit," Peter said, shrugging nonchalantly. "Hey, I warned him about hassling you on the ride home and he didn't listen so he asked for it." He then added softly, "I told you I had your back and I meant it…I'm gonna protect you."

Her heart pounding Angelica gazed up and saw calm, steadfast resolution in the cerulean depths of Peter's eyes. She knew beyond a shadow of a doubt that he was speaking his true intent and the warmth of his declaration filled her to overflowing. Before she knew what she was doing she reached up and planted her lips on his cheek. This innocent action immediately changed the atmosphere around them and when she pulled away their eyes locked. He then cupped her face in his hands and drew to her mouth to his…

It was a gentle kiss at first; a chaste expression of mutual trust and affirmation between two people. However, the feelings of attraction and growing affection that had been developing between them for some time caused the kiss to intensify as passion was ignited. The two young adults felt sensations surge throughout their bodies as the kiss deepened further; urging them to give in to carnal desire. Not entirely innocent, earlier in their teens both Peter and Angelica had explored some forms of sexual expression; she having gone all the way with her former boyfriend, but they were new creations in Christ and something inside was speaking to them, deep in their hearts. So slowly and reluctantly they pulled away…

Feeling guilty Peter took responsibility. "I'm sorry. But I couldn't help myself…the way you were looking at me; I just wanted to kiss you so bad."

"It's okay, I wanted it too," Angelica admitted. "And I didn't want to stop so I'm glad you did."

"Yeah, well, it wasn't easy." He ran a nervous hand through his hair. "And I think before we're tempted further we'd better get back to the village…we both need to get some sleep, it's been a long night."

Taking her by the hand Peter led Angelica back through the brush on the path heading back to the village as the morning sun slipped above the horizon. They walked slowly down the path without speaking and entered the village noticing that the tragic event of the previous night had cast a pall as evidenced by the solemn expressions on the faces of the people milling about.

Angelica stopped suddenly, her face pale and seeing her reaction Peter squeezed her hand reassuringly. "It'll be okay, Angel. They're all people of deep faith…nobody will blame you, especially not Hasani and Disa."

"I hope so," she said dubiously, spotting several of the villagers glancing her way…their sad and confused faces condemning her all over again.

Still holding hands Peter led her over to the women's dorm. They climbed the stairs and headed in, walking down the hall to the door to her room. He opened it, and they entered noticing Leah, fast asleep on her bed.

"Shhh, quiet."

Holding her finger to her lips Angelica and Peter tiptoed over to her bed where she sat down wearily, kicking off her shoes. She lay down as he knelt down beside her…

"Thanks, Pete…for everything," she said, bringing her hand up still holding his.

"It's okay…try to get some rest," Peter whispered, squeezing it.

"You too…You must be wiped," Angelica said yawning.

"Yeah, I seriously need to crash. But I wanted to make sure you were settled in first…so sweet dreams." He leaned forward and they exchanged another brief but tender kiss.

"See you later." Peter got to his feet then turned and let himself out, quietly closing the door…

Later that day, after the midday meal, there was a special memorial service held for the entire village on the stage near the meeting house for Elimu. The worship band played songs of celebration and everyone in the village, including FA attended as Hasani spoke words of comfort and encouragement; giving a stirring eulogy that told of the deep faith and commitment to service of their dear friend who had passed. The worship band played music of celebration; for as true believers of Christ they all knew that his death was not the end…it was in fact the beginning of life everlasting. This was true for Elimu especially, everyone confident that he was alive and well and living in the mansion prepared in the Father's house as promised in John 14:2. Hasani used that particular verse, along with several passages from Job, specifically 1:21 to point out that ultimately it is the Lord who decides everything…and that they would see Elimu again. He then finished with 1 John 3:16-18, verses that absolutely personified the man who passed away…

"…We know love by this, that he laid down his life for us—and we ought to lay down our lives for one another. How does God's love abide in anyone who has the world's goods and sees a brother or sister in need and yet refuses help? Little children, let us love, not in word or speech, but in truth and action."

At the conclusion of the service the five FA youths made their way out of the meeting house lagging behind the rest of the crowd. Once outside, they grouped together almost conspicuously as they glanced at the other villagers. The people were conversing in Swahili, mostly making it impossible to know what they were saying. However, by nature of their periodic glances at FA what they were saying could easily be guessed…or at least speculated upon by a guilty conscience such as Angelica's. But it seemed their sense of isolation was supported by the fact that their offers to help with Elimu's memorial service had been politely declined. It made the group feel very uncomfortable…and even more as if they had failed. Standing in a cluster apart from everyone else, they discussed the situation…

"That was a very moving service," Leah murmured.

"Yeah, not to sound flip, but there wasn't a dry eye in the house," John remarked somberly.

"It's what I expected," Josh stated. "He was well respected; especially in Kuitwa Usiku…he was one of their high ranking officers. He had all sorts of military training and tactical abilities…I really respected him."

"He was a good man and will be missed," Peter pointed out.

Thoughtfully silent up to this moment Angelica said in a soft voice, "When I told him to be prepared before the mission, and looked into his eyes I could tell that he was ready for anything." She sighed deeply then continued, "I couldn't tell him the truth… what would really happen. But I had a feeling he knew…I could see it in his eyes."

Her four comrades stood there expectantly as it seemed she had something else to get off of her chest…

She met the four pairs of eyes focused on her bravely and went on. "I'm sorry if you feel that my not saying anything about Elimu's death was wrong…but I was following the Lord's will. Ever since the beginning when we first got our powers and He chose me to be the Messenger He made it clear…I couldn't reveal everything because of the way we are as humans. At the time, I was unsure how I could pull this off and even now I really wonder exactly what my role is as the Messenger. I mean, knowing something; especially the future and not saying anything could cause people to lose trust in me. And if I were on the other side, I would feel the same way…especially if I lost someone close to me. So I guess what I'm asking all of you to do is to trust me and if you don't trust me, at least trust the Lord. After all, we're all in this together serving Him, right?"

Humbled, the other four FA members stood wordlessly before Angelica until Josh chose to speak…

He said quietly, "You're absolutely right, Angie…we are all in this together for sure. And last night I was out of line. The Lord chose you for something I know I could never do…I'm sorry. And I know I speak for everyone when I say we all trust you."

"Amen to that," John seconded.

"Absolutely," Leah affirmed.

Peter just grinned and threw her a wink which made her smile. She took a deep breath and said gratefully, "Thanks, guys…this really means a lot."

Hasani came over to the group and all five inadvertently dropped their heads, as if in shame. However, in his typical way the chief of the village smiled to put them all at ease…

"I am glad that you all were able to come to the service," he said.

"There's no way we would've missed it," Peter declared. "Elimu was an awesome man, someone we all especially looked up to…He was an example to everyone as to how you should live your faith."

Hasani nodded. "Indeed…He was like my own blooded brother in fact; he was my brother…in Christ. I am certain that he's saving a place for me and Disa at the marriage supper of the Lamb."

Everyone said in unison, "Amen."

Hasani turned to Peter. "We need to meet to discuss what's going to happen in a few days. We have new communiqués from COS regarding Hukumu…Uwambo's grand stand while Abram visits."

"Have you heard from Malensky?" he inquired.

"Yah…If you'll come with me we'll go underground for a conference call to get the latest news."

"Okay…I'm on my way." He turned to the others. "See you guys later."

Before they dispersed, Hasani detained Angelica with a hand on her arm, then laid his hands on her shoulders. She gazed at him quizzically, waiting for him to speak…

He said to her earnestly, "You need not feel badly…we are grateful to all of you, but especially to you as the Messenger. My words this morning were from the Holy Spirit to give comfort to everyone, but especially to you. Do not lose heart."

Her eyes welling up and her voice barely a whisper she said, "Thank you."

Releasing her he turned away to join Peter, who with his head turned towards Angelica gave her an encouraging grin and a thumbs-up. She returned the smile and gesture then headed towards the school. As she headed towards the building housing classrooms a voice spoke to her; a familiar, commanding voice:

Tonight be ready to receive the Shed Blood of the Lamb…alert the others…

The Shed Blood of the Lamb? What's that, Lord…what do you mean? There was no further word so a profound trepidation gripped Angelica…

I wonder what You have for us now…

Meanwhile, Peter had followed Hasani to the rear of the meeting house to the communications shed, which actually housed an array of high-tech communications equipment that had a hook up to a private satellite dish. This was not unusual because Adanech had once been a Tanzanian military base; therefore the government had left quite a bit when it abandoned the base. So Hasani and COS were able to communicate daily with each other in a covert manner, without needing to use a public ISP or cell phone service, and Peter the leader of FA would gather important information on vital COS movement of refugees before missions and would send in reports after each mission. The door to the shed had the electronic lock activated by a security laser scanner over a keypad so he used the same remote laser pen he had given them the night FA arrived to create a beam, opened the door and he and Peter walked in…

Hasani took a seat before the flat screen monitor, turned on the tower and using the software that Josh had designed typed in a password and was immediately linked up to the man known as Malachi Malensky. A scrambled image came up on the screen…

"Hello, my friend," a garbled voice greeted him.

"Hello to you," Hasani replied. "I take it you heard of what happened."

"Yes. I'm sorry to hear of the loss of Elimu…He will be greatly missed; he was a valuable asset to us."

"Yah," Hasani answered. "The ambush was unexpected."

"Was Full Armor there with you?"

"Yes, we were," Peter answered. "But they suddenly came from nowhere…many UWF jeeps, all firing at us. They took us by surprise and completely caught us off guard…I'm sorry."

A brief silence met them. "Sadly, some deaths are to be expected. Remember, we're rebelling against Abram and the one world government. The Scripture tells us that we are to expect to be killed, to become martyrs. Elimu became that, and is now wearing his white robe in heaven where he's waiting for all of us."

Peter sighed deeply then said, "I know this, Malachi…But I and the rest of FA feel like we failed everyone. Especially Angelica."

The gravelly voice spoke encouragement. "Then it's your job as the leader to make sure everyone stays strong. You were all chosen by the Lord specifically for this task." Changing the subject he said, "You must prepare now for the next major phase."

Hasani said, "You're speaking of Hukumu...what do you have for us?"

"The four holding areas in the Sudan, Ethiopia, Nigeria, and South Africa where the mass disposals will take place have been infiltrated...we have managed to infiltrate the guards and our people are overseeing the captives. However, moving everyone is proving daunting because Uwambo has tightened security, due to the successes we've had because of Kuitwa Usiku. Because of the type of man he is, he's not about to allow himself to be humiliated in front of the Supreme Leader by allowing rebels to escape right front of his nose."

"That is true," Hasani affirmed. "Uwambo is a very proud man...too proud...he'll never stand for that."

"That's why we will be counting on you, Full Armor...It's up to you to come up with a way to move all those rebels captured by the UWF using your Holy Spirit powers. That's the only way we'll be able to save all those people's lives."

"I understand...and you can count on us," Peter declared while saying to himself, *I wish I knew just how we're going to be able to do this*...He then recalled Angelica's directive at the briefing they had just before leaving their bunker, back in the States...

"Uwamba has designated four areas as disposal camps...one in the Sudan...one in South Africa...one in Nigeria and one in Ethiopia. These areas have been chosen because they have shown the least resistance to the mandatory ID plantings. Ironically, these locations are also significant because they were all areas which had been places of either great freedom or oppression before the

Rapture. And Ethiopia had ancient significance going back to the days of Noah when his son Ham settled there after the Flood. We'll be rescuing those in the camps."

Now I understand...Our real mission is Hukumu, not what we've been doing all this time. But still, even with our powers how are we going to pull this off?

Hasani then asked, "What about tonight? Are there any movements of refugees headed this way that we need to pick up?"

Malensky then said, "No. After last night's incident I think it would be best to lay low...Just receive people coming in under their own power...by foot or by vehicle. Especially now, with Abram's visit in days. I'm sure all of you could use the night off."

"I'll inform everyone. Do you happen to know how many people are being held at the camps?" Hasani asked.

"According to my inside people each camp has close to 200 people each. My Intel sources tell me that Uwambo is hoping to capture an additional 50 to add at each location, making it a grand total of 1000 people to be executed in front of a worldwide audience and Abram."

Peter was disgusted. "Talk about making the grand statement...What a slime!"

"Yah," Hasani agreed. "Thank you, my friend. We will do what you say and wait for the next communication from you."

"Yes, I'll be looking forward to hearing from you too... Continue to do the good work for the King and be strong." The computer screen went dark.

Hasani and Peter just sat quietly, both contemplating the road ahead of them...

Later on, after the evening meal the team of Full Armor sat in the boys' room as Peter relayed the latest thing that they were being called to do...

"Because of Abram's upcoming visit, we have to figure out a way to move refugees from the four disposal camps in the Sudan, Nigeria, Ethiopia, and South Africa. Remember our briefing before we left home? It's crunch time, people...Our real mission begins in five days."

"Okay," Josh said. "So how are we gonna to do this?"

"That's it...We gotta figure out a way to get to these disposal camps. But first we have to figure out a strategy of how we're going to keep the UWF troops from preventing the escape once we get there. We already know that our powers allow us to protect as we move refugees here to the village. However, getting back to the village and in one piece without inciting a major battle is going to be tough,"

"Yeah, for sure," John said with a sigh. "I know the Lord gave us some awesome powers, but as far as I can see we can't vanish into thin air...or cause others to. And even though I know we have the wheels to get these people here, you know, the UWF will be hot on our tails. With Abram being here, they're sure to have the big guns out. It's a suicide mission, man."

Now is the time to tell them, Daughter.

Angelica heard the Holy Spirit's voice and spoke up. She got to her feet. "Everyone, I have something to tell you…something the Lord wants you to know."

"What is it Angie," Leah inquired.

"He told me that we are about to receive something called the 'Shed Blood of the Lamb'."

"The Shed Blood of the Lamb?" Josh echoed. "What's that?"

Angelica simply said, "I don't know anymore than you do. He said nothing more then to get ready to receive it."

The three others sat puzzled silence until Peter asked, "When are we supposed to receive this?"

"Again, I don't know. He just told me earlier to get ready to receive the Shed Blood of the Lamb and to inform you guys." She shrugged helplessly as if to fend off any backlash.

There was a brief period of inertia with no words spoken then Peter said benignly, "Okay then…I guess we'll know more when it happens, right guys?"

The other three said in unison, "Yeah."

Peter then informed them, "There's no special mission tonight so we can catch up on some ZZZ's. I think we could all use the rest."

Everyone was in agreement and Angelica added, "We should pray because I think we need the Lord's cover for what's to come."

Everyone was the complete agreement so they all got to their feet, joined hands and prayed. There was no set formal prayer… each of them took turns speaking to the Lord their individual and collective doubts, fears, and requests for strength, along with guidance, wisdom, and courage. All five young people; brand new Christians in their own right taking baby steps of faith; seeking the hand of the Father, with implicit trust to uphold them…

It was well over an hour before they had finished praying, feeling a sense of peace that one can get only after knowing they had community with the living God. At the conclusion they all shared and exchanged embraces; warm and heart felt gestures of support and unity as a profound awareness of the task at hand fell over them…

With the group now breaking up for the night both Peter and Josh insisted on escorting Angelica and Leah to the women's dorm. They walked with the girls to the door of their room and went inside…

Peter went with Angelica over to her bed, and Josh, holding onto Leah assisted her. "Well, here you are, little bird…all safe and sound."

Kicking off her shoes Leah stifled a yawn. "Thanks a lot, Josh. Promise me you'll get some rest, you look really tired."

"Yeah, I am…didn't get much sleep last night and haven't really slept well since we got here. And for some reason tonight, I'm really beat."

She gazed up at him and murmured, "Letting go of your emotions can do that."

"Yeah…last night and today were all emotion…I'm drained."

"Yeah…all of a sudden now that I'm here on the bed I'm exhausted." Leah yawned again then curled her legs up and laid her head on the pillow, not even bothering to get undressed.

Josh kissed the two fingers on his right hand and laid them on her forehead. "Sleep tight little bird." He went to the door, glanced over at Peter and Angelica; grinned, shrugged and let himself out.

Over at Angelica's bed, Peter was making sure that she was alright. Aware of their deepened friendship and sensitive to her state of mind due to the latest command of the Lord, he took care of her. Helping her to lie down, he acted the part of a parent putting his child to bed…

"Just lie down and get some sleep," Peter directed.

She protested, "You didn't need to do all this. I was planning to go to sleep anyway."

"Just making sure."

"Okay daddy," Angelica quipped.

Chuckling Peter knelt beside her and kissed her on the forehead. "Sweet dreams and I'll see you in the morning." Turning off the light, he got up and spotted Leah gazing at him with a small smile. Embarrassed, he waved at her and let himself out.

"Pete's really a very sweet guy, isn't he? And it looks like he really cares for you." she remarked to Angelica.

"Uh-huh. Ever since the first day he rescued me, he's constantly looking out for me." She sighed deeply, feeling a small measure of contentment at the knowledge of that fact.

"I think it might be a little more than that," Leah said as she drifted off to sleep.

"Maybe," Angelica said in a noncommittal fashion as she, too finally drifted off.

Nearly an hour later, as both girls slumbered, a golden light that appeared like a flame of fire hovered above their heads. Then, it descended into each girl…

A searing pain stabbed Angelica in her right side, jolting her out of her sleep…She bolted upright with a cry, clutching her side. In her bed Leah likewise shot up, holding her head…

"Ohhhhh!" Both young women moaned in agony as the pain morphed into an intense heat, which gradually subsided, allowing them to come to full awareness. Angelica reached over and switched on the light then gasped as she noticed the bloodstain on her shirt.

"W-what w-was that?" Leah asked shakily as she lifted her head from her hands. Feeling a warm, wet, sensation she looked down at her hands and stifled a scream…

"Angie, Angie…we-we're bleeding! How did this happen?" The partially blind girl, unable to really see what had happened to her was justifiably frightened.

Angelica pulled her hand away, stared at her own bloody side and shook her head *is this what the Lord meant by the Shed Blood of the Lamb?* "I don't know, Leah…I can only guess that this is what I was told about before." She reached over into her backpack and pulled out a mirror, holding it in front of her wound. *It looks just like one of the wounds Christ received during his crucifixion.* Turning her attention to Leah, she got up and brought the mirror over to her friend. Holding it up before her Angelica gently spoke…

"Take a look and see where your wound is," she urged, her hand on Leah's shoulder.

With tears running down her cheeks Leah gazed at her image in the mirror. "Oh my God…The wound is on my forehead, like a crown."

"Uh-huh…And mine is on my side, just like the wounds Jesus received. They're called stigmata…I read about them, when I was studying about different faiths when I was with the Spirit Circle."

"I see," Leah said in understanding. "The Shed Blood of the Lamb…it makes sense." She leaned in closer to the mirror, running her fingertips over the now dried blood on her forehead…

Over in the men's dorm, the boys were experiencing the same thing. All three, with golden flames of fire entering them, were jolted awake by the intense pain; Peter and Josh on their wrists, and John on his feet…

"Yeowww!" He howled, bending forward and grabbing his feet. "Hey guys, I'm bleeding!" He switched on the light and saw that two bloody holes had punctured his feet.

In their beds ad sitting up both groaning their pain, Peter and Josh flexed their arms forward; blood trickling down their forearms from what appeared to be holes the shape of nail marks in their wrists. The dying fire in their wounds decreased to a radiating heat…

Taking in a deep breath to disperse the pain Peter shook his arms. "Maybe this was what Angelica was talking about earlier… I've no other explanation for it," he gasped.

Josh grunted, shaking his hands to alleviate his own pain while John examined the holes in his feet. "It looks like stigmata…the wrists…the feet. Just like Christ."

"Just like Christ," Peter echoed *the Shed Blood of the Lamb*… Then a thought occurred to him. "Let's go check on the girls," he said, reaching for his pants to put on.

The other two did the same and then the three sprinted out of the men's dorm, heading towards the women's dorm. Taking the stairs two at a time, they rushed down the hall and stormed into the room without even bothering to knock on the door. Peter went to Angelica's side while Josh and John flanked Leah…

"Are you two alright?" John asked, wrapping his arm around Leah's waist and examining the wounds on her forehead.

"Yeah," she answered. "I think so."

Examining the blood stain on her side Peter asked Angelica, "How about you, Angel…are you okay?"

"Yeah…What about you, where did you get hurt?"

He held up his wrists. "Right there…me and Josh, right?"

"Yeah," Josh replied. "We were all asleep and then we woke up hurtin' like anything and we got these wounds." He held up his own wrists for emphasis.

"Yeah, that's just the way it happened, only on my feet," John affirmed. "You girls too, huh?"

"Uh-huh…it was just…weird. One minute I'm asleep and the next minute I'm awake, in pain and I'm bleeding." She raised her shirt and exclaimed, "Oh wow…look at this!"

Everyone looked and was amazed as they noticed that the wound had not only stopped bleeding, but now it appeared that she had never been wounded. The only indication that anything had happened to her was the dried blood in the area. Curious now, the other four FA examined their own wounds and found the exact same thing…with the exception of dried blood, the skin in the area of where they had been marked was intact as if they had never even gotten wounded. In complete awe of the occurrence, they sat in stunned silence…

John, always ready with a quick phrase said, "Well, like they say, the Lord does move in mysterious ways."

"Yeah, I guess so," Josh agreed. "And He sure packs heat when He does…Man, that killed." He gazed at Leah and asked in concern, "Especially you huh, little bird."

"Oh yeah…I thought my head was going to split in two." She rubbed the temples gingerly, remembering the excruciating pain.

Frowning thoughtfully, Peter contemplated, "So if this the Shed Blood of the Lamb that we were to receive it explains why it came as stigmata…So we could experience the same pain that Christ experienced as he hung on the cross…which tells me that whatever new powers He just gave us will cause us deep pain somewhere down the line. As the Scripture says to whom much is given, much will be required."

"But I wonder," Angelica said. "What exactly will these new powers enable us to do?"

"Well, I haven't a clue," Josh said eyeing her significantly. "But if anyone would ever know, if the Lord would tell anybody it'd probably be you. You're the Messenger, after all."

She shook her head. "That may be true, Josh, but He still tells me what He chooses to tell me, at His discretion."

Peter spoke up. "Well, whatever they are boys and girls, we'll find out soon enough. And something tells me we'll be using them a lot sooner then any of us think especially with Abram coming to Africa in the next few days."

His grave statement added to the atmosphere of anticipation and sense of heavy responsibility hanging over Full Armor…

The next day FA met with Hasani to strategize the next mission. Based on Intel and communiqués from Malensky and COS Supreme Leader Abram's itinerary was as follows: after arriving in Cairo, he was to go straight to Uwambo's palace in Giza where that night, there would be a grand dinner and ball held in his honor. Every former president, dictator, or royal ruler of the African nations, including the four Supreme Governors of the other regions would be in attendance, before the mass executions of the captured rebels known as Hukumu. It was to be a spectacle of disgusting proportions; a deviant display that celebrated the slaughter of about 1000 innocent people. All of that aside, FA was more concerned putting in motion the plan to rescue those 1000 innocent people by allowing themselves to get captured. Prior to their meeting with Hasani Peter called everybody all together in the boys room at the men's dormitory. It was there that the five laid out their own foundation for the mission by deciding how they needed to be captured. First, they determined to not wear their brooches for the journey for the power that provided the faux TM mark would be negated, making them appear as any other unseeded citizen. They then agreed they would keep the brooches available in their jeans pocket to activate with a touch so their protective powers would be in play for the later part of the mission, the actual rescue. As far as what happened the night before receiving the stigmata, or Shed Blood of the Lamb nobody knew what the meaning was for the occurrence…nor did they dare to speculate…

In the back communications shed with Hasani all five of the youths were discussing and perfecting the strategy that was to be used. First, they shared with him their unusual experience of the previous night, along with what Angelica had been shown prior to them being sent to the village. Since the Lord had shown her the foundation for Hukumu before they even arrived in Africa, Angelica shared with Hasani, the very same thing she had explained to her comrades. Opening her notebook she explained, almost to the letter everything that had been transmitted to them from Malensky and COS, and even the stoic chief of Adanech was mesmerized by the detail. When she came to the part that FA would play, he listened closely…

"When the Lord first revealed the details of this mission to me, he told me that the five of us would be sent to the four places where these disposal camps are." She pointed to the map she had drawn in her notebook, and without even knowing the information that had come from COS, the map showed plainly the exact same locations…

"John is to go to the Sudan, Josh is to go to Ethiopia, Peter is to go to South Africa, and Leah and I will go to Nigeria. Are there any seeding raids taking place near those camps?"

"Yah…UWF is conducting them in areas not far from each camp. It is so much easier to round up those refusing the TM chip." Hasani frowned thoughtfully. "Since these are rather remote villages and small towns, to plant you all to be captured will prove difficult. Your cover here has been that you are anthropology students from Harvard working on your theses, but I doubt that you could use the same cover everywhere and be believable."

"Yeah, that's gonna be tough," Peter agreed. "Not necessarily for me since I'll be in South Africa…But John in the Sudan, Josh in Ethiopia, and the girls in Nigeria are going to be hard to pull off. Unless—,"

"Unless what?" Josh wanted to know. "C'mon, man, don't keep us hanging."

Peter pursed his lips, thinking hard. Then he brightened up, as if a light bulb had appeared above his head. "I think I've got it…Josh, you'll get captured at the airport at Addis Ababa during the inspection…it ought to be easy for you to get in trouble, you have a big mouth," he said, chuckling.

John snickered at that while Josh scowled at him. "Yeah, ha ha." He jabbed John hard with his elbow. "Shut up you idiot!"

Peter then studied John closely. "John, your complexion is swarthy enough that you could pass for an Arab looking for work at a garage. You know, now when you look for a job they ask you to show your chip. If you don't have to one, and you refuse to take one that's when you'll get nabbed; when you refuse to get seeded."

"Gotcha." He gave a thumbs-up.

Peter then turned towards the girls. "Ladies, you'll do the same as Josh…You'll be at the airport in Lagos and when they check you for your chip, you'll get captured." His expression became serious. "I want you two to stick together, hear me? Don't get separated."

"I don't like it," Josh protested. "Two pretty girls traveling together, alone…When they get captured some UWF creep might try to hurt them."

"Yeah, I didn't think about that," Peter admitted. "I don't like it either, but how else can we cover all four areas? I don't see any other way around it; the girls will just have to stay together."

"Yeah, but I still don't like it," Josh insisted and all three men scowled in disapproval.

"Don't worry guys," Angelica assured them. "When I was 11, I took karate…With my mother gone all hours and bringing home strange men who were giving me the eye, I decided I needed to know how to defend myself. I took it up until I was 16 and went to live in the Spirit Circle so I can make sure that Leah and I are alright. Besides, the Lord wants us there so He'll protect us."

"Well, that's true," John agreed

Josh looked dubious but grudgingly agreed.

Hasani cleared his throat. "Well then we need to get you all to the destinations…I'll contact Merci and she can fly you all out in the next two days. Malensky let me know that there are COS operatives as guards undercover at each camp…They can let us know when all of you are there at each camp. The plan then is for Full Armor to shield the refugees using your powers as COS gets them into designated transport vehicles and they escape, to eventually get here." He reached for a cell phone, dialed the number and began to talk to somebody.

All five FA exchanged glances with each other, all thinking the same thing…Just what was going to happen and how exactly were they to accomplish rescuing so many people…And what kind of power was connected to this Shed Blood of the Lamb that they received last night? Peter especially was wondering about this, when he woke up this morning he didn't really feel any differently. But he knew something inside him had changed, not exactly a feeling of surging power, but a definite feeling nonetheless…

Hasani had just finished talking on his cell phone. "It's all set, Merci will fly each of you to the appointed destinations starting tomorrow. She'll take John to Khartoum in the Sudan and Josh to the airport at Addis Ababa in Ethiopia. The next day, she'll take Peter to Johannesburg in South Africa and both young ladies to Lagos in Nigeria."

"Okay then, the plan's all set…You can alert Malensky and his COS operatives to expect us. And we'll see just what we'll be able to do with the Shed Blood of the Lamb." Peter said decisively…

CHAPTER 6—
HUKUMU AND SHED BLOOD

While all of this was going on away in Giza in his Palace Abrafo Uwamba was making his own preparations for the arrival of the Supreme Leader, with all the pomp and circumstance that he could muster. The egotistical Supreme Governor of the South literally licking his chops at the opportunity to not only make a statement worldwide, but to prove to his Excellency Abram that he could be an example of success in dealing with the ongoing rebel problem. The UWCPI global satellite news service, the public relation and news source of Abram's new government was ready to broadcast spectacle round the world and every nation, including Antarctica assuring that every person on earth would see what happens to those who stand in opposition against his Excellency. Cameras and camera crews were already in attendance around each camp waiting for tomorrow's Hukumu, but they were kept at a distance from each facility for security purposes. His own pride was on the line and he had no intention of sacrificing that so he took painstaking precautions; meeting with his assigned UWF commanders to assure that everything for Hukumu would go off without a hitch.

Leaning back in his butter soft leather chair Uwambo sighed, ambivalent; he re-read the report from the ambush that took place a few nights ago in the Rungwa Game Reserve. Reading about the casualty that the enemy had suffered gave him a sadistic smile. However, when he got to the part about the UWF attack jeeps being blown over he cringed. The casualties suffered by the attacking troops were not a lot, but they were serious enough to garner attention. His briefing with the commander of the operation had netted an explanation that sounded something like the plot of a superhero comic book; with descriptions of bright lights and powerful waves of energy. Although, as one of the supreme governors directly under Abram Uwambo had seen supernatural power displayed in great measure by his Excellency, he scoffed at any show of supernatural power by those he considered inferior in many ways.

Be that as it may, it makes no difference…They will have no way to interfere or upset Hukumu, regardless of any so-called powers. With his Excellency here they wouldn't dare and in the face of his absolute power, they may find themselves being blown away…

His cell phone buzzed, and Uwambo picked it up, seeing the CID. "Major Konkosani…I've been waiting for your report. What do you have to tell me?"

Moses replied, "I have important information to tell you… As I've told you before, this village appears to be a haven for rebel refugees. They arrive nightly, all night until sunrise."

"Yes, yes, I know," Uwambo said impatiently. "But I need to know be exact location, so I can plan an attack and as yet you haven't been able to get that information to me. Plus, even with the incident of the other night at the game reserve your report neglected to state exactly what it was that blew that force back. The only reports I've gotten from those troops who recovered after the attack, simply told me that it was as if a bolt of lightning and a great wind like a hurricane blew them back. The only thing you told me was that one person on the enemy side was killed. I'm afraid I need more than that."

A small period of silence met him, then Moses spoke up, "I think there's something unusual being planned…Those five American college students are planning to leave the village and they've been meeting regularly with the chief, Hasani. In my report I did tell you that the three male members were on the mission to the game reserve. So I know they have something to do with the organization of the rebels in moving people to the village."

"Interesting…Please make sure to keep me informed. You know his Excellency, Supreme Leader Abram will be here in a few days for Hukumu and I want to make sure that we rein in these brazen rebel scum and show them who's really in control. And you were the man chosen for your skills to get the information to me that I need to accomplish that."

"I will do my best, sir…I'll work with the region command to help plan a covert ambush and I will find out just what these college students have to do with this. Just trust me."

Uwambo grunted, "Don't fail me, major." He cut off the communication and then brooded, *I need to find out just what this so-called bolt of lightning and blast of wind came from…Have the rebels a new weapon that even we in UWC have never heard about?*

In his hiding place in the storage room at Adanech, Moses wracked his brain, still trying to figure out what it was he saw a few nights ago at the game reserve. Hidden in the chassis of one of the trucks, he had heard when the UWF jeeps began their ambush and leaned out to peak at what was going on…And what he had seen still had him stunned…

It was unbelievable…I still can't get over it. Those three college students held out their hands and a huge light appeared…Then before I knew it, all those jeeps were blown back like a tornado. I'd never been so scared in all my life…Who are these people and what is this power they have? I have to do something to find out…

With a rodent's stealth Moses made his way back out into the village. He then made his way to the men's dorm and his room, looking back and forth to make sure that nobody was watching him. Once inside, he closed the door and went to his bed, pulling out a leather case from his knapsack…opening the case, he took out a micro-transmitter no larger than the size of a postage stamp and a remote, slipping it in his pocket. Moses replaced the leather case, shoving it back into his knapsack then headed out and made his way over to the meeting house, all the while carefully scanning the area for either Ngao or Kuitwa Usiku personnel who always seem to be milling about with a watchful eye. This time seeing neither, he seized the golden opportunity presented before him and made his way carefully to the communication shed. Scanning the area first then seeing the coast was clear, Moses went to the door and using what appeared to be an ordinary laser pointer, overrode the security laser scanner…the door unlocked and Moses opened the door quietly and slipped in.

Once inside the shed, he gazed about him at the large array of high-tech comm. equipment and *marveled they certainly have a lot of high-end technology here…More than I would have expected an average village filled with religious fanatics would have…I admit I'm impressed.*

But the UWF is the worldwide Army and we are second to no one. I'll get to the bottom of everything, and get all the information even if it costs me my life…

Getting right to work, Moses took the micro-transmitter and planted it right above the computer HD monitor, near the speakers. Because the transmitter was as thin as cardboard it practically blended in with the surface of the monitor, making it appear as if it were not even there to all but the most trained eye. He then took out the razor thin Wi-Fi remote and keyed in some numbers to program, activate, and synchronize both pieces of technology. Satisfied, he slipped the remote in his pocket and went to let himself out, scurrying back to his room in the men's dorm.

However, as Moses performed his cloak and dagger operation, he was covertly being observed by none other than Josh; who suspicious from the time he first met him took it upon himself to put Moses under observation. Whenever he saw Moses acting antsy or weird, he would surreptitiously watch every move he made and if necessary, would follow him about. But Moses had to be credited for his ability to be elusive, melting into the crowd as the population at Adanech grew with each nightly arrival of refugees. This time, for whatever reason, Moses had not been as careful as he usually was. Maybe it was because the crowd at the village at that particular time of day was thin that Josh was able to follow him, his own stealth skills impeccable…however the circumstance had presented itself Josh took it, observing every move the UWF spy made and drawing his own conclusions.

Ha, I knew that Moses guy wasn't to be trusted. And I know he's up to something in there but I'd better keep undercover and watch what he's doing Josh hid himself in the brush; his eyes glued to the door of the communications shed, waiting. And he found his patience rewarded when a short time later, Moses let himself out of the communication shed, used the laser pointer to relock the door and made his getaway. Once he was gone Josh extricated himself from the brush and went over to the door of the shed. He used the laser pen that Hasani had given him when they arrived at the village, scanned the pad and entered.

Josh then carefully inspected the shed going over every area, looking for anything unusual or suspicious…any kind of wires or transmitters; any type of listening advice. He took his time, painstakingly going through everything he could think of and was dismayed, and more than a little frustrated to find nothing unusual…

He uttered a curse then said to himself, *this stinks…I know that guy put something in here, did some thing…But I can't find a thing; no wires, no bugs. So what was he doing in here all that time?* Heaving a sigh, Josh too exited the shed, with plenty of food for thought…

Early the next day Merci came into the village in her Jeep to pick up John and Josh and take them to her airfield for the trips to the Sudan and Ethiopia. She planned to fly to Khartoum first, to drop John off, then she would head to Addis Ababa to leave Josh. Before they left Peter briefed with each one…

"Okay guys, this is it. Make sure you're not wearing your brooch and when you guys get captured the COS undercover man at the disposal camps will let us know when you're inside. Once you're in there, I want you to lay low. Don't attract attention to yourselves." This last statement was specifically directed toward Josh and his response was to grunt, sarcastically rolling his eyes…

"Please be careful, you two," Leah said to the boys.

"Will do, sis," John assured her.

Josh put a gentle, reassuring hand on her. "Don't fret your pretty head, little bird…we'll be just fine. You be careful, you and Angie are both gonna be alone and I still don't like that. But I guess it can't be helped."

Angelica stepped forward. "Trust me, Josh…I'll make sure we're both alright."

Josh glanced at her askance. "Okay, Tiger…I'm gonna take you at your word."

Merci started the Jeep, turned it around and Josh and John both waved as they headed out of the village…

The next day, it was Peter and the girls turn to leave…Merci came in her Jeep to pick them up and take them to her airfield where they boarded the Cessna and headed out to the airport in Lagos, Nigeria. Once Merci received clearance for landing, she taxied the plane over to where the chartered flights disembarked. Before the girls got off Peter briefed them one last time…

"Okay you two remember what we talked about. Once they see that you have no chip the UWF will either order you to get implants or arrest you. Just keep your cool during the body search, no matter how creepy it feels…you have to get taken to that disposal camp. Hasani said Malensky have alerted all of his plants in the camp to look out for you. Keep as low a profile as you can, okay?"

Both girls nodded in tacit understanding and Angelica said, "Don't worry…we'll be fine. I'll look after Leah and we won't draw attention to ourselves."

"Good girl…I'm counting on you. And promise me one thing, Angel…if things get really hairy no wonder woman stuff, okay?" He leaned forward and whispered for her ears only, "You're not Charlie's Angel, you're mine and even though I know that you can take care of yourself, you're still a girl and if a 250 pound 6 foot plus guy could still do you some damage."

She nodded. "Okay…I promise."

Their eyes met and locked; as if they themselves embraced however, they merely linked hands. He brought her hand to his lips and kissed it then said to both of them, "Be careful…and I'll see you soon."

"You too."

Both girls headed to the front of the plane to get off, bidding goodbye to Merci, then left. She started up the plane engine, turned around and took off to head to Johannesburg to drop Peter off. The nearly two-hour ride was silent between them, as Peter's head was swimming…Thinking not only about what awaited him, but also about his four teammates and their safety. Right now those four people were the closest to him in the entire world, and even though he knew they all were under the protected of hands of Almighty God, the thought of losing even one of them scared him to death. Although he didn't show it what had happened to Elimu had affected him in a similar manner as that had Josh…he truly wondered if these powers that God had given them could really save the people marked for death in the disposal camps. He had to admit that in his own way he was very much like Josh, doubting his own faith due to the residual sense of betrayal he had felt back when his father abandoned him and his mother; which still clung to him, like a monkey on his back…

*Will I ever learn to truly trust again? Or will I always have a doubt, that someone close to me will betray me, abandon me. And You Lord… even though I love You and I know You love me based on what happened in my life, I still hesitate to trust even You…*He was wrapped deep in his thoughts all through the flight…

Back in the airport at Lagos Angelica and Leah had entered the concourse, lost in the milling crowd of travelers. Because Lagos, Nigeria in the past few years had become kind of a gateway in and out of Africa, they had been less conspicuous. However, they had prepared themselves to be singled out due to the fact that they did not have the TM chip and when told to receive it, they were going to refuse it. Walking along through the busy airport, they got in the women's line for the customary inspection…

As they made their way to where they would be searched Angelica asked Leah, "Are you alright?"

She replied, "I'm fine…The lighting in here is bright so I can see fairly well, it's just my right eye where I can't see peripherally so I don't know what's coming at me from that direction. I'm okay though, Angie, so stop worrying."

Angelica smiled and said, "I'm just keeping my promise to Josh to look after you…If anything happens to you I'm sure he won't go easy on me."

Leah giggled in return. "And if he leans on you, Peter will lean on him. You didn't see what happened the other day when you ran away after Elimu's service…Peter had him by the collar and slammed him against the truck…it was a little scary."

"Really?" Angelica's brows shot up in genuine surprise.

Leah nodded. "Uh-huh."

Angelica appeared momentarily perplexed then remembered what he had said to her. "Oh I get it now," she responded in understanding. "When he came after me, I asked him if he was going to beat Josh up and he said that he did. Even though he had told me that he had done it, and why I guess I still thought he might've been kidding me. I guess he was serious."

"Oh yeah, he was serious," Leah affirmed. "That's why I said to you, he really does care for you and it may even be a lot more."

Angelica nodded thoughtfully then admitted, "Yeah…When he came after me, he was comforting me, hugged me…then he kissed me. And I kissed him back."

"He kissed you?" With a quiet squeal Leah clutched at her friend. "And you tell me now? Why didn't you tell me before?"

"Calm down…it was just a kiss," Angelica reasoned with a slight flush on her cheeks. "Besides, it's not like we're on a date here. We have to keep our minds on our mission and put all the other stuff behind us."

Leah sighed in disappointment, "I suppose you're right…but it just confirms what I've known for a long time…Peter really likes you." Giving Angelica a knowing look she added, "And I think you really like him."

Her blush deepening Angelica just nodded. Giving the conversation a turn, she then asked Leah, "Well, okay, I've confessed…now it's your turn. Have you and Josh kissed?"

Leah hesitated, biting her lip then she replied, "We're close… He's always looking after me. He hugs me and occasionally holds my hand, kisses me on the cheek or forehead. But no…we haven't kissed, not like you have. He never had any siblings so he treats me like a little sister." Her pretty face was clouded, and it was obvious that she had yearned for more than that.

To console her Angelica squeezed Leah's hand. "I think his feelings for you are much deeper than you think. I just think he's one of those guys that has a harder time than usual expressing his feelings. When it comes to getting intimate, especially with a woman he cares about his feelings are intensely personal, shared only with her. You know him better than I do but from what I can see he's very passionate about what matters to him."

"Yes, that's true," Leah nodded, agreeing. "Josh is carrying a heavy emotional burden deep in his heart, something that's tearing him apart. He told me some of it…but he's holding most of it back and suffering in silence. But I can tell you one thing, Angie…He is fiercely loyal to those closest to him and right now that's all of us. And he is totally dedicated to serving the Lord to the very best of his abilities. He's a wonderful man."

Angelica nodded candidly in agreement as the conversation ended. The line moved up to the inspection area where there were both male and female inspectors, dressed in UWF uniforms were thoroughly searching each person. But first, they were checking the right hands or foreheads of each man or woman, boy or girl for their TM chip. Knowing their time was that hand, Angelica quashed the sick feeling of dread inside her stomach. She uttered a silent prayer…*Oh Lord shield us in the protection of your wings…Our mission is about to begin…*

Ten minutes later she and Leah were at the head of the line. They came to a stop before a solidly built middle-aged woman, who commanded them to hold forth their right hands…

Taking the infrared scanner and running it across the front of their right hands she said, "The two of you haven't been seeded yet. If you wait here, I'll get the officer in charge of seeding and you'll be ready to go."

Boldly, Angelica met the woman's icy blue eyes. "What if we don't want to?"

The woman smiled coldly. "Are you telling me that you refuse, little girl?"

"That's exactly what I'm telling you, grandma."

The woman's eyes narrowed dangerously. "Are you asking for trouble?"

"Not at all…I just feel that I have the right to refuse to have a chip put inside me against my will. I have no guarantee that it won't damage my body and I take care of my body," she ran her head up and down, appraising the woman rudely. "Unlike you."

"That's it…you're coming with me." She turned to Leah and demanded, "Do you happen to share your friend's opinion?"

"Absolutely…I agree with her completely." She too, examined the woman's girth and added, "About every thing."

Now furious the woman grabbed Angelica and Leah by the forearm and slapped some cuffs on them. Two UWF soldiers; a man and a woman came over and took the girls to a holding cell, where they waited for a few minutes then were taken through the airport and into a side door leading outside where an armored vehicle with the UWF insignia on the doors was parked waiting…

"Get inside," growled the male guard. "And don't try anything cute or I'll come back there and have a little fun with the two of you, if you know what I mean." His pock marked face leered evilly.

Leah shuddered slightly at the threat, while Angelica snorted in derision. "Yeah, as if…I've taken down bigger guys than you."

The UWF soldier threw his greasy black head back and laughed out loud, amused. "Is that so, blondie? You want a piece of me? That's great because I like my women feisty. It makes for a fun time…I really dig wrestling but I'm a sore loser." He leaned close to her, his foul hot breath, turning her stomach. "Okay baby, hit me with your best shot."

Thoroughly disgusted Angelica recoiled when the woman soldier got between them and pushed her colleague forcibly aside. "Knock it off! It's our job to get these rebel prisoners to the camp unharmed…That means the women are not your personal sex toys."

"Oh come on…they'll be dead in a couple of days anyway. So they might as well take a fond memory to the grave." He leered at Angelica again and added, "Honey, I'll make it hurt sooo good."

The woman UWF soldier then whipped out her Glock 29 automatic, cocked the slide and shoved the muzzle under his chin. "Back off now pervert or I'll blow your freakin' head off," she snarled, her eyes slits.

"Okay, okay!" He obediently backed away with his hands raised. "It was just a joke…I wasn't gonna do anything. Don't get your panties in a wad."

The woman slipped the automatic back in its holster. "Just making sure…I heard all about what you tried to do this to some other girls who were being taken in…and I'm making sure that you don't do it on my watch." She assisted Leah and Angelica in the back of the vehicle. "And I think I'll ride back here with them just to make sure."

She reached and slammed the door shut, leaving her comrade to grumble a curse and stomp over to the driver's side. He got in, slammed his door started the vehicle and took off with a roar.

Once inside, she addressed Angelica, "That guy's a real slime. Rumor has it that he raped two girls that refused taking the chip. So you're lucky that I am here with him because of it were anyone else, he would've been all over you and your friend." The woman leaned forward in interest. "Did you mean what you said to him?"

Angelica shrugged and replied, "It was the truth…I know karate." Remembering Lucien and Bacchus; Ichabod's henchmen from the Spirit Circle and how Bacchus had tried to molest her as she waited for her ill-fated execution she added grimly, "A guy made the mistake of hitting on me once and I made him pay for it. Believe me, I'm not afraid of anybody."

"Oh, I believe you." The UWF soldier eyed her speculatively then asked, "Then why are you refusing to take the chip? You know, everyone eventually will have to have it…it won't hurt your body, if that's what's stopping you."

"That's not the reason," Angelica said. "It's just the principle… Neither one of us agrees that any government has the right to keep track of us by putting a chip inside of us."

"But you know why they're doing it, don't you? It's because of the Great Vanishing. Didn't you lose somebody close to you when that happened? Two billion people just disappeared, leaving nothing but their clothes…something or someone took them away. They just want to make sure that nothing like that ever happens again."

Feeling like the woman was trying to corner her Angelica shrugged and said, "They don't really know what happened… where those people disappeared to. In my opinion ID'ing everybody is a power trip…another way for this government to control us."

The UWF soldier's eyes never wavered. "You really like to buck authority, don't you?"

Knowing that she was being goaded Angelica, simply answered, "We just stand up for our principles…we'll even die for them."

The woman soldier sighed, "Well, I'm afraid that's what's going to happen to you. Your principles are what's going to get you killed."

Leah then spoke up quietly, "We know that, officer…and we're fine with that."

Heaving a deep sigh the UWF soldier shook her head and there was no further conversation as they headed to the camp. About twenty minutes later, the vehicle pulled up to a fenced in complex that had barbed wire and armed sentries. The driver stopped momentarily to get clearance, and then pulled forward to a large gray cement building. He killed the motor and came to the back to open the gate…

The woman UWF soldier got out first and reached in to pull Leah out first, then Angelica. Her male counterpart resumed his harassment of the blonde FA by blowing her a kiss, earning him a glare. Another UWF soldier stepped forward to take hold of both girls…

"These girls the new rebels?" he asked gruffly eyeballing both young women. "They're just kids. They refused to be seeded?"

"Yeah…And they both know what's going to happen to them," the woman replied, almost regretfully.

"Hmmm…I see. I'll just take them down to the holding area." He turned around, holding each girl's forearm.

"Need any help?" Angelica's nemesis suggested hopefully.

The camp guard, an older man snorted, "No, thanks…I've heard all about you and your kinky inclinations so I'll take care of them."

"Aww, man…everyone wants to spoil my fun," the soldier whined as the three walked away.

As they walked down a long dimly lit corridor the camp guard guided them with a firm, but strangely gentle hand…not what they expected as Angelica and Leah exchanged quizzical glances. They turned right down another corridor and stopped before a tempered steel door. Taking out a set of keys, the guard reached and unlocked their handcuffs, freeing them. He then further surprised the girls by laying his hands on each of their shoulders…

Looking right at them, he said, "I know who you are and what your purpose is."

Incredulous, Leah said, "You do?"

"Yeah…I'm with COS…my name is Saul and I'm honored to meet you. You're both with Full Armor, aren't you?"

Angelica nodded. "That's right. I'm Angelica and this Leah."

Saul nodded a brief greeting. "We've been waiting for you to get here…We've been briefed on who you are and what abilities you have and know that you're here to help us save these people."

"Yes," Leah said. "We'll do our best to keep these people safe and help them escape."

"Thank the Lord," Saul said fervently, but in a low voice. "We have to succeed at this…if we don't; in two days the world is going to witness a brutal slaughter of 1000 innocent lives. If we can get them to Adanech, they'll at least be safe for a while."

"I'd like to know," Angelica murmured. "How are we going to accomplish this? I know we can shield you using our powers, but how are we going to escape?"

Saul replied in a soft tone, "Because this is a military installation it has underground facilities and escape tunnels that were installed in the event of an aboveground nuclear attack. My undercover colleagues from COS and I have devised a plan to get everyone out to waiting transport vehicles, using the escape tunnel, which here happens to be an old sewer passage…wide enough to move all of the refugees quickly from each holding cell this one here; Cell East and the other, Cell West. It's a moonless night so we'll be able to get to the transports without being seen since the hatch leading out of the tunnel is far away from the floodlights surrounding the camp."

A beep on his communicator interrupted the conversation. Saul clicked a button and the voice commanded, "Guard 3 you are needed outside for a new prisoner arrival ASAP."

"You'd better get inside."

He went over to the steel door, keyed in a combination on the side panel and the door slid open to a large, windowless room the size of the gymnasium with fifteen rows of ten cots…150 total; with about three quarters occupied with frightened and confused people. Taking hold of the girls' forearms, he led them past several occupied cots to two empty ones…

Angelica and Leah went over to sit on the cots. As they did, Saul knelt down as if to do a last-minute search and whispered to the girls, "I'll inform my superiors that you've arrived and as soon as I get the word from them, we'll begin the operation tonight at lights out…11 PM."

Wordlessly, both young women nodded. The guard rose and turned, heading back to the door to leave. To give the appearance of typical captives, Leah and Angelica, both looked around them with nervous expressions then lay back on the cots.

Angelica closed her eyes, her thoughts on the upcoming rescue operation when the same, calm voice spoke with quiet authority echoing in her ears…

Daughter, the time is at hand to use the Shed Blood of the Lamb.

She replied silently *the Shed Blood of the Lamb*, Lord? Inadvertently, she fingered her right side where she had received her wound.

Yes…You are able now to whisper in your spirit with each other. This power will enable you to speak back and forth without anyone else hearing you.

I can speak, Lord…To everybody? She couldn't help but be incredulous. *Just like I'm speaking with you?*

Yes, Daughter…Do it now.

*All right, Lord…*She spoke to Leah. *Leah? Can you hear me?*

Over on her cot Leah turned and looked at Angelica…Her friend just smiled and nodded *go ahead Leah, answer me…*

With her periwinkle eyes wide in wonder Leah responded, *Angie? Am I really hearing your voice in my head?*

Yes…The Lord just spoke with me and told me that this is the power of the Shed Blood of the Lamb.

So we can talk like this among each other?

*That's what He told me so I'm gonna try to talk to Peter…*She then spoke his name *Peter? It's me…can you hear me?*

Angelica heard nothing at first…Then she heard Peter's baritone answering in surprise *Angelica? Is that you? What's going on and why can I hear you? It's like you're in the same room with me.*

She couldn't help but smile *the Lord just let me know that this is because of the power because of the Shed Blood of the Lamb…He said that we can now talk among ourselves without anybody else hearing.*

Oh wow…So all of us can do this, not just you? he asked.

Uh-huh…I was just talking to Leah…Go ahead and try it, then let me know.

Okay…I'll get back to you.

In wonder Angelica spoke to the Lord, this is amazing Lord… *We'll be able to speak to each other any time?*

Yes…It will help you to be wise as serpents, yet stay gentle as doves. And when the time comes soon you will see what else the Shed Blood of the Lamb will empower you to do. And never forget, Daughter I am always with you.

Angelica been heard Peter speak to her, his voice as clear as if he were right beside her it *works, Angel…I just talked to Josh, and he said he was going to Leah and John…this is really wild. So how are you guys doing…are you okay?*

Yeah, we're okay…The guard that brought us into the holding cell is working with COS and he told us that we're going to escape underground.

He said he's going to contact his superiors, I think everything's going down pretty soon. How about you…are you okay?

Yeah, I'm okay…I connected with the COS operative right away, as soon as I got here. He told me the same thing, that we're to get everybody to an underground tunnel…Then out to a transport truck to head to Adanech. And he told me another interesting thing…COS discovered that all of these disposal camps are identical in design…Military bases with established underground escape routes. So the plan is good for all of us. It's all gonna happen tonight because tomorrow is Hukumu.

I see…Leah and I will be ready Angelica thought a moment about what else Lord had told her and said to Peter, *the Lord also told me that the Shed Blood of the Lamb will be giving us additional abilities. What kind I don't know, He didn't tell me…just that we would be empowered by it.*

Wow…I guess I shouldn't be surprised by anything the Lord does to use us…I'm real curious see just what kind of abilities He meant. I'll talk to Josh and John and tell them what you just told me and you tell Leah.

Okay.

I'll talk to everybody tonight just before everything happens. The COS man told me that the movement would happen after lights out…That's about 11 PM here.

Same here…It's about four hours away.

Okay then…Let's all stay in touch. Keep a low profile and take care, Angel.

You too.

Angelica than spoke to Leah, sharing everything Peter had told her and was heartened to know that Josh shared the same information with her based on his own meeting with the COS operative at the camp in Ethiopia, which John affirmed with his own COS connection at the camp in Khartoum. So it appeared everybody in FA was on the same page. Now all that was left was the waiting…Four hours until they would be called to help accomplish an escape similar in scope to what Moses did for the Israelites in the book of Exodus. It was both exciting and frightening at the same time.

To take her mind off of the impending mission, Angelica gazed around her at the people within the holding cell. There were singles, and families; men and women, boys and girls all frightened by the uncertainty of the future and even more so by the probability of the loss of their lives. Because most of those rebelling against the UWC and getting the TM chip implant were Christians, there were scattered murmured prayers in various African languages made clear by the name Jesus Christ; invoked fervently and uttered reverently. She and Leah exchanged glances, then nodded in understanding. Bowing their heads, they too joined the rest of the group in sending their petitions to Almighty God…

It was a long four hours, but finally a guard entered the room and shouted, "All right all of you rebels, pipe down with all your babbling! It's lights out now so you better get some sleep. Tomorrow you'll have one last chance to change your minds and if not, then you'll all die. Your foolish choice to still believe in a old book full of lies and the fairytale of a God will be your end and then you'll have no one to blame but yourselves."

He threw the switch, extinguishing the lights in the cell then left closing the door with a thud, plunging the room in total darkness. There were murmurs and cries throughout the room; the people fearful and disoriented by the situation and circumstances and Angelica, her heart filled with compassion, prayed for them to have peace. About fifteen minutes later, the door opened again and the guard that had escorted Angelica and Leah to the cell entered, turning on the lights…

He announced to the room, "Everyone keep quiet and form a line…You're leaving here now…"

About an hour earlier back in Adanech, Hasani was in the communication shed getting the latest information on the mission from Malensky. The COS leader informed the chief that Full Armor had been successful in getting captured and had arrived at the disposal camps, and were inside with the other refugees. Contact had been made with the interior COS operatives in each camp, and the rescue operations were nearly ready to commence. On his side, Hasani promised to have meals and shelters for be expected 1000 refugees that would be arriving in the village…

"So transports carrying these rescued refugees should arrive there in the next few days," Malensky stated in the garbled voice over the computer. "They will be escaping through the underground tunnels at each facility."

"And Full Armor will use their powers to shield them…The plan is well thought out and I pray it goes without mishap," Hasani said.

"We've taken all precautions to make sure this goes off without a hitch…our people have infiltrated deeply into the UWF at the camps and remain in touch with the regional command. I have the utmost confidence in our people."

"Yah, and with Hukumu taking place tomorrow and the ball tonight all attention is going to be at Uwambo's palace in Giza, where Abram and the rest of the supreme governors will be holding court with all the former national leaders around the world. It appears they won't expect a thing."

Malensky responded, "Yes…As I am updated of their progress, I'll be contacting you. So stay available…Out."

In his room at the men's dorm Moses had the Wi-Fi remote receiver turned on and thanks to the tiny bug he planted heard every word spoken between Hasani and Malensky and simultaneously transmitted this information to UWF soldiers guarding the disposal camps. He also spearheaded the strategy to eliminate Adanech with the UWF top regional commanders. As Uwambo's right hand man in this mission, the regional commanders all took direction from Moses and measures to thwart the operation were immediately drawn up and carried out. The plan was simple…First render such a large number of people helpless, using the nerve gas sarin then execute them. They were traitors to the UWC anyway and bound to die… it was the fate of all rebels. UWF soldiers and guards were immediately dispatched to halt the rescue operation and UWF troop battalions stationed in the surrounding areas of Tanzania were put on standby for attack on the village. And when that was completed, Moses relayed the entire plan of action to Supreme Governor Uwambo as he prepared himself for the evening's festivities…

In his bedchamber Uwambo's valet was helping him with his tuxedo jacket when the phone rang. Pushing the servant aside, he reached for the phone eagerly…

"Major Konkosani…I trust you have good news for me?"

"I do indeed, sir…I've spoken with the UWF region command for each camp after discovering the enemy's next move. Trust me sir, Hukumu will go off without a problem, I guarantee it. The five college students from the village have been dispatched and planted inside each camp, where they are assisting undercover rebel forces and helping the captives to escape. They are heading out and down the underground escape routes in each camp."

"And what do you plan to have the troops do to stop them?" Uwambo inquired.

Moses replied smugly, "The region command for each camp site has already informed the guards of the enemy's movements. And at each camp, they are preparing a warm welcome."

"Excellent!" Uwambo crowed. "Good work, major…Just make sure those captives are not slain tonight…We're saving their execution for tomorrow's Hukumu. And what about the village? Have you taken care of that?"

"Oh indeed, sir…The regional commands have been alerted and will move upon my word," Moses assured his superior. "Their destruction is at hand, the plan we've drawn up is that the region battalions will attack the village using sarin to render them immobile…then everyone will be slain for treason and rebelling against the UWC."

Uwambo was exultant. "You couldn't have given me better news. Just keep me in formed as things develop and when everything is complete, report back to me."

Moses responded, "As you wish, sir. Do not worry and leave everything to me."

Back in the camp at Lagos, Angelica and Leah were assisting Saul and five other COS operatives in getting all of the captives out of the cells in down into the escape tunnels in Cell East, while the same thing was taking place over in Cell West. The girls assisted the COS guard in helping to keep the people calm and quiet, so that their movements would go quickly and without mishap. The underground tunnel path actually led from beneath each holding cell over to the western far end of the base and came out approximately 200 m past the high-voltage security fence surrounding it. Over in the surrounding woods, transport trucks were waiting.

Yet, traveling through the tunnels was daunting…although it wasn't completely dark in the tunnel the dim lighting gave an eerie feeling, adding an additional sense of fear to the already frazzled nerves of the harried captives. Saul and two guards were leading in the front and had three other colleagues policing the rear while Angelica and Leah were in the middle of the crowd, maintaining order and offering encouragement by keeping calm. The girls' seemingly extraordinary placid manner in the face of such danger and uncertainty acted as a security blanket, immediately bringing peace to the refugees. Cool heads were truly prevailing here as they made their way to the main escape tunnel. The main escape tunnel was much wider, having once been a main sewer line…so when the group from East met the group from West at over 200 people strong they made a sizable throng; all heading out and away from the death camp…

As they made their way down the tunnel Angelica's mind was in a whirl; her thoughts swirling in a maelstrom fueled by anticipation and anxiety…wondering when exactly their confrontation with the UWF was going to happen. Curious about her colleagues in the other camps, she communicated with them. She spoke first with Peter…

Peter…Are you there…what's happening with you?

Angelica? We're all heading out of the camp with the refugees, me and the COS men…How about you, are you girls okay?

So far so good…We're in an underground tunnel heading out of the camp, no sign of enemies yet. How about you where you are?

We're fine so far…Seems like most of the UWF boys here decided to celebrate Hukumu early…They're all passed out dead drunk, according to the COS undercover men so we've been able to get out of here are rather easily…But I don't like it; it seems like a setup so I've got my guard up. I've been checking with John and Josh and they tell me almost the same thing…

That the mission's going almost too smoothly, like they're being allowed to get away. I told them the same thing I'm telling you…watch your backs…

*Will do…*Her communication with Peter was then interrupted by the sound of many footsteps echoing in the passage, approaching from the way they were heading. Angelica gasped as the noise became louder with the voices of men shouting…

Saul shouted, "We've got company! Everybody stop for a minute and keep calm!"

Confused and frightened the refugees began to murmur excitedly and some began to scream just as an entire line of UWF troops rushed forward, brandishing AK-47 assault rifles. They came to a stop, forming a barrier and simultaneously cocking their weapons aimed them at the group…

"Halt right where you are!" barked the UWF commander, his own weapon at the ready. "Just what you think you're doing with those rebel prisoners?" he demanded of Saul, then his eyes widened as the soldiers behind them lowered their weapons in shock. "What the—!"

As this was going on in the middle of the crowd both Angelica and Leah noticed that the sites on their body that had received the wounds of the Shed Blood of the Lamb began to glow in a golden light. At that very instant, a golden light like a shield enveloped the entire body of refugees…in the twinkling of an eye, Angelica, Leah, and the entire 250 refugees disappeared right before the eyes and gun sights of the astonished UWF forces…

In Adanech, the usual group of Kuitwa Usiku workers were gathered by the meeting house, under amber glowing pole lights making their nightly preparations for refugee arrivals. With folded blankets piled up and ready to be used Hasani, Disa, and Chiaga were anticipating the groups being rescued from the disposal camps, but they knew that the wait could be long, depending upon the progress made and whether or not the rescues were successful. They oversaw the preparations as Merci Fofana drove up in her jeep. She parked over near the stage by the meeting house and joined the couple…

"Habari za jioni," they said in unison.

"Hey Mama…Papa," she greeted using her nicknames for them. "What can I do to help tonight?"

"With everything you've done up to now…you have done more than enough," Hasani pointed out. "You've flown all over since yesterday for this most important mission…dropping off Full Armor so we can rescue all those captives in the camps to halt Hukumu."

"Humph!" Merci snorted in disgust. "Hukumu…justice coming from a criminal like Uwambo, who coldly murders helpless people like he did in the uprising before the Great Vanishing…it's a joke…a tragic one."

"Yes, but that is why he was chosen by Abram as his supreme governor…to be ruthless and gain control over all," Disa stated the hard fact. She then brightened and added, "But the Lord and His Full Armor will make sure everyone gets here safely."

"Hmmm," subdued, Merci lowered her head and commented, "When I picked up those five to first bring them here to Adanech I thought they were just students from America. I had no idea that they had so much power…amazing." She added softly, "Seeing that made me finally believe in the one true God and His Son."

Hasani came forward. "I believe that's why they came…to show us the one true God…The God who is love, and who has never left us or forsaken us…yet possesses power inconceivable to us humans, which we were blessed to have seen in those five incredible young people. They are His chosen vessels."

"But why? Why us? And why now?" Merci asked. "If I hadn't seen it with my own eyes. I never would've believed that power like that could come from a human in reality…more like a fairytale with sorcerers' magic."

Disa nodded solemnly as she stated softly, "It is not for us to try to figure out the mind of God or His ways. He chooses to use His power in many ways, but He is sovereign, and the choice is His. Perhaps He has given His power now because of the time we are in."

Hasani declared, "Yah…We're in an extraordinary time, like the time of Moses. God revealed His power through Moses, when he led the Israelites out of Egypt, and He's doing the same thing now, leading the lost here using His power through Full Armor."

The three of them then gathered together and Hasani called Kuitwa Usiku over to pray…and they readied themselves further by sharing together Scripture verses for encouragement; specifically Ecclesiastes 3:1-8…

"For everything there is a season, and a time for every purpose under heaven: a time to be born, and a time to die; a time to plant, and a time to pluck up what is planted; a time to kill, and a time to heal; a time to break down, and a time to build up; a time to weep, and a time to laugh; a time to mourn, and a time to dance; a time to throw away stones, and a time to gather stones together; a time to embrace, and a time to refrain from embracing; a time to seek, and a time to lose; a time to keep, and a time to throw away; a time to tear, and a time to sew; a time to keep silence, and a time to speak; a time to love, and a time to hate; a time for war, and a time for peace."

At that very moment the village was flooded with golden light; as if midday had come in the middle of the dark, moonless night. Then, the captives from each disposal camp materialized right out of thin air…one group after another, all accompanied by Full Armor. Every face on every refugee bore a stunned expression but neither was more stunned then those on the faces of the five young servants of the Holy Spirit…they truly had no idea what had happened…

Over in Giza, in the supreme governor's palace, the chandelier lit grand ballroom was crowded with dignitaries and potentates from all around the world; former royalty, dictators, and presidents and their spouses had gathered from near and far. They had been invited to wine and dine; the sumptuous buffet laden with the richest and finest of gourmet fare and best spirits, but mostly to be front row witnesses to the ultimate demonstration of the stranglehold of power that the Unified World Community now claimed over the Globe…a vulgar travesty of human rights viciously crushed; all in the name of unity. So clad in Hugo Boss, Armani, Vera Wang, and Christian Dior and frosted with Harry Winston, Tiffany's, and Cartier the gaudy and arrogant danced and dined; stuffing themselves all the while paying fawning homage to his Excellency, UWC Supreme Leader, Isaac Abram. He presided over the gala with his best diplomatic and impersonal smile…holding court like any enthroned Monarch, flanked on one side by his executive secretary and lover Thora Blackmon and on the other side by his top advisor and spiritual guide Ichabod.

The evening had begun at about 8:30 with the first early arrivals; officials of lower ranking and security staff. Then the more important of the guests began arriving announced by a majordomo at the door…followed at last and certainly not least by the infamous Quad; the four Supreme Governors of the four regions; East…Jiang Tao-Wei, West…Maria Elizabeth Rondalle, North…Sergei Rodrinka, and the host himself; Abrafo Uwamba, Supreme Governor of the South. Then arriving fashionably late at 9:30, Abram made his grand entrance amidst thundering applause, descending the long, red carpeted staircase in a benign, yet regal manner. During the course of the evening, he mixed and mingled…making the rounds like any good politician, dancing with homely wives while their obsequious husbands all literally bowed and scraped. After about of an hour of this circus Abram stifled a yawn as boredom set in…

Gowned in scarlet raven-haired Thora nudged him and asked in her throaty voice, "Having fun, dear? Or should I slip you a No-Doze to take with your next glass of champagne."

Abram chuckled and replied, "It's really not that bad… Making my appearance here is part of my duty now. But I do admit these things become quite tedious. There's just so many times my feet can get trod upon before I've lost feeling in them."

Leaning over and nuzzling his ear Thora murmured, "Then why don't you just make your apologies and we could slip up to your chamber? It's a beautiful desert night, no moon but full of stars…we can make love on the terrace of the balcony like we did last night." She held onto his arm and planted a soft, nibbling kiss to sweeten the offer.

Becoming aroused Abram groaned softly and said, "Just a little longer, my love. Because of who I am, I cannot leave too early. But we'll make our excuses soon…be patient."

Heaving a petulant sigh she pouted but acquiesced, just as they were joined by Uwambo. The Supreme Governor of the South approached Abram with a wide smile; in his best sycophantic form…

"Your Excellency, I'm sorry I've been so busy to attend to your needs. Are you having a good time, my lord? There's quite a good turnout here." He seemed harried; anxious.

Abram favored his underling with a warm, albeit insincere smile to reassure him. "Do not worry, my friend. You are to be commended; this is quite an excellent gala…the perfect introduction to your Hukumu. I'm sure everything will go as we planned."

"I-indeed," Uwambo stammered, on edge. He gave a shaky smile that did not reach his eyes, based on the UWF reports from what happened at the game reserve a few days earlier, which were still uppermost in his mind.

Extremely astute, Abram's eyes bore into Uwambo. "Abrafo, my friend…I am well aware of the extraordinary events that took place at the ambush at the Rungwa Game Reserve a few days ago. Even though it was not from your own lips did you really think that I would not find out about it? I'm a bit insulted…To think one of my own close associates would doubt my ability to keep my finger on the pulse of what's going on in the world as its ruler, well I don't know what to say." The supreme leader shook his head regretfully.

The subordinate shook his head quickly and vigorously. "Oh no, my lord…I—I just did not want to trouble you. I have the situation well in hand and my man Konkosani is making sure that the rebels will not get away with anything else."

"Hmmm…I'm curious, though, Abrafo…From the report I received from the UWF commander in charge of the ambush it appeared that a bolt of lightning and great wave like a hurricane wind blew all of his attack forces away from the rebels that were trying to escape. Did you know that this had happened?"

"Of course, my lord…Konkosani is in place undercover at a rebel stronghold…a village known as Adanech. He told me that he was at that mission to Rungwa Game Reserve and witnessed a bright bolt of lightning and a wind like a hurricane during the ambush."

"So he reported the same thing to you that I heard…Anything else?"

Uwambo hesitated, then sheepishly replied, "No my lord… He did say how there are five American college students there at the village and that they seem to be involved in every mission since they arrived. They were accepted immediately by the chief, Hasani. Konkosani himself has had a hard time getting even a little bit close to the chief and those close to him."

Abram scowled thoughtfully then asked, "Did he find any weapons of any sorts? Anything at all suspicious?"

Uwambo replied, "No, my lord…Every report he has sent me has no mention of any type of weaponry there at all."

Abram stared off out the window, past the crowd of revelers and stated, "The past incidences involving these rebels have been peculiar. The reports from the UWF forces trying to intercept these rebel movements tell of some great force of energy…a bright light then a gust of wind or something, like a tempest thwarting any attempts at capturing them. There's some force assisting these rebels—,"

He was about to say more when a UWF forces adjutant corporal came rushing right over addressing Uwambo. "Sir, sir… We just received reports from the disposal camps…mass escapes were taking place of the captives that were to die tomorrow. And as they were confronted by our troops…they disappeared!"

"What on earth are you talking about, man? What do you mean disappeared?" Uwambo demanded.

"E-exactly what I said," he stuttered, unable to believe it himself. "I just got a report from each commanding officer at each camp telling me the same thing…that the populations of rebels that were to be executed tomorrow for Hukumu…have vanished right before their eyes!"

"Is that so?" Supreme Leader Abram interjected as the subordinate turned and noticed the world's ruler standing before him. The man fell down to his knees in fear, quaking before him.

"Yes, Your Excellency…It's exactly what I was told; the rebels to be executed tomorrow have vanished." He raised his head slowly, cowering.

Abram turned to Uwambo. "Well, Abrafo? What do you intend to do about this? Your Hukumu has been thwarted apparently."

Off to the side, the other three supreme governors appeared to be smirking…especially Jiang and Rodrinka; both of whom boasted military superiority, and although they had been displaying similar troubles in their own regions, during weekly supreme council meetings they insisted they had a better handle on them. In the last meeting they had all had both those men had expressed doubt in the whole concept of Hukumu when Uwambo presented it…

Look at those smug expressions…they think I'm a fool Inside Uwambo began a slow burn; however, he composed himself and presented a confident air to his leader. "Your Excellency, I assure you that Hukumu will take place as scheduled…It just won't take place the way we had originally planned. But I give you my word, it will take place. So if you'll excuse me," he bowed and dismissed himself, then gestured to the subordinate to accompany him.

Abram watched as the two men push their way through the crowd of dancers at the ball and looking over to the side summoned his assistant and advisor Ichabod, who made his excuse to a lady he was talking with and came over…

"My lord?" he inquired.

Abram commanded, "Go off into another room and find out if there are any spiritual waves of energy that you can detect… There have been some new vanishings…something on a far greater level within the spiritual realm is taking place and I want you to find out what it is."

Ichabod bowed. "As you wish, my lord."

Meanwhile, having headed over to his command center, Uwambo grabbed the shoulders of the subordinate UWF adjutant corporal and growled, "When did you get these reports? And what else do you have to tell me?"

"N-nothing, sir…I came to you as soon as I heard. Maybe they came back for more."

"They?" Uwambo echoed.

"The aliens that took everybody else!" the man wailed, adhering to one of the varied and most popular of far-fetched theories of causes linked to the occurrence of the Great Vanishing.

He looked around, terrified…as if he himself was about to disappear. Seeing that, Uwambo shook his head and dismissed him as a fool. "Don't be ridiculous!" He snatched a wireless transmitter and began barking orders to the top regional commander, then reaching for his cell phone he dialed Moses Konkosani…

At Adanech, there were various levels of confusion; everyone stunned by what appeared to be a miracle; multitudes of people appearing from nowhere. Even those like Hasani and Disa, with great faith in the power of Almighty God were flabbergasted by seeing another tangible supernatural occurrence happening right before their eyes. From around the corner of the storehouse Moses watched incredulously, momentarily frozen in shock…

I must be dreaming…This can't be happening. People just don't appear out of nowhere as if out of thin air. But here they are right before me, all the rebel captives that were supposed to be executed tomorrow!

At that very moment his cell phone buzzed and seeing Uwambo's CID Moses immediately picked it up…

"Major…we have a grave situation…the rebels have literally disappeared from the camps."

Considering his state of mind at the present Moses spoke in a surprisingly calm voice. "I know…they are here at the village."

"They are there?! B—but how? When?"

"It's not important…I anticipated something like this and have acted accordingly."

"You anticipated this?!" Uwambo croaked. "Why didn't you tell me?" From his end Uwambo felt cornered…Shocked by the news and facing the fact that his great opus; his Hukumu had just gone up in smoke, he was in a quandary. *What am I going to do? H-how am I going to tell his Excellency…What am I going to tell him and everybody else? The media, the press, and especially the Rebel Faction…They won't make a fool out of me!*

Moses hastened to reassure his superior. "Don't worry, sir… the regional commanders and I have devised a plan. The rebels will be dealt with, our forces are standing by. They are at the ready…just say the word."

They are at the ready, are they? Well, we'll see who has the victory here his mind whirling Uwambo took a deep breath to compose himself, then said, "Do not summon them yet…Wait for me to contact you again at thirty seconds before midnight and when I do countdown to begin the attack exactly then."

"As you wish, sir."

The communication broken, Moses then contacted the four UWF commanding officers in charge of the troops poised from four directions surrounding the camp. For a final time he went over the tactics and strategy for the attack utilizing his own absorption of tactics he learned from Sun Tzu's *Art of*

War to create with the commanders an inescapable trap. When everyone was satisfied that the plan was complete, Moses hung up and went back to mingle in with the crowd at the village… and wait…

Meanwhile, Uwambo made a call to the UWCPI Bureau to alert them of the change of plans for Hukumu…directing them to send all of their coverage and cameras to a place in remote northwest Tanzania upon his word, he gave specific instructions to make the broadcast global on every station and in every language. He then arranged with those UWCPI reporters covering his gala to get the technical personnel to activate the HD screens he had installed around the ballroom with a satellite hook-up to the helicopters sent to fly over Adanech to broadcast the attack…synchronizing everything to happen at the stroke of midnight, local time. Satisfied, he hung up the cell and then made his way back into the ballroom where the party was still in full swing. He spotted Supreme Leader Abram, with Thora Blackmon and strode confidently over to them. Addressing the world ruler, he was practically gloating…

Still irritated by the news of the enemy's latest move like a trump card having been played Abram glared at Uwambo and demanded, "Well, Abrafo…what tale do you have to tell me now?"

Uwambo flinched then met his superior's eyes with a calm assurance. "My lord…as I said before Hukumu will go on as planned…just at a different time and place. But all will still bear witness of our unshakable authority over this world."

Abram was dubious. "Indeed? Would you like to share with me exactly what's about to happen?"

Uwambo smiled and replied, "Better yet, my lord. When the time comes I'll show you…and the entire world. Just be patient…it won't be long now." He turned and gazed at the elaborate clock on the ballroom wall…It was a quarter till midnight. *Midnight, the witching hour…the perfect time for the Cinderella's golden coach and horses to turn back into a pumpkin and rats…and those miserable rebels to be crushed…*

Eagerly, he indulged in a glass of Dom Perignon and kept his eyes glued to the hands on the clock…

In the middle of Adanech curiosity of what had happened drew all of the village population to join the newcomers, swelling the number in the square to nearly 2000. However, the crowd remained mostly silent…still in a state of shock over what had happened. And the same was true for Full Armor…the five young adults were still, marveling over the way that they had been used this time. They made their way up to towards each other and gathered in an area just over to the side to meet up…

Coming together Josh, John, Leah, and Peter all gazed at Angelica with expectant expressions of wonder…seeking an explanation from her but she knew as much as they did…nothing. So she headed them off at the pass…

"Look, before any of you ask me what that was that just happened let me be the first to tell you…I have absolutely no idea."

Tentatively Leah asked, "The Lord said nothing to you about this power, Angie…nothing at all?"

She shook her flaxen head. "All He told me was that we would see what else the Shed Blood of the Lamb would empower us to do."

"Well, I guess it just did…I never would've figured that we'd be able to do something like that," Josh pointed out, still amazed by what he had witnessed. "I thought it was freaky when we could talk to each other in our heads…getting these people here using what looks like magic well, that was scary."

Even John, who always had a ready word of wit in tense situations was noticeably somber in his response. "It just proves what we've always been told and now know…that the power of Almighty God is absolute and immense. The fact that He's using us to display that power is unbelievable."

Peter nodded affirming what he said. "We are His tools…His Full Armor. We'll do what He tells us to do, when He tells us to do it." He added enigmatically, "No matter the outcome."

They all nodded in unison, then made their way up to the front of the crowd, most of whom were still without words as they tried to determine what had happened. Hasani, Disa, Chiaga and the rest of Kuitwa Usiku were lined up, standing before the throng waiting for the right moment as they too were striving to gain courage and composure. Shaking himself to awareness, the village chief and his wife stepped forward to address the new crowd of people with a welcoming and reassuring smile. His voice booming and carrying, he spoke…

"My dear friends…Welcome to Adanech. You don't have to fear anymore for you are safe here. My name is Hasani and this is Disa, servants of the living God and rest assured that you can come to us if you have any concerns or questions. We have hot meals, blankets, and beds for all of you. So please make yourselves comfortable."

Disa then came forward and added, "Those of you who are hungry if you'll make a line, the meeting house is set up to serve you some meals…You can rest in there as well. Those of you who are tired our people will show you to the dormitories."

Hasani then said, "I now wish to share with you a word from our Lord…from Hebrews 12: 1-3…

"Therefore, since we are surrounded by so great a cloud of witnesses, let us also lay aside every weight and the sin that clings so closely, and let us run with perseverance the race that is set before us, looking to Jesus the pioneer and perfecter of our faith, who for the sake of the joy that was set before him endured the cross, disregarding its shame, and has taken his seat at the right hand of the throne of God. Consider him who endured such hostility against himself from sinners, so that you may not grow weary or lose heart. And let me add this, Psalm 23…The LORD is my shepherd, I shall not want. He makes me lie down in green pastures; he leads me beside still waters; he restores my soul. He leads me in right paths for his name's sake. Even though I walk through the darkest valley, I fear no evil; for you are with me; your rod and your staff—they comfort me. You prepare a table before me in the presence of my enemies; you anoint my head with oil; my cup overflows. Surely goodness and mercy shall follow me all the days of my life, and I shall dwell in the house of the LORD my whole life long."

At those passages the stunned silence evolved into a murmur as the entire village including the 1000 new refugees began to come to life...the words spoken galvanizing them and comforting them as they began to get used to their surroundings. The members of Kuitwa Usiku then came forward and began to organize the crowd in orderly groups to eventually head towards the meeting house...

At the back of the crowd Moses was observing what was taking place all the while keeping an eye on his watch...Uwambo had contacted him and told him that he was to give the signal for the attack to begin at precisely midnight so he was watching as the minutes were taking away. However, in the deepest reaches of his dark heart a tiny little flicker of something that would've resembled guilt in any other person possessing a conscious rippled. Maybe it was that when he was younger his mother and father insisted that he attend Sunday services which he dismissed as soon as he reached 13, considering all faith but especially the Christian faith silly. Or perhaps it was what he had witnessed since arriving at Adanech; the feeling of peace and unity everyone possessed even in the midst of dark threats hanging over them as they rebelled against the UWC...courage that even he, as a battle tested soldier envied. Whatever it was, Moses was experiencing a touch of ambivalence; excited yet regretting what was about to commence...

Just two more minutes...Two minutes to total annihilation. Do these people even care? I wonder. I remember when I was a child in Sunday service and I'd hear all these words, the same words I've heard tonight. I thought they were silly words about a powerful God; guiding and, watching over us. But watching these people, seeing them appear from out of nowhere, and hearing these words really makes me wonder...

In the ballroom in Giza Uwambo kept his eye on the clock, as if he were on Times Square in New York City counting down the seconds to the New Year. At the thirty second mark he pressed a button on his transmitter, relaying the signal to Moses Konkosani…

Now the time has come…let the endgame begin…

Moses felt a vibration in his pocket, and reached for his remote transmitter. He looked at the face of the device and saw the signal to countdown to midnight to start the attack. He glanced around him at the expressions on the faces of the people would just arrived and was very surprised to see that with one or two exceptions, most of them had peaceful looks; as if they possessed total and complete trust in whoever or whatever it was behind their circumstances…in this case it was a steadfast belief in the Almighty God. It drew from Moses a growing sense of grudging respect. However, his role was clear; his die had been cast and he pushed the button on his remote to alert the UWF forces lying in wake. He then retreated behind the storage building, and slipped on a gas mask to block the nerve gas and observe the oncoming onslaught…

Over by the meeting house the first group of new refugees arrived at the door lining up, getting ready to enter and have the meals that were prepared and waiting for them when a loud roar, almost like a freight train approaching sounded from around them. All of a sudden, the village was flooded with light as jeeps and other combat vehicles rushed in, crashing through brush and jungle, cutting off the roads both leading into the village from the north and the south as well is coming in from the thick jungle that surrounded them from the east and the west; all blasting grenade launchers into the crowd. Multiple explosions took place followed by clouds of vapor that billowed up and around everyone…the smoke grenades camouflaged high concentrate of the nerve gas sarin…

The five members of Full Armor were stunned into momentary inertia by the surprise attack, and then realizing what was happening immediately touched their brooches still hidden in their pockets to activate their powers to fight and protect. However, they were dismayed when nothing happened…

"What the—what's going on? We can't do anything!" Josh snapped in fury and frustration.

"I don't know!" Peter barked back, then was completely bowled over while he watched his and each one of his comrades' Shed Blood of the Lamb stigmata marks begin to glow as a shield was drawn around them individually to protect them…alone…

When the grenades first went off the crowd began screaming in panic, but as the gas began its vile work screams began to fade as people one after the other collapsed helplessly, unable to move or speak. And the heart, soul and lifeblood of the village; Hasani, Disa, Chiaga, Merci, Anna, the rest of Kuitwa Usiku, and Ngao along with each and every refugee who had hoped to find harbor and safety in a village named She Who Has Rescued fell, crumpling to the ground. Now the main event was about to begin as the UWF forces came streaming into the village on full attack…

At the ballroom in Giza Uwambo had arranged for the several HD widescreen monitors to power up around the entire room. After contacting Moses at just thirty seconds before the stroke of midnight he made his way up to the main dais and spoke into the Wi-Fi microphone pinned to his lapel to get the crowd's attention, clearing his throat…

"His Excellency, Supreme Leader Abram, esteemed colleagues, and honored guests…May I direct your attention to the screens set up for your convenience?" Responding in sheer curiosity, the crowd made their way to each screen set up murmuring. When they were all settled, he, the other three supreme governors, Abram and Thora all headed over to the nearest screen. As each monitor flickered to life, displaying in bright blue he spoke again…

"As you are all aware tomorrow was to be an event known as Hukumu…The Swahili word for 'administration of justice', it was to show the world and most specifically the treasonous Rebel Faction that refusal to submit to the absolute word of his Excellency and join the rest of us in the United World Community would not be tolerated. Refusing to do the right thing, and take the TM chip so we can protect our own and keep tabs on each other so another catastrophe like the Great Vanishing will never happen and send us into chaos again is the highest of criminal acts…and as you know, all criminals deserve punishment. That is Hukumu…"

A smattering of applause echoed through the ballroom as Uwambo sported an expression of pseudo-regret. "…but unfortunately, in spite of all our painstaking preparations and security I'm sorry to say tomorrow's event will not take place.

The rebels have managed to pull off an exodus at each disposal camp, and the captives have escaped—,"

A collective gasp of dismay, followed by a growing outcry of outrage rippled through the room, but Uwambo just smiled and raised his voice above the commotion…

"My dear friends, please…all is far from lost. Let me reassure you that I have had my finger on the pulse of what goes on here in the South Kingdom all along and I have anticipated a move by the enemy like this…and we have acted swiftly to counteract it. So please turn your attention to each screen."

At that moment the large clock on the wall began chiming to announce the midnight hour…And at that moment each HD screen came to life and the pictures of the happening taking place was the very definition of a massacre…a surreal and deliberate display of coldly calculated cruelty that rendered the entire festive ballroom throng absolutely silent as they witnessed the spectacle unfolding right before their eyes. Even Abram, whose eyes were usually the same placid, unemotional windows to his black soul reacted with amazement at the methodical ferocity of the attack on Adanech. His eyes widened perceptually as he along with everyone else saw the grenades explode within the crowd, and how one by one, each person fell. Then came the second phase of attack; the UWF forces advanced in a line from all four directions surrounding the rebels, and they proceeded to slaughter each and every one. Using AK-47s and even machetes, they ruthlessly shot people in the head or decapitated them… strangely targeting the head specifically.

With his eyes still on the screen, Abram leaned over to Uwambo and asked, "Abrafo," how is it that we're witnessing this now? Did you arrange for the UWCPI to cover this?"

Uwambo flashed a Cheshire cat grin. "As I told you before, Your Excellency…I had this all under my control. For the last ten days I had a man undercover in the village, giving me reports of what was going on, how the enemy was moving. And he was the one who worked together with regional UWF forces commanders to plan this assault. He is a top man in the UWF covert special forces and a tactical genius, Major Moses Konkosani." He then announced to the entire room in a voice ringing with pride…"This, my friends, is Hukumu!"

There was throughout the ballroom a soft buzz that graduated into a steady hum of approval, indicating that everyone was appreciating the vast display of power and authority shown against the troublesome rebels. There were even frequent cheers as the ball became a venue reminiscent of the ancient Roman Coliseum where Nero's lions were slaughtering Christians, with all the spectators relishing the mauling as the witness provided by the UWCPI television cameras in helicopters hovering above gave them a birds eye view.

"So this is Hukumu…It's quite the sight," Maria Rondalle commented.

"This was planned by Major Konkosani, huh?" Rodrinka was intrigued. "This is quite impressive and certainly not what I had expected."

"Indeed," Jiang approved. "I see that this Konkosani has employed the genius of Sun Tzu in his attack by closing in from all sides…nicely done."

Uwambo basked in the glow of his colleagues' praises, but nothing pleased him more then when Abram himself placed a hand on his shoulder. "Abrafo, what can I say? This is…quite remarkable. And as we're seeing it now it is being broadcast around the world. Am I right?"

"Yes, Your Excellency, that's right. All programming was preempted so everyone would be able to see my Hukumu… It's just tonight instead of tomorrow." His eyes narrowed as he added, fiercely, "The rebels weren't going to get the best of me."

"Hmmm…So I see. I'm interested in seeing how the rest of this plays out." Abram continued watching as the attack continued. As he watched on the screen Uwambo, in the meantime took out his cell phone to get a status report straight from the battlefield…

At Adanech, the UWF troops were hard at work literally going through the crowd of weakened and helpless refugees… men, women, children…they did not discriminate, each one lost their lives with a shot in the head or decapitation. With vicious precision they methodically made their way through the crowd like a buzz saw. The only ones spared were the ones that were invisible to the soldiers' eyes…Full Armor. And those five young people watched with incredulous eyes, something they had never imagined they would ever experience. Yet, with morbid fascination the party of five could not tear their eyes away…

Leah, the most sensitive of the group watched through her bleary, tear-sheened and partially blind eyes. *Dear Lord t-this is dreadful! How can this be happening…and why?*

On the other side of the spectrum, Josh, the most volatile, was livid *you gotta be kidding me, Lord…This is a joke…Or maybe we're the ones who were the joke with our so-called powers, unable to do anything to stop this. So what's the deal?*

John fought tears as he watched some of his new friends; friends who he had played praise music with, worked on vehicles with, and protected during missions with powers that were now failing him were ruthlessly mowed down. And, although he had the most easy-going and practical personality of the five and always rolled with the punches even he found this situation intolerable *wow…just wow…I guess when we saw what our powers could do we felt we could do anything, but obviously that's wrong…We are just the same as we always were, flawed, imperfect and human, even with these powers…But I can't accept this…*

Peter, who because of his biblically rooted background recalled the scripture in Revelation which foretold of lives lost; martyrs who refused to take the Mark of the Beast and immediately saw the similarity between the current world situation and the mandatory planting of the TM chip. *Well, here it is…biblical prophecy coming true. Despite our powers we can't kid ourselves anymore; we're in the front lines of this battle. And we better gird ourselves up for what's to come…*

As that thought, he gazed over at Angelica and examined her face…The bleak expression on those delicate features chilled him. *Look at her…Just looking in her eyes I can tell how much she's suffering. She saw this all before we did; she's been tormented all along, far more than we have been. How many nights was she tormented with the same scene playing in her head, over and over again?* He desperately wanted to reach towards her, but knew that he could not…not now…

From his hiding place behind the storehouse Moses Konkosani peeked around the corner and watched as his plan came to full fruition. But as he watched the inhabitants of the village being systematically mowed down even he, as a hardened soldier felt a growing sense of horror and disbelief. *This is brutal…These people aren't even armed. Yet the UWF troops are just slaughtering them, fighting them as if they were armed…*

He heard the sound above him of helicopter blades and saw approximately 5000 feet above him a UWCPI news camera chopper filming the entire debacle. Moses shook his head as he realized that, Uwambo had covered all the bases…Even though the disposal camps were emptied of captives and rebels, they had not really escaped. Hukumu…Administration of justice; UWC justice, Uwambo's justice had been administered…swiftly and brutally. And all the world was witness, just does Uwambo had planned. His cell phone buzzed in his pocket and he answered the call of the supreme governor…

"Major Konkosani, give me a status report…Thanks to the UWCPI cameras, I can see what's happening. But I want to hear directly from you as my commanding officer for this operation."

Quashing his maudlin mood Moses replied immediately, "It's exactly what you see, sir. The UWF troops have come in and are executing the rebels that escaped the camps."

"So they did end up at that village," Uwambo mused. "But how? I only received the report and hour ago that they disappeared from each camp…How the devil did they get there?"

Moses took a deep breath. *How do I explain what I saw?* "Well, sir…They, uh just appeared here."

In the ballroom, Uwambo nearly choked and said incredulously, "They just appeared there?!" His statement drew the attention of his three other Quad colleagues and Abram, who all looked at him sharply. He shrugged shaking his head at them and waited for further explanation…

"It's just as I told you, sir…one minute nobody was there and then there was a flash of light and all of a sudden over 1000 people appeared out of nowhere. I still can't get over it."

As he listened to his subordinate, unable to explain what happened, or make it any clearer Uwambo himself felt cornered. Jiang, Rodrinka, Ms. Rondalle, along with the supreme leader of UWC surrounded him with questions and their eyes, listening, along with him.

Firmly pinned on the horns of a dilemma he commanded, "Konkosani, when the battle is complete I want you to report immediately to me to give me a full report of what you seen both tonight and all the while you have been at that village. When everyone there is confirmed dead, you are to dismiss the troops that are there and we will send a special reconnaissance team to go through that village from tooth through nail. Those rebels escaped from the camps in some way using some sort of unknown weapon and I won't rest until we find it. So signal me when the battle is complete and report here on the double. That is all."

He cut off communication and was immediately addressed by Abram. "So Abrafo…What exactly happened tonight? How did those rebels get to that village?"

Feeling like he was on trial with all eyes on him, Uwambo had no other choice but to tell the truth. "My lord it appears that these rebels from the disposal camps that disappeared appeared in this village, the same way…out of thin air."

His three colleagues burst into laughter and Rodrinka, scoffed, "So these rebels, these criminals suddenly disappeared from the camps, then reappeared at this village? Preposterous!"

Jiang affirmed, "It is unbelievable. The most advanced weapon could never cause people; flesh and blood to disappear and reappear. Even the most advanced technology cannot evaporate then regenerate the cells of one human, let alone 1000…it doesn't exist."

"It's true," Ms. Rondalle pointed out then added, "however, we see it here right in front of us. It's highly unlikely that that village had so many people there before tonight so they must've come from somewhere."

Uwambo found himself at a loss to offer any explanation that made sense. However, he was saved from that by Abram, who addressed the other three supreme governors. "My friends unbelievable or not, this did happen. We can no longer refute the evidence that in this world now there exists supernatural power. Whether it is that power that the rebels are using or that they developed a new super weapon that is the stuff of classic science fiction television programs or novels the course we have before us is clear…The Rebel Faction is the enemy of the Unified World Community and we must fight them and defeat them…no matter what."

Chastised, the other three nodded in agreement as Abram turned to Uwambo. "Abrafo, when Major Konkosani reports to you inform me immediately. I will delay my departure from the South Kingdom until I too can speak to him." He abruptly turned away and headed off, melting into the crowd as Uwambo, Jiang, Rodrinka, and Ms. Rondalle continued watching the attack to the bloody end…in high definition…

Meanwhile, within the center of the village the din that had arisen when the attack began; the sounds of war cries and victims' screams of agony gradually faded as each life seeped away like the blood from their bodies. Soon the only sound within the village was the troops' voices as they whooped and yelled in triumph; still drunk with blood lust, celebrating their victory, waving at the retreating UWCPI helicopters who been there the whole time and had captured the entire thing and broadcast it around the world. The commanding officers, allowing their subordinates to blow off steam stood by conversing with each other as they gazed about at the village set up…

One captain of the guard; part of a special service squadron immediately recognized the building set up as a former military base. He took note of the many dormitories and the sophisticated looking storehouse, then spotted Moses still glancing at the activity from around the corner. Not recognizing him at first, he drew his automatic 9mm Beretta…

"You hiding there…Come on out and show yourself now!" he demanded, then withdrew his weapon, saluted, and apologized profusely when he saw that it was Moses. "Major Konkosani, sir…forgive me, I didn't know that was you."

Moses strode forward with an air of authority returned the salute and reassured the captain, "That's quite all right, captain." The other three captains of the guards called the troops in order, and they all lined up at attention before Moses saluting smartly. He stood before them and addressed them sharply…

"At ease." They all relaxed to Parade Rest before him. "Good work, men. On behalf of Supreme Governor Uwambo and his Excellency, Supreme Leader Abram. I want to commend you on successfully completing Hukumu. On the supreme governor and his Excellency's orders, we are to retreat, effective immediately."

"Begging your pardon major sir, but shouldn't we go through this village? Surely there is evidence of weapons or some other means that should be confiscated," one of the captains of objected.

Seeing the practicality of the suggestion Moses, inwardly agreed, but acted upon his superior's command. "Negative… We are to retreat immediately for debriefing. And I will be going with you to report to Giza immediately."

"Yes sir."

The four captains acquiescing ordered the troops back into their vehicles and Moses joined them. Then, as they came into the village all of them left, leaving behind a pile of corpses… the only live ones remaining were the five invisible people that made up Full Armor, who had borne witness to one of the most heinous atrocities either had ever seen. Still stunned, they slowly came forward…

Leah walked on shaky legs…And as she had spotted some of the people that she had worked so closely with in the kitchen among the slain she collapsed, immediately drawing the attention of John and Josh, who rushed over to her…

"Sis?" John knelt beside his sister and grasped her elbow to steady her. "Just hang on, okay."

"Take it easy, little bird," Josh said softly from her other side, wrapping an arm around her waist and holding her close.

"I-I was just in the kitchen the other morning preparing breakfast with everyone…a-and now they're g-gone. Why didn't our powers work to save them?" she sniffled, then buried her head in his chest.

"That's what I'd like to know," he muttered, looking up to glare over in Angelica's direction.

However, whatever harsh words of blame he had died on his lips as he saw her kneel beside the prone and lifeless forms of Merci and Disa. He watched as she ignored the bloody flow from her friend's fatal wound and cradled the wife of the village chief, Hasani in her arms, her expression of agony plain to see as she leaned down to speak to her…

"Forgive me, Disa…Please forgive me. I saw this…I saw this from the beginning…but I couldn't tell you anything. I was told not to say anything." She sobbed and said over and over, "I'm sorry…I'm sorry."

Peter, who had come to stand beside her was about to kneel down and offer her comfort when they were flooded with a bright golden white light. He gasped and jumped back as glowing ghostly orbs emerged from each corpse and slowly drifted upward, ascending up and away into the sky.

The other trio got to their feet and watched in awe. "Oh man, now what's happening?" Josh wanted to know as they were suddenly surrounded by a sea of rising orbs of light…

It was eerie…odd yet wondrous. Like being in a field of snow in the winter when the temperature becomes warm and a fog develops, rising from the thawing surface, creating a curtain… or a forest mist wafts up from the grass at dawn in a meadow. Having been witness to many displays of supernatural power Full Armor stood there amidst this latest one reverently; silently enveloped in the phantasmagoric circumstance…

After an indeterminate amount of time, the strange experience drew to a close as the lights of life from the broken bodies at last had completely ascended above, leaving Full Armor standing among the earthly bones, flesh and blood. Having borne witness to the vast display of godly power in multiple instances coming back to back the five were in a state of inertia; immobile and stupefied…overwhelmed by the sights they had seen and a myriad of emotions churning inside each of them. Even Peter, who felt responsible as leader to jumpstart the team into any kind of action could not get a grasp on his own feelings…

Wow…I don't know what to say or to do at this point…I know we need to probably head back home, but leaving all our friends…and all these people that we were trying to rescue here in this mess without doing something about it is just…wrong. What can we do…what should we do? Bury the bodies? Burn them? I'm sure that the UWF will be back here so if we're gonna do anything we've gotta move now. But look at us; nobody's been able to move a muscle…

He glanced around at his four teammates, all of them just standing there, not moving or saying anything…dazed with blank expressions on their faces like zombies and Angelica, whose shirt front was stained with Disa's blood. With everything that had happened Peter felt conflicted as he was confronted with one glaring fact…Although they have been given great abilities and been privy to a display of power that could only have come from heaven's throne, they were still merely human beings with limited capacity to comprehend such inconceivable spiritual power.

With everything in him, Peter began to snap himself out of it…however the sound of approaching vehicles helped him and the others come back to reality. As they got closer, the girls both paled suspecting the worst.

John just stared while Josh turned his head towards the road leading out of the village. "Who the heck is that coming now?"

Four dark-colored Range Rovers rumbled into the village square and parked, brakes squealing. Doors opened, and about a dozen men dressed in dark jeans and T-shirts bearing the Hebrew symbols םש ידלי came forward, looking slowly around them at what had once been a crowd of 2000 refugees and villagers. They made their way over by the meeting house, where Full Armor was standing and a tall young man, with a head of black, wiry curls and a goatee stepped forward, offering his hand to Peter…

"Peter Roccque of Full Armor?" he inquired.

Taking his hand with a wary look, Peter answered, "That's right…who are you?"

The man smiled, his black eyes keen, yet friendly. "My name is David Malensky…I head the South region of the Children of Shem. We came here to pick you up and to offer our assistance by my father's order, Malachi Malensky." He gazed about, with a look of sadness and added, "We can't just leave the village like this because the UWF will be back to finish their dirty business. We have to get rid of the bodies."

Nodding, Peter agreed, "Yeah, I was thinking the same thing…But how do we do it? You know, the UWF will see from their satellite if we burn them. But we're gonna have a hard time burying over 1000 dead people."

"I agree." David Malensky then gestured to his colleagues, and they went back to the vehicles to retrieve something. Turning towards Peter he asked, "Do you know where the communication shed is?"

"Yeah, it's back behind the meeting house…Why do you want to know?" Josh demanded.

"Is that the meeting house," he said, pointing to the building diagonally across from where they all were standing.

"Yeah," Peter replied. "Come on with me and I'll show you." He addressed the rest of his team. "You guys just stay here, I'll be right back."

John and the girls just nodded while Josh asked abruptly, "What you want with the communication shed…what you planning to do back there?"

David held up a hand. "Chill out. We're going to get rid of any evidence that the UWF could use against us. You can be sure that they're going to be back and soon, I want to make sure that there's nothing here to lead them to us when they return. In the meantime, you four go to your rooms, get all your belongings, get over to the vehicles and wait there for us to come back. We'll all be leaving ASAP."

With no further explanation he and Peter then turned and headed down towards the communication shed, leaving Josh, John, Angelica, and Leah to do as they were bidden.

"Well, we better do as he said," John said.

"Yeah, okay," Josh grudgingly agreed.

Taking the girls by the arms they all headed away from the field of slain refugees. And as the four turned and headed towards the men's and women's dorms Josh couldn't help noticing over in the distance, where the other men from COS were taking out drums of what looked to be gasoline from the back of their vehicles. On edge and curious, he wondered if they were in fact planning to burn down the entire village, not just the corpses of the slain…

To me it looks like they're just gonna torch this place…Makes sense though, before the goons from the UWF show up. So that explains why this guy Malensky went back to the communication shed, he's probably going to get all of the hardware and software; all of the technology out of there before the UWF can take anything. So, we'd just better help the girls get everything together and get out of Dodge…

In the communication shed, Peter assisted David as he systematically took down every piece of technology and equipment; the computer, the monitors, the radio and the controls to the satellite dish…he left no stone unturned. When they were finished the shed was absolutely empty. The only thing left were empty shelves, the desk and chairs and a few crates of wires and cables. They took the packed crates and boxes and lined them up outside.

"Where are the vehicles they were using?" David asked.

"Over there."

Peter pointed to wear the transports were parked. Beside one of them was a Jeep with a short truck bed. David nodded in approval.

"I'll use that…are the keys in it?"

"Yeah, they're under the front seat."

"Good."

David strode over to the Jeep, got in started it and drove it over to where the boxes and Peter were waiting. They loaded the bed of the Jeep with the boxes then drove out to the village square, carefully skirting around the carpet of slain bodies as the COS men systematically went from structure to structure, pouring gasoline at the base of every building. When they got to the back of the crowd; or the pile of corpses is that once was, the crowd, David parked the Jeep near the Range Rovers…

He gestured to Peter. "Come on, and help me with the boxes…We need to load them in the back and get ready to leave."

"Okay."

Peter followed him to the back of flatbed of the Jeep, and they began to take the boxes out to put in one of the Range Rovers. They finished just as the other four members of Full Armor came forward, carrying their belongings, John, carrying not only his knapsack but Peter's as well. Peter stepped came over to address his friends…

"Did you guys get everything?"

John nodded and replied, "Yeah…I picked up your gear as well." He handed Peter his knapsack.

"Thanks, man." He peered at Angelica, noticing that she had not changed her shirt but noticing her fragile emotional state he deferred from saying anything and just wrapped his arm around her, holding her close.

He looked off into the distance, into the village and noticed that the COS men that had come with David still pouring gasoline on everything, and were now pouring it over the sea of dead bodies. Drifting back into his nostrils, the pungent odor was beginning to overwhelm him. Then he watched as with torches the men from COS began to set the village on fire…beginning with the farthest dormitories and working their way over to the garage, the storehouse, the men's and women's dormitory that Full Armor had been living in, the meeting house, and last but not least, all of the pile of slain village members, refugees, Kuitwa Usiku, including Chiaga, Merci, Disa, and Hasani. The flames instantly became a controlled conflagration; a funeral pyre that was cremating the earthly remains of the throng of believers. Their grisly task done, the COS men emerged from the blaze like shadows as they made their way back to the Range Rovers, carrying the empty gasoline drums…

David stepped forward, addressing his colleagues, "Everything is taken care of…including, leaving no evidence of how the fire was started?"

"Affirmative, chief," a COS man named Nathan replied.

"Good work…now when the UWF shows up here, they'll be too late to find anything leading to us in COS. But I'm sure they're going to see the flames from their satellite so we better roll on out of here."

All the men nodded in agreement and were turning to go when Leah spoke up. "So that's it?" she questioned, her first words since the entire ordeal took place.

David looked at her with curiosity and said, "What do you mean? We can't stay here, we have to leave or will get caught by UWF troops."

Angelica then stepped forward and stated with quiet conviction, "I think she means that we just can't leave the remains of our friends here without saying a prayer…as much for ourselves as for them."

David nodded in acquiescence. "You're absolutely right, Messenger," he said.

She arched a slim brow. "You know all about me?"

He nodded solemnly and replied, "We know everything about all of you." He then gestured to his men to join Full Armor and they formed a circle holding hands. "Would you like to lead us?" he asked her.

She nodded, taking hold of Peter's hand on one side, and Leah's hand on the other. "Heavenly Father, we are here today to offer up prayers for our deceased friends, our brothers and sisters who have left this world and come to You. We ask You to receive them and bring them into Your house and before Your table where we know we will meet with them again one day. Please help us to deal with the grief we're feeling at their loss and prepare and equip us for the missions and the battles ahead of us as we continue to fight the good fight and bring more to sit at Your table. In the name of Jesus the Savior and Lord we pray. Amen."

"Amen." Everyone said in unison, then began to make their way slowly to enter the vehicles as the flames crackled in the background.

The Range Rovers all turned around and headed single file on the narrow road leading out of the village. Seated beside Peter in one of the vehicles, Angelica couldn't help but turn around and stare at the blaze in the retreating distance consuming the village…that which was once known as Adanech…She Who Has Protected…

After about half an hour they came to the airfield that once belonged to Merci Fofana. Her Cessna Caravan, Rallidae-1 sat silently in the early morning light, as if waiting for her to return. Parked near the plane was another Cessna Grand Caravan, its propellers spinning and ready for takeoff. The Range Rovers and the Jeep flatbed from the village all pulled up to the waiting craft…

David, who was sitting in the front seat of the Jeep, exited and with two of his men began to load all the boxes and crates bearing all the technology from the communication shed into the plane's cargo area. One of the COS men, known as Levi who was driving the vehicle with Peter and Angelica gestured to the plane…

"All of you five are to get on the plane…We're flying you to Cairo, then you'll take a British Airways jet to London, then another jet will take you back to Boston." He handed them tickets.

Peter opened his mouth to ask a question, but Levi continued his instructions. "Daniel is aware of what's happened and is expecting you. So please hurry and get on board."

"So Malensky let him know what happened at the village?"

Levi simply nodded so Peter and Angelica exchanged glances, shrugged and did as they were told…joining the other three who were already boarding the plane. As he began to follow Angelica to climb up the stairs to get into the craft, Peter turned around to address David Malensky, who was at the bottom of the stairs, watching them board…

"Thanks for the help," he said, offering his hand to shake.

David shook his hand and said, "No, Full Armor…Thank you."

Humbled yet bewildered Peter nodded and got into the plane. Making his way to his seat beside Angelica he pondered about that last statement…

He's thanking us, huh? For what? We rescued over 1000 people…even more than that if you want to count all the people that we brought to the village during our missions with Kuitwa Usiku and they all are dead. Even with our powers, we couldn't protect them. I know what it says in the Bible but it was still hard to watch all those people die right before my eyes…

At that thought he turned and looked at Angelica, who had laid her head back on the seat, staring blankly out the window at the sun beginning to rise on the eastern horizon and realizing how he was wrestling with the tragedy that had occurred, he then thought about how she had probably also still wrestled with this. Even before they had arrived in Africa, she had lived with the vision of what had happened, probably every day and night, with the extra added burden of not being able to tell anybody; not able to share the almost inconceivable pain that she had borne as she suffered in silence…

Filled with a deep tenderness Peter reached for her hand and held it in both of his. "It's over, Angel…It's all over so now you can rest."

With an inherent weariness Angelica turned her head to face him and stated in a foreboding manner. "Yes, it's all over, Peter…but only for now."

Her grave words sent a chill skittering down his spine as the plane lurched forward to take off and start the long journey that would take them back home.

As the sun rose Moses Konkosani arrived at Uwambo's palace in Giza, just as the last of the partygoers were filing out of the ballroom. Still drunk from the freely flowing champagne, they swayed and stumbled, their evening finery looking garishly out of place in the early morning light. Moses ignored them as he made his way into the palace in search of the supreme governor. He strode through the foyer, past the ballroom and down the main hallway until he came to the oak double doors of Uwambo's office and study. Knocking on the portals, he was surprised when they opened right up and shocked when he saw who it was in the room. Immediately he fell to his knees before the Supreme Leader himself…

"Y-your Excellency…m-my lord." Moses was beside himself, not knowing what to do or think.

Abram offered a congenial smile. "Major Moses Konkosani… Moses, please get up because I am humbly in your debt." He offered the covert UWF officer his hand.

Gaining his composure Moses got to his feet and took Abram's hand. "Your Excellency…I don't understand—,"

"Don't be modest, my friend…last night's victory over the Rebel Faction is directly tied to you and the fabulous job you did. If not for that I'm sure that we would have experienced a major setback and political blow because of those rebels." He gestured to the leather sofa by the window. "Let's have a seat and chat some more. They appear to be very well organized." Abram wasted no time and immediately began his probing.

They both sat down and Moses began. "Yes my lord, they are. From what I saw at Adanech, they appeared quite well organized. But unfortunately I could not get as close to the chief as I wanted to…the circle surrounding him was quite close knit." Moses thought for a moment and then added, "There were five college students from America that had arrived in the village almost a fortnight ago, who from the moment they arrived, became quite close to the chief."

"Five college students from America?" Abram echoed, intrigued. "Tell me more about these college students."

Moses took a moment and searched deep within his mind for every piece of intel he had gathered and stored regarding Full

Armor. "I picked them up and drove them to the village when they first arrived…three men and two women, anthropology students from Harvard…or that's what they said they were."

"I see," the Supreme Leader intoned thoughtfully. "Please go on."

Moses swallowed nervously, unsure as to how to say the rest. "Well…They accompanied a village group known as Kuitwa Usiku on nightly missions, which brought rebels into the village, fleeing the scheduled seedings. Unfortunately, because I was never able to infiltrate into Kuitwa Usiku I was never at any of the missions until I stowed away on the mission that took place at the Rungwa Game Reserve…and I saw what I saw."

"Ohh?" Abram leaned closer, as he reached in his pocket and pressed the button on a tiny transmitter. "And what was that?"

Moses took a deep breath and continued, "The rebels were getting ready to leave after loading the rebels on the transports for their escape when the UWF troops' assault began. I was hidden in the chassis and looked out to see what was going on when I saw the three male college students stand in front of the transports grouped together. Then I thought I was dreaming when I saw blue white light shoot right out from their hands and the huge waves of energy they created blew all of the attack vehicles back as if they were hit by a tornado."

"Is that so?" Abram asked. "I had reports on that incident and questioned its validity…I mean, it sounded like the stuff seen in a comic book." He chuckled, shaking his head and chided amiably, "Supernatural power coming from ordinary people to blow back an entire army…it's absurd!" Then changing his tune, he leaned closer to Moses and looked him directly in the eye, pinning him with eyes like daggers. "But you saw it happen, didn't you? Both then…and tonight when all those rebels from the disposal camps just appeared at that village. Am I right?"

"Y-yes, my lord…I saw both incidences with my own eyes," Moses admitted; an icy finger of fear running down his spine at the Supreme Leader's intense stare.

Seeing the reaction of the covert officer to his interrogation Abram leaned back with an easy grin and a friendly pat on the shoulder to put him at ease. "Relax, my friend. As I told you before I owe you a great debt. It was because of your brilliant plan to attack the village that those meddling and troublesome rebels have received their justice…just what they deserved." And he drew Moses closer. "Because of that, I'd like you to head up the UWF regional command here in the South Kingdom as brigadier general."

Moses was overwhelmed. "Your Excellency!"

Abram continued, "You'll head up the South UWF division and report directly to me on the same level, power wise as the Supreme Governor. So can I count on you, General Konkosani?"

Before Moses could respond the door to the office slammed open and Uwambo rushed in, agitated. "This can't be happening! Those rebel scum, how dare they!"

Startled, both Moses and Abram stood up. "What's wrong, Abrafo?" the Supreme Leader wanted to know.

Uwambo, livid and forgetting that Abram was there addressed Moses. "Konkosani, when you retreated from that enemy village you were supposed to send out a reconnaissance team immediately to go through the village in order to retrieve and confiscate anything leading us to the head."

Moses was dismayed. "I did that, sir. As soon as I got to the regional headquarters I had the team sent out."

"Is that so? Well, I just received a report that is very disturbing that I need you to explain."

Abram demanded of Uwambo, "What happened?"

Now, remembering that the world leader was in front of him, Uwambo became effusively apologetic…the model sycophant. "Forgive me, Your Excellency…It seems that the village that was the rebel stronghold…Adanech…is gone."

"Gone? What you mean gone?"

Uwambo swallowed nervously and replied, "I just received a report from the regional UWF command…They sent a reconnaissance team to the village and found it ablaze. It appears that the rebels got there and set the place on fire to keep us from finding out or discovering anything about them. Damn them to hell!"

"Hmmm." Abram stood there with his lips pursed. "It appears that the Rebel Faction is better organized than any of us realized. They were probably nearby, waiting for our troops to retreat…then came in to destroy any of the evidence that the village might've given us…very impressive."

"Impressive…ha!" Outraged, Uwambo was insistent and decided to pin the entire blame on Moses. "This is your fault, Konkosani! You should've prepared and figured that something like this could happen and had a reconnaissance team ready to move in right after your retreat. Now a golden opportunity to find out more about these rebels…has gone up in smoke… literally! All ashes!"

Cognizant of the offer that his Excellency presented to him Moses responded with the air of authority that was afforded to him in his prospective new role. "I believe I made the right decision and I stand by it, Uwambo."

"W-what did you say to me?!" Uwambo was apoplectic as Abram stood benignly aside to watch the drama.

"You heard me."

"Why you—how dare you speak to me; your superior in that way in front of his Excellency…that's insubordination!" Uwambo snapped.

Moses gave a serene yet steely smile. "Indeed, it is…or it would be if I were still your subordinate. However, his Excellency just rewarded me for my hard work and our victory tonight by promoting me to brigadier general in charge of the South region UWF troops. Which means that I am on the same level as you as the leader of the military and therefore not your subordinate."

In a high rage, Uwambo turned to Abram and protested, "Your Excellency, this can't be true! If Konkosani truly did his job the rebels would never been able to burn down that village before we got there." He blanched as he saw the glacial orbs of the UWC Supreme Leader impaling him…

"Is that what you think?" Abram inquired coldly. "Then you're either too proud, blind, or a fool. To think that the Rebel Faction is just a bunch of helpless, harmless simple minded religious fanatics that adhere to an old faith system is folly, pure and simple. And to blame one of your best people for the fact that you had the wool pulled over your eyes is very disappointing to me." He then turned towards Moses and asked, "Well, Major Konkosani…I take it you're excepting my offer of this position?"

He said with a bow, "Your Excellency, I humbly and gratefully accept this honor and I promise to do my best."

Abram smiled and nodded as he said, "I am quite confident that you will. You can immediately take command." Laying a hand on Moses' shoulder, he added, "I'm expecting great things from you for the future of the UWF and the UWC, General Konkosani. So carry on."

"Yes, Your Excellency."

Moses then turned smartly around and strode out past the stunned silent Uwambo, who just stood there in suspended animation. Having felt blindsided and foolish he was trying to gather his thoughts and salvage what was left of his pride when Abram spoke to him…

"Abrafo, if you don't mind I require the use of your office for a while longer…So if you wouldn't mind leaving and closing the door behind you to give me my privacy, I would greatly appreciate it."

"Yes, Your Excellency," he meekly complied.

Duly dismissed like any lowly underling, Abrafo Uwambo, Supreme Governor of the South Kingdom slowly turned and exited, leaving Abram alone in the lavish office. He reached in his pocket for the transmitter, pressed a button and a side door opened, ushering in his right hand man, Ichabod. The spiritual seer and clairvoyant came before Abram and bowed deeply…

"Yes, my lord."

Abram wasted no time. "Did you hear what Konkosani said…about the supernatural power that comes from these five college students?"

Ichabod nodded and replied, "Indeed I did…I have felt the stirrings of spiritual energy getting much stronger in the last few days. I have absolutely no doubt that a great power has been cultivated and planted in these five and I can even feel a familiar and nostalgic presence from my naughty little runaway girl and her two brave knights." He smiled as he added, "I'm greatly looking forward to confronting my dear old friends."

"Then that's your task…Tracking them down, finding them, and the source of their power…then eliminating them," Abram commanded, his expression fierce.

Ichabod bowed again. "As you wish, my Lord." He exited quickly, leaving the Supreme Leader to darkly brood as he stated his resolve…

These five are a problem…a potentially persistent thorn in my side. And that thorn must be removed and crushed…as soon as possible.

EPILOGUE

It was almost 1 PM the next day when Full Armor found themselves at the cave entrance that led into the abandoned APL bunker that they called home. The journey that had started in Merci Fofana's abandoned airfield in Tanzania took them into Cairo, then out to London in Heathrow…then finally to Logan after yet another delay. By the time they were on the plane for the final leg home all of them were like the walking dead; numb and oblivious to their surroundings. When they got off at Logan, two men came up to them and introduced themselves as members of COS…then escorted them to a nondescript Jeep SUV and drove them to Walden Pond where they hiked through the woods until they reached the cave that hid their secret place. Entering the cave, the five travel weary and heartsick young adults then trudged down the shaft and into the subterranean stronghold where they were greeted by their mentor Daniel Roccque, A.K.A. Brother Danny. Having prepared for their arrival back home, he had their bed rolls, extra blankets, and hot food waiting…

"Welcome home my children." He stepped forward and addressed the five youths standing bedraggled and exhausted in front of him. "You did well."

"Thanks," Peter said, the only one able to respond while Leah burst into tears. John wrapped an arm around his sister to comfort her while Josh took his backpack and hurled it across the room in impotent fury…

"We did well…Yeah, right!" he snapped sarcastically. "You know what happened so cut the bull and tell us the truth…we blew it big-time. We have these huge big-time powers to protect and in the end we couldn't protect anyone. So don't tell me we did well because in my opinion we sucked!" He threw himself down on the floor and buried his head in his knees as if in agony.

John heaved a sigh and looked extremely uncomfortable. "It was kind of hard to take…Seeing all those people, people we came to know in the short time we were there die right before our eyes. Just like Josh said…we couldn't protect anybody."

Giving into the despair around him, Peter nodded as well. "There's just no way to sugarcoat it. Our job on this mission, at least the way we thought was to protect these people and guide them to the village…not lead them to their eventual death. We did blow it."

At his candid yet grim statement Angelica, who up to this moment had just been standing there still clad in the t-shirt stained with Disa's blood under her jacket silently dropped her knapsack then headed straight for the prayer room, closing the door with a solid thud and isolating herself once more. The atmosphere in the main room of the bunker was thick and heavy with the cloud of disappointment and failure hanging like a shroud. Full Armor, full of chinks from the spiritual battle they had just come through was beset with doubts…

Brother Danny watched with a paternal eye over the children that had been entrusted to him and wanted like any father to gather them to his breast and comfort them. However, he knew that they were chosen for great things; and to whom much was given, much would soon be required. So to draw them out of their misery, he decided to challenge them…

"So you all blew it, huh? Is that what you think?"

Taking a seat on the floor next to Josh he gestured to Peter, John and Leah to join them. When they did, he continued, "Serving the Lord is never easy…It requires strength, resolve, and perseverance to fight the good fight. Mistakes are a given and should be expected because we are human, no matter what power God gives us to fight. And you five have been doubly blessed; to be chosen by our Lord to have incredible, amazing supernatural abilities and powers, at this time to perform this task."

Josh raised his head and stared at Brother Danny. "We're blessed are we? So how come I don't feel that way?"

"How do you feel, Josh?"

"How do I feel?" he echoed, incredulous. "You're kidding, right?"

"No, I want you to tell me," Brother Danny persisted.

Josh sighed heavily then replied, "Like I got a sucker punch… outta nowhere square in the gut, knocking the wind out of me and by the time I could get up and give it back the guy that hit me was gone…leaving me hurting and frustrated." He ran his hands through his hair and added, "As Christians I just don't get what it is we're supposed to do anymore."

"That about sums it up for me too," John said, and Leah simply nodded, sniffling.

Brother Danny nodded. "Hmmm…I see…And it's understandable, really. Death is a hard thing to face, no matter the circumstance and especially the death of anyone close to us. But as Christians, we are taught to believe that death has been defeated at the cross, by Christ." He reached for his Bible, which was conveniently nearby. Flipping through it he reached First Corinthians chapter 15 turned to the passage he wanted and began to read it…

"So when this corruptible shall have put on incorruption, and this mortal shall have put on immortality, then shall be brought to pass the saying that is written, Death is swallowed up in victory. O death, where is thy sting? O grave, where is thy victory? The sting of death is sin; and the strength of sin is the law. But thanks be to God, which gives us the victory through our Lord Jesus Christ. Therefore, my beloved brethren, be steadfast, unmovable, always abounding in the work of the Lord, forasmuch as you know that your labor is not in vain in the Lord….This is the hope that we all carry, my children." He then turned to another verse, Revelation 13:15…

"And he had power to give life unto the image of the beast; that the image of the beast should both speak, and cause that as many as would not worship the image of the beast should be killed…This is prophecy, happening right before our eyes. The beast is the Antichrist and the Antichrist…is Isaac Abram. So you'll have to expect with each upcoming mission you will encounter people that you will grow close to and who you'll lead to the Lord…will be killed. How will you handle that? What will you do?"

The four youths sat there quietly as the truth had a chance to set in. Finally, Peter spoke in a quiet yet determined voice…

"We'll do what we have to do…What we're told to do; go where we're told to go and use the powers we were given to protect and get God's people to a place of safety until the appointed time. Prophecy is prophecy and destiny is destiny as long as they know Christ."

Daniel regarded his son with growing warmth in his heart *as the leader of Full Armor he's really taking his role in this seriously. He's a much better man at his age than I ever was.* Yet he felt impelled to toss the gauntlet, "Even if you watch many people die?"

"Yeah." Peter nodded and looked off into the distance, as if deep in thought then added, "There was something we saw at Adanech, just before we left everyone after they were killed. We saw lights ascending from their bodies, going straight up into the sky. It was…amazing. I'm sure that those lights were their souls, going into the presence of the Lord."

Brother Danny just nodded, to affirm his statement.

"That was really something," John said, still in awe as he remembered the event. "With everything we experienced, using our powers then getting the Shed Blood of the Lamb…following what we saw after everybody had been killed was a mind blower. We're kind of shell shocked."

"The Shed Blood of the Lamb?" the older man inquired.

Peter replied, "Yeah…one night we all were woken up with a sharp pain and received wounds that were stigmata. Angelica had told us earlier that night that we were to expect to receive the Shed Blood of the Lamb. So we got the wounds of Christ… Josh and I got them on our wrists, John got them on his feet, Leah got it on her forehead, and Angelica got it on her side, then the next day the wounds disappeared. But the real unbelievable thing was how it was used. We were able to move all of the captives from the disposal camps as if by magic to the village… then, we were all able to disappear right before the eyes of the UWF troops."

"The Shed Blood of the Lamb, huh?" Brother Danny raised a brow feigning surprise. But inside, he knew the source *You had much more in store for them didn't You, Lord…But as I said to them once before to whom much is given, much will surely be required.* He got up and said briskly, "You'll have to tell me more about that at another time, but for right now it looks like you all need to have something to eat and to get some rest." He glanced at the group and noticing that one was missing, he added, "All of you."

The four looked over to the closed door of the prayer room and the air was pregnant with meaning…they knew why Angelica had headed over there, and why she once again closed herself off from everyone. And as guilty as all of them were feeling, it wasn't even a fraction of how she must have been feeling at that moment…because as God's designated messenger it was her slender shoulders that had borne the greatest weight…

Leah said softly, "I hope Angie's all right."

Josh and John both nodded gravely while Peter made his way over to the door…

When she entered the prayer room, Angelica's heart was heavy after having seen her visions become reality…gruesome, horrifying reality. Before leaving for Africa, they had been at the least disturbing thoughts and at the worst, terrifying nightmares. Now, her mind would not give her rest, playing back scene after scene…remembering Disa's ready smile and her friendship as they worked side by side in the village school with the children. She was a true woman of God, who handled her life in Adanech with a gentle yet steely strength that Angelica admired and the respect that she had shown to her as the Messenger was always genuine, humbling her. She grasped her t-shirt, staring at the blood of her friend…

Everybody at Adanech was fantastic…But especially Disa, she always had such amazing peace and faith. When she taught at the school, she wanted to instill every child they had there with the truth, that no matter what was going to happen that they were precious in the eyes of God and His arms would always be around them. I wish I could tell her how much she encouraged me. Her peace was with her to the very end, on her face, even when they shot her in the head…

At that thought Angelica finally shattered…All through every incredible occurrence that had happened in the last 48 hours her eyes had remained dry and inside she was numb. Since arriving at Adanech she had pledged to keep a firm handle on her emotions; making sure she did not cry openly in front of people and since her childhood had been so difficult she was expert at that…she didn't break easily. However, seeing the faces of those she had seen in her visions, long before she set foot in that village…interacting with them, laughing with them and when Elimu died, grieving with them she had become as much a part of that village as if she had been born there. The thing that had impressed her the most however, was the sense of peace, love, and joy among the villagers…they truly embraced the Lord and accepted what ever He had waiting for them. Then, when she and Leah had been sent to the disposal camp in Lagos while they were in the holding cell she had seen how everyone there had the same quiet peace and acceptance in their uncertain future. So for Disa, Hasani, Merci, Chiaga, and all those people at the disposal camp that she and Leah had transported to Adanech… she finally succumbed and allowed her emotions their release. Collapsed, crumpling to the floor and burying her face in the makeshift altar made from the only bench in the room where she had prayed for hours since entering the bunker Angelica cried; deep, heart wrenching sobs that convulsed her entire slim body. She cried for Elimu, whose stoic strength and conviction overcame any fear he might have possessed as he willingly went on the mission that ended his life and the pain that had pierced her heart at the time that she had pushed back came forth with a vengeance, making the tears flow like a storm deluge. It was as if time had stood still…and she was sucked into a waterspout; a whirling vortex of pent-up emotion, threatening to tear her apart…

Angelica was immersed so deep into her misery that she did not hear the door softly open and close. Nor did she sense that another person had entered the room; a strong, reliable presence that reached for her from behind, with the familiar warmth she had come to depend upon. Sitting on the floor behind her Peter's corded arms encircled her and pulled her close, up against the security of his broad warm chest, resting his head against her back as he shared her anguish. Slowly becoming aware of him she eagerly accepted the comfort he offered, straightening up and turning into him, wrapping her arms around his torso and burying her face in his broad shoulder to continue crying while his own arms locked around her. They said nothing to each other, words were not necessary at this point…just the simple mutual expression of affection and understanding that had been forged between them as they clung and gave comfort to each other.

As he held Angelica Peter silently pondered; his mind fluctuating between the recent memories at the village of Adanech and the losses they had experienced there and what he had just heard from Brother Danny as they had talked outside. The Scripture verses that their mentor had read resonated deep in his spirit; as they did at the village…coming to mind when he witnessed the souls of the slain ascend to heaven. He knew that the road that lay before Full Armor, the road they had all just started walking upon was long and arduous…a marathon that will have them end up with battle scars; bruised and battered in body, mind, and spirit. However, it was also a journey; a Pilgrim's progress that would lead them to the ultimate reward…eternity in paradise at the marriage supper of the Lamb. The next couple of days and possibly weeks, there will be sadness, frustration, guilt, and anger as they all tried to make sense and put into perspective in human terms what had happened during the mission in Africa. But he also knew that with God's supernatural power that He had given them and the infinite love that He had borne them, He will guide them every step of the way as He calls them again into the fields. And the Full Armor of God with renewed strength will go out and glean again…for Him.

END

CPSIA information can be obtained at www.ICGtesting.com
Printed in the USA
BVOW031952310512

291513BV00001B/24/P